MEGACROC

A NOVEL BY

JULIAN MICHAEL CARVER

SEVERED PRESS
HOBART TASMANIA

MEGACROC

1
THE MENACE OF THE WETLANDS

The young woman had suffered a horrible death. It had been much longer and violent than any other animal attack he had seen before, or from any serial killer, for that matter.

Sheriff Jacob Dawson bent down over the malformed earth, studying the grisly scene that saturated the grassy knolls, concealed by the rhythmic motions of the sawgrass. As he lowered his head closer to the scene, he found the pungent smell too nauseating to bear. He trotted awkwardly backwards, doubling over a log and throwing up all over a knotted old tree stump, grateful that none of the other deputies had noticed.

Sluggishly, he wiped his lips before staring back at the frightening face frozen in time.

The first thing he noticed about the woman was her icy blue eyes that seemed to lock with his, no matter where he stood. Her pale head remained completely unscathed, connecting with her slender neck down to her torso until the skin transitioned into exposed, decaying organs near the shredded belly button. Her legs were missing, although a foot was found nearby, closer to the watery edge of the swamp a few yards away. Both arms had been recovered by search teams deeper in the nearby high grasses, although mostly bone was all that remained. One of the rigid fleshy hands still had a gold band on the bloated ring finger. From what remained of the body, Dawson concluded that she was in her late twenties at the time of death – barely older than his own daughter.

He regained his composure as more police officers and crime scene photographers began to arrive through the grasses at the hilltop, roping over the scene with yellow tape reading *Police Line – Do Not Cross*.

Dawson doubted that they needed to put any tape up at all.

The scene was so isolated, so dense, that it was unlikely any civilians would be coming along. The Palm Grove police cruisers had to park a mile back on the main road and hike to the scene on foot, cutting through the jungle with machetes while fending off nasty summer mosquitoes. As the familiar sound of clicking Nikon cameras flashed around him to document the findings, he found himself staring out at the remote landscape, noting how cut off from civilization the area really was.

And yet, the swamp region was dangerously close to the southern edge of Palm Grove, just a few miles from the development of the Sunset Ridge housing plan, still in mid construction. The realization of the close proximity to the new housing site sent a shiver down his spine.

It was a sweltering hot afternoon in the Southern Glades, about a half-hour south of Homestead and just over an hour south of Miami. All around him, he was dwarfed by tall exotic plants and drooping trees, most of which dipped down into the murky green bog that trimmed around the shore. Just ahead, he could see a trickle of bubbles coming from the depths of the swamp before breaking lazily on the surface. He figured it must be one of the alligators.

The gators were everywhere down there.

The rustle of boots on grass behind him made him turn. He relaxed when he saw it was Deputy William Bolasco, one of his friendlier recruits and transplants from Orlando. He had a soft spot for Willie, thinking of him sometimes as more of a son and protegee than a subordinate. Dawson made a point to wipe his mouth again, assuming there was more residual vomit that he missed.

"Willie," he managed, trying to sound confident in the presence of the female corpse. "Didn't expect you to arrive this fast. Where's Berman? Adrienne?"

"En route, last I checked," Bolasco replied, stepping beside the sheriff and studying the marshes that dispersed before them in all directions, sprawling out ahead around various pockets of interwoven jungles.

"Good, very good. What about Ryan and Clarence?"

"They should be arriving soon, too."

Dawson saw that more of his units began to arrive, appearing through the tall cattails as they padded carefully along the animal trail that snaked to the cove. A young female photography intern threw up over a bush beside the main trail before she checked her camera batteries and resumed her task. Several officers nearby chuckled and nudged each other, amused by her youthful innocence.

"This is the fourth one this month," Bolasco muttered under his breath, sipping his Starbucks coffee in a white cup. "Jeez, it's worse than the Miami Strangler."

"You were too young to remember that," Dawson replied, managing a smile.

"Well, I was old enough to catch the TV recap," Bolasco laughed, indulging another drink. "I don't think there's much to gain from this one that we haven't learned from the others. Alligator attack – a nasty one. Same old thing if you ask me."

Over the past month, starting from the week after the fourth of July, three people had vanished in the Everglades, only to be found later, usually in scattered pieces near the highway to the Keys. One victim, Jonah Levine, was barely old enough to drive, identified by relatives which expedited the dental records confirmation process.

The attacks were concentrated near the bottom edge of the Southern Glades, where the mainland met with the Florida Keys. The bodies were unnaturally mangled, usually contorted to nightmarish angles and discarded all over the shoreline and interim swamp pools.

"I don't know, Willie," the sheriff admitted. They turned and began to walk along the edge of the water, discussing the animal attacks as they went. "Honestly, I suspect we have something bigger on our hands. A real man-eater."

"Something bigger?" Willie asked, his voice rising. "Like a croc?"

"Perhaps."

They stopped just shy of another piece of evidence: the woman's foot. The area had already been taped off, and forensic analysts were bending over the shredded appendage, preparing to collect it in a protective evidence bag. Willie spilled coffee on himself, cursing, padding the damp spot on his knee with his hand as the steam billowed upward.

"What makes you say that, sir?"

"Well, mostly it's just a hunch," Dawson admitted. "But honestly, it's what we saw at the second crime scene, back in mid-July. You remember him, don't you?"

"Sure," Willie replied as he finished drying his leg. "Big guy. African American, if I recall correctly."

"Not just big," Dawson corrected, "He was six foot nine. A real athlete, with arms like a horse. I doubt any small, sluggish alligator could have got the jump on him."

"You sure about that?" Willie asked, careful to watch his challenging tone with the sheriff. "Those little peckers are fast. They lie in wait and ambush. They're opportunistic. Hell, there's probably a hundred just watching us right now, I'll wager."

"He wouldn't have been exploring down here if he wasn't prepared to deal with those dangers," Dawson suggested. "Everyone knows the stories of coming to the Everglades alone, even tourists. It's a jungle out here. The animals are at war. Everything's a territory dispute. And now, with the invasion of the Burmese python in South Florida, the competition is even more fierce."

The Burmese python was native to only Southeast Asia. However, in the past twenty years, the snakes had become a dominant invasive species in the Everglades. The serpent's uprising had been so rapid, that the U.S. Department of the Interior banned the further importation of the species, hoping to prevent the invasion any further and eventually reverse the damage.

"So, you're thinking a croc then?" Willie asked, stepping around one of the investigators that was shining a light over the murky water's edge.

"A big croc," the sheriff added. "This is the southernmost edge of the state. We're right in the middle of their territory. It seems only natural that there may be a few ill-tempered alpha males in the area that may try to strike at passersby."

Willie nodded, silently admitting that the sheriff may be right as the deputy turned to survey the investigation. American crocodiles were known to inhabit this part of Florida, and were significantly larger than their alligator counterparts.

The area was now saturated with law enforcement officials. Evidence bags had been produced and samples of the victim were being collected by forensic scientists picking through the brush. Several of the other evidence samples had already been collected and taken back to the main road, which remained barely visible through the tall grasses waving in the oceanic breeze.

"Hey sheriff," called one of the other deputies, Sherwin Graham, from the far side of the swamp. "Hey, you should see this! For what it's worth, I think it may back up your crocodile theory!"

Dawson raced over to the other edge of the bog, with Willie right on his heels, cupping at his overflowing coffee cup. Graham was coupled with another forensic photographer, who had his Nikon D500 pointed into the grass at something unseen. Their faces were static, studying something low to the ground in the shrubs.

"How's this for your theory, sir?" Graham smiled, pointing to the earth.

Dawson looked down. From the corner of his eye, he could see Bolasco's jaw drop as he arrived hastily beside him. Dawson was surprised when he felt his own lower lip sag as he studied the mark on the muddied bank.

Imprinted on the ground was a massive crocodilian footprint, hardened in the harsh sun.

At first, Dawson thought it might have been a joke from one of the deputies. Such a track this large couldn't possibly be authentic. But when the sheriff examined the perfect cylindrical bevel of the toes and claws, he knew that if it was a prank, it would've taken some time to mold and carve out all the intricate details.

The track was easily two feet wide. Dawson noted the scale of the claws had to be six to eight inches in height, that tapered off into five formidable jagged points. In the drying surface, additional dimples and imperfections were visible, although some had crumpled apart in the baking sunlight, scattering to the bowled middle of the print in fragments.

"Holy shit, sheriff," Bolasco said, kneeling down beside the mark. "You might be onto something. I've never seen a crocodile this size before."

"Croc?" Graham laughed. "That's no croc! That's a tyrannosaurus footprint, obviously."

The photographer laughed, after adjusting the focus on the camera and snapping another image.

"Hell, you're not kidding," Bolasco said. "Hey, Graham. Snap a pic for me, will you?"

He handed Graham his iPhone and bent down next to the track. After easing his hand over the imprint without touching it, he nodded to Graham.

"How do you work this effing thing," Graham mumbled, shifting the smartphone sideways as if it would make the device perform better.

"Here, Numbnuts. Press this!"

Bolasco handed the phone back to his colleague after activating the camera app.

"Say cheese."

"Yeah, yeah."

Graham pressed the button on the touch screen several times, before handing the smartphone back to Bolasco. Dawson leaned over to the deputy, admiring the image. The crocodile track dwarfed Berman's hand.

"That will be a good reference image," Dawson noted. "Willie, send that to me, please."

"Yes, sir."

"I think there's a dinosaur loose in the Glades, boss," Graham noted.

Dawson frowned, eyes locked on the photo before he finally broke the spell, only to find himself staring in a trance at the actual footprint just in front of his boots. Slowly, his gaze wandered to another track of equal size, half submerged in the swamp shore. Through the green film, Dawson saw a third track underwater, distorted from the refraction of the underwater world and eroding under the current.

Bolasco and Graham looked at the trackway in awe, following Dawson's stare out into the bog.

The monster crocodile was close.

"You just might be right," he nodded, before turning back to the trail and heading for his squad car, a mile back in the wilderness. He began to make a mental list of items to retrieve and contacts to call.

There was much to be done.

2
PALM GROVE

The Palm Grove Police Department was situated on the corner of Main and Fifth Avenue, just a few minutes north of the Southern Glades and the Sunset Ridge housing project. The two-story building had once been the town hall, but after the 1980's, the building was reconfigured into the police barracks.

The building was the crown jewel of Main Street. Erected at the turn of the century in the early 1900's, the structure had been designed to reflect ancient Greece-Roman architecture. Four tall Grecian gray columns guarded the front, before rising to the roof. Images of ancient warriors were carved into the wall above the columns, looking out onto the visitors that arrived through the front entrance. The building remained one of the last surviving buildings from the early 1900's in Palm Grove. Many of the other buildings had already been torn down or given face lifts.

Sheriff Jacob Dawson sat behind his desk, facing out his window.

The sheriff's office was the corner room, which stared out on Main Street. One of the columns obscured his view of Fifth, although he could see the traffic coming in and out of the bend. Palm trees lined the road, rising up out of the old wobbly sidewalks where they were planted by a garden club thirty years ago. Tourists and shoppers walked under the green fronds, making last minute shopping trips before the businesses closed for the day.

Across the street was a store called Lenny's Hardware, a family business that served as a staple in the community for over fifty years. Above the faded asphalt roof, was the company sign on a large white pole. The mascot was a cartoon American crocodile. The croc was angled toward the intersection, holding a big thumbs up to the passing traffic. "Meet me under Lenny's Croc" had long been a saying in Palm Grove – everyone knew the place.

Jacob stared blankly at the sign, pondering the grim scene from earlier in the day. By now, the sun was beginning to set over the other side of the building, casting long skewed shadows over the road beneath the window. The passing of time didn't stop the dead woman's face from haunting his memory.

He fumbled with the idea of a monster crocodile loose in Palm Grove, or the Southern Glades for that matter. American crocodiles were known to be in the area, especially along the bottom edge of the state, and were often significantly larger than the American alligators. But a crocodile that large?

Impossible.

But yet, the colossal footprint remained ingrained in his mind. After they drove away from the swamp, he finally received the picture via text message from Bolasco: the deputy's hand engulfed by the gigantic track. Dawson scanned over the image again and again, trying to find any imperfection that may lead him to rethink his theory and conclude it was just a joke.

But a joke that detailed would be hard to pull off. And Dawson was observant; he would have observed one of his subordinates kneeling down and carving the track. And then there was the photographer next to Graham. Clearly, the cameraman didn't think it was a fake; he snapped a dozen pictures of the mark.

Eventually, Dawson swiped the image away, content with what he had seen. The Everglades were a vast array of exotic landscapes that ran practically the width of South Florida. There could very well be large crocodiles or alligators that had yet to be discovered, avoiding brushing shoulders with mankind.

A shadow passed over Dawson's face.

Through the blinds of his office, he could see Bolasco approaching, crossing around the aisles of outdated desks of the secretaries. The sheriff perked up when he heard the crinkle of a McDonald's fast food bag in the deputy's hand.

"Hey, sorry I'm late boss," the deputy announced, peeking his head through the door. "I bring a peace offering."

He held up the brown paper bag with the beautiful golden arch logo. The delicious smells of fast food wafted throughout the room as Bolasco shut the door behind him.

"You're forgiven," Dawson smiled. "Pull up a chair. Three McDoubles?"

"And a medium fries," Bolasco replied, sliding over a chair in front of the sheriff's desk and setting the bag down on the tabletop, careful not to get any grease on Dawson's documents. He ruffled through the food before pulling out three neatly wrapped burgers and passing them to the sheriff.

"Good job, Willie."

They began to wolf down the food. Most of the officers had skipped lunch that day, given the recent surprise dispatch in the Everglades. Dawson was particularly hungry. When Bolasco offered to run to pick something up, the sheriff immediately thought of double cheeseburgers. Their frequent fast food runs had become ritualistic. Next time, it would be Dawson's turn to pay.

"Hell of an afternoon," he stated, munching down some French fries.

"Indeed," Bolasco agreed. "If it wasn't for those fishermen, the body might have been swallowed up by another gator. It was by God's grace that they were fishing in that area."

"Doesn't make any sense to me," Dawson asked. "How do these people keep getting snatched? You can't be telling me that they're just hiking through and get pulled in. Crocodiles and alligators are fast, but not that fast. Most people could outsmart them in a race. I'm toying with the idea of closing the area to fishermen until we figure out what's happening."

"Ambushed on the road, and dragged, maybe?" Bolasco suggested, sipping his large Diet Coke.

"But still, Willie. A mile? And honestly, it's probably more than a mile. Shit, in that heat, it seemed like a half-hour past before we made it back to the body. I'd say it's more than a mile and a half. That's a hell of a way to drag a body, even for a strong animal like a croc."

"Yeah, but you saw that track, Sheriff," Bolasco said. "If that's the animal that's been picking off our residents, it has to be as big as a boat. And with a foot like that, I'd hate to encounter the real thing. It must be thirty feet long!"

"Thirty feet?" Dawson smirked, skeptical of the deputy's guess.

"Well, maybe twenty feet. Twenty-five tops."

"Well, I guess I have no room to talk – I honestly thought it might be that big when I saw the track. And honestly, I'm still unsure how big I think it is. But the size is irrelevant. Either way, I'm considering bringing on an expert for this case. A consultant. We're gonna have to corner this beast eventually, before the town thinks we're just sitting on this with our thumbs up our asses. I'd say we plan a boating expedition to the swamp as soon as next week."

"Who did you have in mind, Sheriff?"

Dawson spun around his computer monitor, pressing a button on the back that caused the screen to jump back to life. Bolasco took another swig of the drink as he read over the website headline and article. Dawson could see the officer scrolling down the page in the glowing reflection in the deputy's glasses, assessing the sheriff's recommendation."

"Michael Robinson. The gator guy from Redland?"

"He's just up the road," Dawson replied. "Why not?"

"Well, you know I don't have a problem with it. I've heard he lives and breathes crocodiles, so he probably knows everything about them. But from what I hear, I think Jeff hates him."

"Berman? Why?"

"Ancient history. Apparently, the two go way back. I've heard they were pretty good friends back in high school. They graduated from somewhere up near Miami. Somewhere along the line, the two had a pretty dramatic falling out."

"About what? A girlfriend?"

"I'm not sure, but probably. Isn't that what always happens in high school? Everyone loves someone but that someone loves someone else."

Dawson wrinkled his nose, but finally understood the sentence and agreed.

"Is he still here?"

"Berman? Yeah. Just saw him downstairs."

Dawson turned towards his office landline, picked up the phone and dialed 1-1-4 on the button set.

"Cindy? Oh good, you're still there. I – oh, thanks. Yeah, it was a hell of a day. Yeah, be thankful you were here on the phones. What I saw out there I'll never be able to unsee – really messed up shit. Listen, Berman. Is he still down there? He is? Good. Please send him up, and head on home. No problem. Have a good night, Cindy."

Moments later, the familiar click of leather boots clattered towards the corner office. Through the blinds, an officer approached, offering a quick courtesy knock before entering.

"Berman. Come in, please."

The officer entered the room, standing rigidly beside Bolasco.

Jeffrey Berman was a handsome deputy in his mid-thirties, joining the force a few years earlier after he finished police school. After joining the Palm Grove Police Department, he immediately moved up in the ranks due to his bravery and dedication, although many in the department found him irritating and impulsive. One of his trademarks was his thick blonde hair that he molded with pomade to produce an Elvis style pompadour. Aside from his devilish looks, he remained a reliable officer on the force. Dawson admired Berman's methods of getting the job done, no matter how ballsy or controversial they may be, and was one of his favorite deputyies to bounce ideas off of.

"Did you want my last cheeseburger?" Dawson offered, clearing his throat.

"No thank you, sir," Berman shook his head. The deputy was a health and fitness nut. When he wasn't on a case or doing paperwork, he was hitting the gym or running at the high school track.

"I'm assuming you're all caught up on the situation in the Glades?" Dawson asked.

"Yes, sir. Sorry, I got to the scene a little late. There was some trouble up town. Domestic dispute."

"How did it get resolved?"

"It was over when I got there, sir."

"Take a seat, please."

"Sir."

Berman scooted up beside Bolasco, resting one of his legs over his knees. Dawson swiveled his computer monitor to face the deputy. On the screen, the website headline read: **Local Alligator Zoological Preserve to be Featured in upcoming Florida Trend issue.**

"The Redland Crocodilian Sanctuary," Berman said, after reading into the article. "Yeah, I know the place."

"Bolasco tells me you're familiar with the owner, Mr. Robinson."

Berman turned to the other deputy, who looked away, embarrassed.

"Well, sir," Berman began, fidgeting in his seat. "Yes. I guess you could say I know Mike. We used to be friends a while ago in high school. To be honest though, we sort of lost touch through the years. I have no idea what he's up to now, other than operating his crocodile enclosure up in Redland."

"I think we may need to bring on an expert in this case," Dawson went on, spinning the monitor swiftly back around to the original side. "I'd feel more comfortable if it's someone that we know. I've read about Mr. Robinson. His business is thriving and his expertise seems promising. It certainly seems like he knows the crocodiles very well."

"What do you have in mind, sir?" Berman asked.

"I'm not entirely sure," Dawson went on. "The Palm Grove community has already demanded that we apprehend some kind of killer crocodile after the Jonah Levine killing. Off the top of my head, I'm toying with the idea of leading a small team into the Southern Glades and trying to find the croc."

"What are we going to do with it after we catch it, sir?" Berman asked. "I guarantee Robinson won't be happy about shooting it, if it's an American crocodile. I hear they're nearly endangered as it is."

"Let me think on that," Dawson said, spinning in his chair to face Main Street again. The cartoon from Lenny's Hardware seemed to provoke him, causing the sheriff to complete the 360 spin and arrive back at the deputies.

"Head up there tomorrow, Berman – as soon as your shift starts. Tell him I would love to meet with him about a problem we've been having down here. Who am I kidding – he probably has heard all about it. The news has been covering it extensively. It'd be great if we could talk to him about locating this elusive animal to his facility, but I won't get too carried away until I meet him in person."

"Yes, sir. Is there anything more that you need from me?"

"That's all for now. Go hit the gym, kid."

Berman managed a subtle smile before leaving, closing the door gently behind him. When his silhouette slipped around the corner, Bolasco turned back to the sheriff.

"Well this ought to be interesting," said the deputy.

"Why's that, Willie?"

"I'm pretty sure that he's deemed Michael Robinson his arch rival, ever since high school. I've heard him complain and bitch about the man many times. Who knows what's gonna happen?"

3
MORNING COMMUTE

Michael Robinson stepped out of his rickety screen door into the hot Florida sunlight that baked his front yard. Fishing through his pockets for his set of keys, he found them wedged under his bulky wallet that he hastily shoved in the same pouch. He cursed, struggling to dislodge his wallet simply to unlock his vehicle.

He lived in a small yellow ranch that he painted himself a few years back, with a front yard that looked out onto a curve that wrapped around the neighborhood. The backyard he loved even more, fenced in and leveled off, sitting at the edge of a wooded area.

It was a quiet neighborhood, just the way he liked it. He moved there for an easy commute to his business but it was also far enough away from the busy lifestyle of living near Miami. He found the only drawback being the close proximity to neighbors. Fortunately, they didn't bother him too often. He hadn't spoken more than ten sentences to them since he moved in and their property was only a few feet away on either side.

As he opened the door to his Ford Taurus, he winced as the back of his neck met with the leather interior. The car was parked partially in the sunlight, and the hot rays had already absorbed into the seats. It was going to be a hot couple of days. On the news app on his smartphone, notifications were going off about storms arriving throughout the week. Michael hoped they would provide at least momentarily cooling relief from the heat wave that was torturing the area since mid July.

He started the car and pulled out of the driveway, careful to keep his neck away from the scorching leather chair until the AC had fully kicked on. By the time he whisked out of the neighborhood, he relaxed and leaned back, coasting slowly to admire the beautiful morning scenery along his commute.

Michael first moved to the Redland area of Miami ten years earlier, buying the small ranch home, a fixer-upper at the time, towards the back of a quaint neighborhood. He was really fond of the area, loving the tropical charm and the convenient location just south of the city, away from the nightlife that he had come to outgrow. For the first year, he lived in a bachelor pad studio apartment. But after Michael started the crocodilian refuge, he knew it would be a lifelong commitment and decided to make the move a little more permanent, tired of throwing away money on rent.

He turned left on the highway heading westward toward his facility which sat near the western edge of town, only a few miles from the eastern border of the Everglades. As he passed a fenced in vineyard to his right, Michael turned on the radio. The vintage tunes of Frank Sinatra's *My Way*, came crooning out of the speakers.

Mike listened for a little minute, before turning the radio to an AM station, catching a news report halfway through from NBC 6. He liked listening to current events before starting a work day. It made him feel more up-to-date.

"...victim has been identified as a Caucasian woman in her twenties, found where the other bodies had been recovered, deep in the Southern Glades. This marks the fourth victim of a crocodile or alligator related fatal attack this summer. Here is a brief interview earlier with Deputy William Bolasco at the scene where the body was discovered."

There was a short pause. The voice on the radio changed from female to male, and the audio now contained background noise that sounded like the rustling of boots over wet grass. The incessant hum of insects was heard swirling around the microphone, indicating it was somewhere in the wilderness.

"Well so far we have confirmed that it is an alligator or crocodile that's been responsible for the Everglades deaths over the summer," revealed the man named Bolasco.

Mike's eyes drifted over the dashboard, scanning over the swaths of swampland that rolled by to his right, nestled near a recently renovated apartment complex. He stared just long enough to catch a large brown limpkin take off in flight across the water. He scanned the watery surface for an alligator, as if to put a face to the monster in the radio broadcast, but found none.

"Is there anything else you're allowed to tell us about the situation?" a male reporter asked over the radio static.

"Well we suspect that the crocodile may be catching the victims on the nearby road in an ambush-style of attack and dragging them back here. There's no other reason that we can figure out why all these victims would be coming back to this remote area where their bodies are being discovered."

"That road's a pretty long distance off," the reporter stated.

"It is, yes," replied the officer. *"It's easily a mile, so we're dealing with a pretty strong predator. I'd advise anyone traveling through the Glades just south of Palm Grove to avoid walking near the swamp, especially near heavily dense areas where visibility is low."*

"What steps are you taking to defuse the situation?" the reporter asked.

"Well temporarily, again, we advise anyone traveling through the Southern Glades to be cautious and mind the edges of the roads if traveling by foot. I know the Palm Grove Police Department will be meeting throughout the week on the best course of action on how we're gonna deal with this. For now, all I can say is to be cautious of the wilderness."

"There is a rumor going around that this is some monster crocodile on the loose. A beast of mythical size. Is there any truth to that claim?"

There was a moment of silence before the officer spoke again.

"I'd be interested to know who the source was, and cannot confirm the legitimacy of those claims. All we know at this point is that the culprit is some kind of crocodilian, based on the bite marks and the way the bodies were found."

"What about the claim that the suspected croc is over twenty-five feet long?"

"As I've said. I'm not sure where these claims are coming from. I cannot confirm that at this time."

Mike glanced down at the radio screen in the console, as if watching the report on a television. The voice changed back to the female news anchor overseeing the report at the station. The news story reminded him of the films *Lake Placid* and *Blood Surf*, which both featured killer crocodiles of unfathomable size, leading to many fatalities and jump scares throughout the story lines.

Of course, neither of those films had any basis in reality. They were pure fiction, conceived to strike terror into viewers through typical Hollywood special effects and animations. Mike found himself smiling at the naivete of the news reporter for encouraging such a ridiculous concept. There were no Godzilla crocodilians in the Everglades. If there were, he would've known about it by now.

"Well, there you have it," replied the confident voice of the female news anchor. *"A fourth victim found in the Glades yesterday afternoon. Demonstrations will be taking place today outside the Palm Grove Police Department as growing unrest in the area continues to swell. A spokesperson for the demonstrations told NBC that the protests are primarily to put pressure on local law enforcement to act fast before another victim is discovered. I'm Audrey Donerson for NBC 6. Now, for*

local Miami traffic..."

"Monster crocodile," Mike said aloud, laughing to himself.

The reports were startling. Four deaths in the same area in the same season was serious, but the idea of a giant monster movie in Palm Grove made him roll his eyes. He remembered hearing something about these attacks weeks earlier on the radio, but was only half listening, shrugging them off as isolated incidents that couldn't possibly be related – especially from an animal that didn't exist.

Mike shrugged off the idea, turning the radio back just in time to hear the end of the next song before turning into the parking lot of his zoological sanctuary.

4
THE REDLAND CROCODILE SANCTUARY

The parking lot to the facility was nearly empty, as usual, except for a few of the employees' cars that were parked on the far side of the building. Michael saw that the front door was already unlocked and open. A tall black standing fan patrolled back and forth, cooling off the lobby. His receptionist, Sherry Williams, must have already arrived and begun the morning chores.

Mike parked his Taurus in his usual spot, far from the front of the building under a tall shady sabal palm on the edge of the parking lot. The tree provided adequate shade throughout the day, minimizing the scolding damage that his leather seats would inflict on him by the end of the afternoon. And on a beautiful sunny August day like this, the vehicle would be a sweatshop by day's end.

A refreshing breeze whipped into his shaggy hair as he approached the front of his business. The Redland Crocodilian Sanctuary was built on the site of an old pharmacy. At the time that Mike attained the property, he barely had enough funds to build one alligator pen. Thankfully, some grants came through, as well as some charitable handouts from the Redland community and generous lone benefactors. Within two years, the current welcome building was completed, and Michael hired a staff of nine employees to help him with his passion: saving crocodilians. The primary objective of the zoo was to help bring back Crocodylus acutus – the American crocodile – from its conservation status of 'vulnerable'.

The main facility seen from the road was merely the reception area for visitors who wanted to observe the animals. It was an octagonal-shaped modern building, harboring a small waiting room with brochures and takeaways, a small gift shop, an employee lounge and break room, and an overlook platform that looked out on the lower building and zoo, as well as the tangled terrain beyond. The front of the facility was built to mimic the sleek look of a museum, comprised of modern white large bricks and tall dark-tinted windows.

From there, the building fed down a hillside via an enclosed stairwell which led to Michael's office and the filing rooms. The lower offices looked out on the outdoor animal pens. There were six pens altogether; two for the American alligators, two for American crocodiles, and two for dwarf caimans, which were a relatively new venture to the facility. Each outside pen connected to an interior sanctuary with proper heating and cooling installed for the wildlife. All in all, the sanctuary would have been a hefty investment if not for the funding he received for his wildlife conservation efforts – funding he hoped would continue to roll through.

A white transparent gator icon awaited him on the frosted glass door that hung ajar. Mike eased through the opening, the wind of the fan whipping over his face.

The lobby itself was a work of art. All around the sides of the walls, stained bamboo stems bordered the white painted walls. Above, track lighting spotlighted various alligator drawings and finger paintings that children and schools had submitted, and were rotated out periodically to make room for more pictures. In the center of the room, behind the circular counter, stood a large fossilized skull of a juvenile gryposuchus. Gryposuchus was a large crocodilian that resembled a modern-day gharial, originating from South America during the prehistoric Miocene epoch. It had been the most expensive online purchase that Michael ever made, but proved to be well worth the investment. The fossil was a conversation piece among the visitors. Michael considered it a victory when his employees began to pronounce the extinct animal's name correctly.

His lively receptionist, Sherry, greeted him. He could smell her freshly brewed coffee.

"Hi, Sherry."

"Mike."

Sherry Werner was a jovial woman in her late fifties. She used to work as a librarian in Homestead, but applied for the sanctuary after becoming intrigued by Mike's job description on Indeed. In her pink flannel shirt and curly blonde hair, he thought she made a pleasant, friendly first sight when visitors stopped in. Michael was surprised to hear that she'd been through two marriages.

"Any calls yet?" Michael asked. "I was a little late in the shower this morning."

"Just the usual wrong number call for the Sunglass Store," she smiled.

Sunglass Store was a Miami chain. Unfortunately for Michael and his business, the number for the crocodile zoo and the major sunglasses

18

retail chain was very similar. Calls for sunglasses inquiries and cancellation orders were a daily occurrence. They were so frequent, that Michael considered utilizing a robotic answering service to inform potential callers about the correct number.

"When will that ever stop," Michael joked. "Is anyone else here yet? I thought I saw a few cars."

"Just Sandra and myself at the moment."

"Where's she at?"

"I think she's down in filing. Something about a mix up in one of our utility bills from another address. I'm not sure what she was talking about."

"Okay, I'll go touch base with her. Thanks, Sherry."

He stepped around the circular reception area and proceeded down the stairwell that fed deeper into his facility. The stairs emptied out into another hallway that led straight ahead into his office. Both sides of the hallway were lined with tall windows that looked out into the tropical hillside covered in palms. Michael often found himself scrubbing feverishly at the glass to keep it looking immaculate for the visitors. With the sleek corridor and lush surroundings, it made him feel like it was his very own Jurassic Park.

At the end of the scenic hallway, he heard the familiar clunking of filing cabinet drawers.

To his left, he could see the door to the filing room was open. He could see Sandra, trying to force one of the clunky old filing cabinet doors shut. The drawer was full. Additional filing cabinets would need to be acquired soon.

"Good morning, Mike," she said, stepping into the corridor and closing the door to the filing room.

"Hey," Michael replied with a hearty wave.

Sandra Castillo was a young Hispanic woman in her early twenties, studying Biology at the University of Miami. She started as part-time help last summer, helping Sherry answer phones and greet visitors. A few months into her employment, she requested that Mike let her help with some of the animals, although she was still hesitant involving their handling. These were opportunistic crocodilians, capable of snapping her like a twig if she wasn't careful. He thought about it for a while, but eventually let her help with feeding and cleaning the interior enclosures, once the animals were in the exterior pens. He agreed that she shouldn't directly handle them, being that they were too dangerous, and she happily understood Mike's reservations while acknowledging his gratitude.

"What's up? Sherry said something about a utility bill?" he asked.

"Yeah. It's Michael Robinson's chiropractic business down the street. It's another electric bill from them. I put it in the filing cabinet the other day to be paid, but when our actual bill came, I realized they screwed it up. Typical."

Mike laughed, impressed by her dedication to correcting her mistake.

There was a chiropractic firm down the road, with a Dr. Michael Robinson heading up the clinic. When the electric company billed the Redland Crocodilian Sanctuary, the statement was usually made out to Mike, leading to the mix up. It was a fluke that Michael had been lazy about correcting. The post office must have mismatched the bills.

"First the Sunglass Store, now the chiropractor," Michael laughed. "Thank you for going to retrieve it for me. I know our organization system isn't the best here. I'll drive this down to him after close of business."

"No problem," Sandra said. "Well, I think all the caimans in Pen 5 are in the outside enclosure. I'm gonna go see if I can sterilize the inside."

"Be careful," Michael warned. "They're pretty dark, sometimes it may seem like it's empty, but there may be a few stragglers. Even with the security lights on, it's still dark."

"I'll be careful; see you down there."

"See you soon," he called after her as she began to descend the stairwell that fed down to the outside gully to the animal exhibits. Mike pulled out his keys and unlocked the door to his office.

It was a large room, covered in textured wallpaper and various art prints of crocodilians. The tall windows that lined the hallway were also installed in the office, looking down to the American alligator enclosure and eventually out to the outlying houses of Redland.

Mike sat down in his chair, looking down at the landline that sat on the desk, grateful that the voicemail light wasn't flashing for once. After retrieving a generic soda drink from the mini fridge under his tabletop, he stood up again and observed the animals below.

Through the landscaping vegetation that had been planted along the hillside, he could see the American alligators wandering around in their muddy pen. One large male sauntered along in the moistened grass, stepping over a decorative log as the sprinkler system shot over its scales like a machine gun. The bulbous neck of the creature was so thick, it brushed against the faux wood. A few younger gators swam away nearby in a lagoon, staying out of reach from the approaching alpha male.

Buck was the twelve-foot-long alligator's name. Michael first rescued Buck from a canal up in Orlando a year earlier. The visitors frequently enjoyed when Michael would pull him out of his pen by the tail so Sandra could clean the interior enclosure. It was a show they would put on once a month which frequently drew a lot of spectators. What surprised the audience the most of the charade was how easy Michael would handle the gator. Buck was usually cooperative for the show, as long as he was fed a reward at the end, usually a large fish. The show was accompanied with lessons in alligator safety, facts, and teaching kids how to properly sound out the creature's complex scientific name: *Alligator mississippiensis.*

Buck continued to walk, eventually passing out of view behind a hedge of bushes just below Mike's office window. He quickly jotted down a note in his phone as a reminder to consider teaching Sandra how to subdue one of the gators in case he wasn't around in the event of an emergency, then decided Charlie might be a better choice based on his bravery. So far, the sanctuary had operated without incident. Mike intended to keep it that way. He shuddered at the idea of the potential liability ramifications if a crocodilian snapped on an employee – or a visitor for that matter.

Every enclosure was connected to an adjacent interior pen that the animals could transition between freely, which allowed the faculty to seal off either side from time to time for maintenance. Most of the pens were accessible through rear utility access hallways that ran around the back of the enclosures, inaccessible to visitors who could only move around through a decorative mulch trail that Michael had filled with information boards and crocodilian factual posters. Around the border of the zoo ran a tall board fence that Michael had erected years earlier. One of the sections was cracked partially from a fallen tree during the prior spring.

He cursed to himself for not fixing the crack sooner. Although there wasn't any danger of the crocodilians ever reaching the visitor trail to escape through the crack, Michael himself found it annoying that his employees poked fun at his laziness in repairing the damage. It really had become an eyesore, ruining the scenic experience by the alligator pen. He debated putting up a hedgerow in front of the fence, which might make that side of the sanctuary more visually appealing while also solving the problem of the crack. One day he overheard a few teenagers plotting to sneak in, using the crack as a step to hop the fence. Thankfully, they chickened out. He camped out near the gap in the fence that night, hoping to catch them, but no one jumped over.

Falling back into the chair, he waited for his computer to boot up and scanned the wall to the left. His diploma from the University of South Florida hung in a beautiful black frame just below the recess lighting, where he graduated with honors, receiving a Bachelor in Animal

Biology degree. Beside his degree hung another valuable, framed achievement: an official certificate from the Association of Zoos and Aquariums. This was the second time Michael earned the accreditation from the AZA. It was a process that had to be repeated every five years to stay accredited. It was essential for him to maintain his status. The grants and funding from the certificate were crucial to the continual survival of the sanctuary.

Michael liked to display his achievements. It was important to keep his motivation up and convince himself that the business would continue to thrive, despite the burdening costs of operation. After all, it was South Florida. Down there, people didn't have to go to a zoo to find alligators. They could just check their swimming pools.

He snapped to reality once he heard the static hum of Sherry's voice coming through the speaker on the landline.

"Hey, Mike. Heads up! A cop is here to see you. I've just sent him down."

Mike sat stunned for a minute like a deer in the headlights as if he had done something wrong – some unseen forgotten crime that had come back to bite him. The only time the sanctuary had a police visit was nearly two years earlier in September, when there was an armed robbery across the street.

He heard the boots clicking along the corridor just outside, briskly approaching his office. They stopped briefly, as a second shuffling of feet interrupted the visitor.

"Can I help you?" Mike heard Sandra say. She must have doubled back to ask him a question, Mike thought.

"I'm looking for Michael Robinson's office," came the male reply.

"Oh, right this way," Sandra said.

The officer's voice sounded familiar. Mike listened again as they approached, before scrolling through a website on his computer monitor in an attempt to look busy. His office door crept open, and Sandra's face slipped through.

"Mike, there is an officer, uh..."

"Berman," came the officer's muffled reply, just outside of Michael's view. "Jeff Berman."

"Ah. There is an officer named Jeff Berman to see you."

Sandra slipped back through the door, and a tall, athletic police officer stepped through into the office. That's where he'd heard the voice before.

"Hey, Mike," Berman began. "It's been a long time."

5
BERMAN

At first, Michael wasn't sure how to react. Seeing his old high school friend was like seeing the ghosts of the Marley brothers from The Christmas Carol.

Just in front of him, standing in the office in Michael's crocodilian refuge, was Jeffrey Berman. Berman was one of Michael's closest friends from his years at Miami Senior High School. Just the thought of realizing how far back it was since those days gave him a headache. How long had it been? Fifteen years? It had to be more than that. Time and life had made him forget.

He looked the officer over, realizing that he was even more in shape now than he was when he was playing high school football.

Age had been good to Berman. His defined arms seemed to contour perfectly to the officer's uniform. His chiseled jawline hung forward like a Roman centurion bust. Michael noted that his old friend still kept his primary hairstyle: pompadour. For a moment, Berman's senior picture in the yearbook came back to haunt him. A few awkward seconds had passed before Michael realized he hadn't said a word. He didn't want the officer to remember him as being rude during their impromptu reunion.

"Jeez, I'm sorry," Mike said after a long pause. "Hey, Jeff. It has been a long time, hasn't it?"

"Seventeen years."

Berman always had a sort of graceful cool about him, and he still maintained that confidence after all these years. His high school status as quarterback had solidified his status as a lady-killer. It was a reputation Michael assumed he carried into adulthood.

Michael, on the other hand, spent most of his time with his nose buried in the school science textbook. After school, his free-time had been spent earning volunteer hours at the nearest humane society. Weekends were even more hectic. Saturday and Sunday were usually a blur between catching up on homework and splitting up family time with his two divorced parents. There was hardly any room for chasing girls.

"Well, it's been a long time, Jeff. How have you been? Looks like

23

you've been taking good care of yourself. A police officer now? That's pretty great of you, Jeff."

Berman remained silent for a moment, striding slowly around the room like a ghostly specter while ignoring Michael's flattering comments. The officer was very interested in the wall art, or at least faked interest. He read over the diplomas and certifications on the wall, grinning in brevity at what he saw.

He paused after each framed qualification, mentally reading the print. Michael noticed that the officer took special interest in the zoo and crocodile related achievements.

"Looks like you've been doing well too, Mikey," Berman replied. He kept his hands in his pant pockets, except for his thumbs, which rested on top of the pocket opening. The stance reminded Michael of a 50's greaser or an old-fashioned gangster character like Marlon Brando.

There was a genuine tone in his voice. Berman was impressed by the amount of accreditation that Michael's zoo had earned. But at the same time, there was something else. A darker emotion – a bitterness perhaps.

"Well you know, just a few pieces of paper," Michael replied, trying to shrug off his life accomplishments as nothing important. But after the words came out, he was worried that they sounded too prideful. He was beginning not to like the meeting, feeling unprepared and vulnerable. He wished he would've known about Berman's arrival sooner. If he had prior knowledge about the reunion, he would've told Sherry to call him in a minute for an emergency meeting, forcing Berman to leave early.

"Just a few pieces of paper?" Berman asked, pointing to the wall. "It looks like you have quite a few important qualifications going on up here. What's this?"

The officer leaned forward, reading through one of the larger and more artful diplomas.

"An accreditation from Association of Zoos and Aquariums. I've never even heard of that. That sounds pretty important. You have it hung a little crooked, but still."

Michael shrugged, managing a slight smile and confused how to respond.

"You always were a humble son of a bitch, weren't you Mikey," Berman laughed, walking over to the window to study the roaming alligators below the hillside.

Michael wasn't sure how to read the officer's mannerisms. Was it a compliment or an insult? Against his better judgment, he decided it must have been a Berman compliment, satisfying both sarcasm and degradation.

"Yeah, the AZA. They're sort of a necessary accreditation for our business. We can secure grants and funding through their organization that would otherwise be difficult to get. Hopefully, we can maintain our accreditation with them."

"Shit!" Berman exclaimed, ignoring Michael's explanation. "Look at them go down there. They're hard to see from up here. What are they? Crocodiles?"

"Alligators actually," Michael corrected him. "American alligators."

Berman was watching another one of the larger female alligators, Olga, tear apart a fish that one of Mike's interns had thrown towards her from a secured window. Several other alligators waded over to the area, including Buck, who nearly pushed a few of the smaller ones aside as he stampeded happily towards the flying food.

"Like ravenous dinosaurs, if you ask me," Berman observed. "Look at them go."

"They like to eat, that's for sure," Mike replied, watching the alligators converge at the feeding platform.

"Do you have any other kinds of alligators here, Mikey?"

"No, just American alligators. The only other kind would be the Chinese alligator, which are very endangered at this point. It would be tough to get one of them here. They're practically extinct in the wild and from another part of the world, so I'm sure the conservation laws would be very strict in owning one. But I've thought about looking into it."

Berman nodded, keeping his eyes at the enclosure below.

"What's the biggest one you have?"

"At the moment, the largest alligator is Buck. He's a twelve footer. The visitors tend to like him. The bigger and scarier, the more they love them, or so it seems."

The intern, a young male teenager named Charlie who was one of Michael's more recent hires, skittishly tossed the food towards the hordes of hungry jaws that snapped around him. Eventually, the teen relaxed once he realized that the bars prevented the alligators from snagging onto him. The sounds of the clamping primeval teeth still made the youth a little nervous, before Michael saw him relax and shrug off the carnivorous chomping, trying to put on a tough guy act.

"Well, that's sort of what I wanted to talk to you about, Mike."

Finally, Michael thought. There was some point to Berman's visit after all.

"You mean you didn't drive all the way up here to swap high school stories?" Michael joked, taking a seat at his desk.

"Not exactly," Berman said with a trace of seriousness as he stepped away from the window and back toward the office doorway. "I'm sure you've been following the news down in Palm Grove. Or at least, you must've heard a little about it, right? Our little problem in the Everglades."

"A little," Michael confessed. "The crocodilian killings in the Southern Glades. They're starting to become a big problem down there, from what I heard on the news this morning. Another victim. I hear the people are starting to worry."

"Correct," Berman said. "Anyway, my sheriff got to sniffing around the internet and found your business profile on Indeed or one of those websites. He wants you to come down and meet with him, given your expertise in dealing with these creatures and their habitat. Obviously, we know a little bit about gators from various house calls and golf course run-ins, but not much about crocodiles. We suspect this may be the work of a large American crocodile."

"An American crocodile? And what's leading you to assume that?"

"Just the size of the tracks we found near the latest attack," Berman replied. "They were fairly large. Plus the fact that the area towards the edge of the state is known for the presence of crocodiles."

"Right. American crocodiles inhabit the bottom edge of Florida in sparse areas. It's the only state you'll find them in. How big were these tracks?"

"Well, I wasn't really –"

"Are there any crocodile nesting sites near the area where the body was found? What is your long-term plan with these attacks?"

"Look, Mike," Berman cut in, impatient and slightly annoyed, "I'm just the messenger. The sheriff's the one that suggested that we consult an expert, and you're the first name that popped up on his web search, so you've got the golden star for now. He wants you to meet with him right away, preferably today if you have time. For now, I'm just the errand boy. I can drive you down to Palm Grove, if you'd like."

For a second, Mike felt a slight glimpse of their former rivalry returning. He frowned. The officer's abrupt agitation told him that Berman was still scarred from their past. Their bygones hadn't become bygones after all.

"Today I have a pretty busy schedule," Michael said bluntly. "As much as I'd love to help you with your case, Jeff, there are a few managerial duties I have to get done. We have several enclosures that are in need of some housekeeping. I think the new caiman might be arriving today and there's a summer youth trip that's planning a –"

"Mike, hey Mike! You up here?"

A youthful shouting rang out from the hallway. Charlie ran into the room, knocking over the waste basket in his careless flight, almost crashing into the police officer in his clumsiness. Berman caught and steadied him before the teen collided into anything else.

"Shit, Charlie! What?"

Michael could sense the distress in his voice. Something was wrong.

"It's Sandra!" Charlie sputtered out. "One of the adult caimans has her cornered in Pen 5!"

6
CUVIER'S DWARF CAIMAN

Charlie led them down the stairwell from Mike's office to the enclosures. Mike couldn't help but think, thank God there aren't any visitors here yet. A trapped, frantic employee was all he needed for anyone to see. They'd probably stream it all over social media.

The quickest route down to the caiman pens were the farthest from the lobby. They sprinted out of the hallway that emptied out below the stairwell, into the harsh blinding sunlight of mid-morning. The fresh mulch trail that Mike replenished himself laboriously weeks before wound through the pens like a nature park, taking them past the various crocodile and alligator pens. He led them past more small sitting areas and a lunch pavilion, to a decorative cavern with fake cave paintings. Behind a patch of jungle fronds, Michael flipped open a hidden access panel and punched in a clearance code. A hidden door opened into a utility hallway, leading into the managing entrances to each crocodilian pen.

Once Berman shut the door behind them, Mike could hear Sandra's screams reverberating through the dim passage. They raced around the corner, passing under a large sign that read: Cuvier's Dwarf Caiman – Pen 5. The door to the pen was open.

"Sandra!" Mike called out. "Sandra, we're here!"

They ran into the interior pen. Beside him, Mike could feel Berman tense up, placing a hand on his service pistol in his holster.

Sandra Castillo was trapped against the far wall.

Sinclair, a medium-sized male Cuvier's dwarf caiman was feet away from her, jaws raised in an aggressive stance as it slowly approached. Sandra trembled, scooting along the concrete wall, hoping to reach the exit where the others were waiting. Sinclair countered, stepping to the left as if to head her off. Like a bear trap, the jaws snapped shut and then open again, making Sandra quickly second guess her strategy before backing up again to the corner.

Cuvier's dwarf caimans were first noted in 1807 by Frenchman

Georges Cuvier. They were the smallest of the crocodilians in the Western Hemisphere. Normally praised as being not as aggressive as their larger crocodilian counterparts, Sinclair was one of the more temperamental males in Michael's zoo. Unfortunately, Sandra caught him in one of his mood swings.

Several other caimans congregated towards the sealed entrance, attracted to the commotion inside but powerless to investigate further than the glass barrier allowed.

"I'm sorry, Mike," Sandra cried, her voice quivering. "I was in here cleaning and it just happened. I think he must have been waiting inside one of the pools. They're pretty hard to see through, even with the lights on. Gosh, I don't know why he's being so nasty."

She could barely keep it together. Her voice rose and fell, as each step from the caiman encouraged more yelps, more tears.

"It's okay, Sandra," Mike said in a soothing voice. "Caimans are mostly nocturnal. Maybe he didn't get enough sleep last night."

It was a poor attempt at a joke, but it made Sandra smile, which was all Mike wanted. She needed a distraction, a momentary relief from the horrific situation.

"Mike, do something!" Charlie ordered in a panicking voice.

Charlie had to go – Michael had already made up his mind. Having him around was tiresome and nerve-wracking. The kid had a mouth on him, and only momentary respect for adults and authority figures. Michael regretted hiring him, but couldn't find a good enough excuse yet to let him go. Now he felt stuck with the teen. At least today he proved himself useful in alerting Michael to the caiman situation.

"Charlie, go up to Sherry and tell her to stall if there's any more customers. Gently tell her the situation, and not to admit anyone in until it's resolved."

"Are you serious? Mike, by the time I get up there, we could –"

"Charlie. This isn't a debate. Do as you're told."

"*Ugh,* okay," Charlie grunted in agreement, running out the door and back out into the zoological courtyards.

"It's okay, Sandra. Sometimes Sinclair gets like this. He's very much an alpha male, I think he's just trying to show some strength since you probably woke him up from a nap. Adult caimans can be hard to control once they're riled up."

"Shit, Mikey, I have my SIG," Berman pressed him. "I can end this pretty quick..."

"No!" Mike replied angrily.

He wasn't sure why the officer had suggested such an action, especially when police routinely helped solve crocodilian problems without using lethal force.

"I can resolve this myself, Jeff."

"Okay, Mike," the officer scoffed.

Sinclair snapped his gaping jaws again, thrashing his head once to both sides, making sure Sandra was stuck against the corner. The caiman had no intention of letting his target escape, studying the way she moved, pivoting to keep her guessing and disoriented.

"Mike," Sandra mumbled uneasily.

"Okay, hang tight. Here I come."

He eased along the wall, slowly approaching Sinclair from the side. Behind him, he could feel Berman watching with interest. Mike could hear the officer's hand coming off the SIG holster as the deputy leaned back and watched the spectacle unfold.

When Michael appeared in Sinclair's view, the caiman turned to the left, away from Sandra and towards the newcomer. He waved his hand along the wall, telling Sandra to sneak out the other way. She eased out of the corner, slowly at first, before bolting out of the way, past the caimans who snarled on the other side of the glass barrier to the outside. She ran past Berman to the corridor, where she stopped behind the officer who continued to observe the encounter.

Sinclair snapped once at Michael, who jumped back once to avoid the crocodilian rows of jagged teeth. Once the mouth closed, he grabbed down on the snout, preventing Sinclair from lashing out again. The caiman thrashed its head back and forth, before finally accepting the situation.

"Wow, Mike," Sandra said. "You did that so fast."

"Watch out," Michael said, pivoting and backing up slowly. "He'll try to snap at me once I let go. He's got a mean temper today."

Once he heard Berman and Sandra backing out into the hallway, he let go of the caiman, quick enough to avoid another bite as they dashed back into the outer hall and sealed the entrance. Behind the door, they watched through the bars as Sinclair approached, agitated at their escape. The caiman turned, whipping his tail against the door before wading back into the pool as if to triumphantly admit he scared them away,

"I'm sorry," Sandra apologized, wiping her eyes with her shirt. "He just kind of jumped out at me. I thought all of them were in the outer pen."

"Don't worry about it, kid," Mike said, patting her back to calm her down. "It's happened to me a handful of times. Hell, just last week. The trick is to approach from the front, where their eyes can't see you as well. Once they have you from their side view, they know you're there. Take a break to calm down. I'll be up to check on you in a bit, okay?"

"Thanks, Mike."

"No problem. Here. Here's a buck for the break room. Get yourself a Diet Coke. I know how much you love those."

She accepted the dollar and waved goodbye, walking back out into the exterior mulch trail and heading back to the entrance building. When the door shut behind her, Michael exhaled in relief. Another micro-crisis averted. That could have been disastrous.

"Well Mikey," Berman said. "I must admit, I'm impressed. You're definitely the right man for the job. Please, let me escort you down to Palm Grove and we can figure out this whole mess of shit we've got ourselves in –"

"I don't know, Jeff," Michael interrupted. "Are you sure I'm the man your sheriff is looking for? I know a thing or two about crocodilians in captivity, but I'm certainly no Steve Irwin."

"Well the boss is expecting me to deliver someone who has some expertise," Berman went on. "If I show up empty handed, he's not gonna be happy. Please Mikey. Just a consultation. I'll even buy you lunch after the meeting. If I remember correctly, you were a sucker for a hot dog. There's a good place I know right down from the police department."

Mike hesitated for a second, finally giving in. Maybe he could be of some help after all.

"Well, I do love a good hot dog."

7
UNREST

It took about half an hour to drive down from Redland to Palm Grove. Michael told Sherry that he would be taking an early lunch break that might run long, leaving immediately with Berman in his squad car. She seemed worried about the officer's sudden visit, but he assured her that there was nothing to worry about, dismissing her anxiety without delving into all the details about why he had to hurry off to Palm Grove. Sherry understood, making a note that any appointments that Michael had that day had to be moved back or canceled altogether.

During the drive, Berman was surprisingly quiet, refusing to divulge any additional information about the case.

After a few unanswered inquisitive comments, Michael got the hint and tried to shift the subject, making a few jokes about their high school days, which Berman usually responded with a brief courtesy laugh, that encouraged neither friendliness nor camaraderie. One topic that did come up was the good times in study hall, where Michael first met Berman when he tutored the star football player in freshman science.

"You were always a whiz at bio," Berman noted in brevity.

Finally, Michael thought, happy that the officer was finally engaging in conversation. Berman's participation would make the drive go faster.

"Hey, when you got the hang of it, you were pretty good," Michael replied. "We brought your score up two whole letter grades in just a few weeks. Remember?"

"I still hate the proteins," Berman grunted. "What a boring lecture and an even more boring reading assignment."

With a slight turn, the car exited the off ramp and proceeded into a more rural area. As Berman pulled the police cruiser around a tall monument and through an intersection, Michael noticed the sign: **Palm Grove – Welcome to the Edge of the Sunshine State.** The community had been using their southward location on the mainland as an interesting tagline, cleverly ignoring that the Florida Keys were the actual edge of

Florida.

He remembered traveling through the downtown area of Palm Grove a handful of times since he moved to Redland, usually for day-long vacations or for backpacking excursions through hiking trails in the Everglades. The town was a snapshot of small town America, consisting of a main street with little shops and markets, accompanied with outlying suburban neighborhoods and rural communities that ran up to the jungle's edge.

He recalled reading a Crocodilian information book from the Palm Grove Library one time before a dinner date, finding it interesting how the author described the hunting rituals of caiman and gharials in the wild. Coincidentally, he wished that he would've skipped the date and kept reading.

But visiting with Berman after all these years was shockingly not as brutal as Michael thought. The reunion itself wasn't terrible – just one-sided comments from Michael's part with moments of awkward long silences. But thankfully, throughout their ride, the police officer hadn't mentioned their lengthy feud that began nearly twenty years ago during their senior year, which resulted in their permanent severance of their friendship.

A few times throughout the years, Michael had tried to bury the hatchet and reconnect with Berman, but his friend was nearly a ghost. He didn't even have a Facebook account or a Twitter profile, which in today's day and age meant you were practically off the grid. Additionally, Berman wasn't at any of the high school reunions despite his immense popularity of years gone by.

As they drove down Main Street, Michael noticed a large band of people congregating near an intersection, armed with crudely made picket signs with gripping statements sharpied onto construction paper.

"Great," Berman commented in agitation. He drove the vehicle slowly, inching the car closer to the protesting mob. "I didn't expect this shit to have such a big turnout."

The bulk of the protest was calm and bound to the sidewalk, but there were a few pockets of brave kids that stepped closer to the road, hoping to get a reaction from passing cars while impressing their friends. A few of the younger protesters noticed the officer approaching and pointed, yelling complaints and waving their custom signs. A few of their friends took note and spun their signs to face Berman's car. The traffic light above changed red, forcing the officer to brake right in front of the intersection.

"Perfect," Berman frowned.

Two protesters crossed the street, sprinting over the crosswalk. They hovered outside Michael who was sitting in the passenger seat, failing miserably at avoiding their eye contact. The first protester swung her sign in front of his window, which featured a detailed marker illustration of a crocodile chewing on a police SWAT vehicle. The vehicle was lodged in the creature's jaws, with the officers falling out the back of the vehicle to the ground below. Palm Grove was in the background and foreground, depicting the animal in the center as a crocodile of unfathomable kaiju-like proportions.

The protester continued to repeat her waving motion, swinging it back and forth inches from Michael's face on the other side of the glass. When Michael refused to react to the sign, the protester angrily brushed her red hair over her shoulder and resumed pushing the sign up to the window.

"Wow, Jeff," Michael said, turning slowly to admire the signage artwork, fixating on the hideous yet telling illustration. "It's really hit the fan down here. Looks like you got one hell of a problem."

"Yeah, it would seem that way," Berman answered, coasting through the intersection as the light finally turned green. "Reminds me of Frankenstein, towards the end of the film when the villagers got their torches and pitchforks. These pricks are out for blood down here."

Michael could see his former friend turning red in the face in anger. A vein bulged in the officer's thick neck. His fingers rasped impatiently at the steering wheel, and his muscles under his blue shirt flexed. Berman was getting frustrated. Michael wasn't sure if it was better to be in the car or out with the protesters.

"Is that the police station they are around up ahead?" Michael asked in an attempt to get the officer to relax. "I think I heard a little bit about this on the radio this morning if I remember correctly."

"Yeah," came a dull reply. "That's our home base."

Berman left the first two protesters behind, cruising past the centralized mob that converged on the police barracks. Most of the ruffians were younger, probably in high school. Several were middle-aged adults or parents, and two or three were retirees. A trio of male teenagers stepped onto the street as the car flew past, swearing and raising their signs in a show of defiance.

"When will they stop, officer?" a charismatic young voice called out. "When will the killings stop? What is Palm Grove PD doing to stop it?"

The voice melted away as the cop roared past.

"They act as if we're just sitting on this whole case," Berman stated. "Meanwhile, we're going over the countless options on how we're planning to deal with this. It's not like we can just ride right into the swamp, identify the killer croc, and get it the hell out of here. I can't wait until those little shits are back in school in a few weeks. No respect for law enforcement. And it gets worse with every passing generation."

Michael sensed that his former friend's years in law enforcement had taken a toll on the officer's approach to coping with civilian unrest. The arch of Berman's brow was evident in his disdain for unruly crowds and ballsy teenagers. He shuddered at the thought of how Berman might deal with actual criminals.

Berman whipped the cruiser to the right, taking a narrow road bordered with thick hedges which fed back to the rear of the barracks to a hidden police parking lot.

The lot was edged out on all sides from the outside world, sometimes with the tall hedgerow and in other areas with a border wall. The noises of the crowd were nearly muted to silence with all the barriers in place. Michael contemplated quietly having a similar wall built around his facility for additional animal security and peace of mind. It would probably work a lot better than his board fence, which was already showing signs of dilapidation.

Berman pulled up to an empty spot near the rear entrance and shifted the car to park. Several police officers stood nearby smoking cigarettes, offering a wave to him as he pulled in. He reciprocated with a firm courtesy nod, although his face indicated he was still annoyed by the volatile mob that besieged the front of the barracks.

"Finally, peace and quiet," he said to Michael, unbuckling his seat belt and turning the engine off. "Okay. The sheriff's office is up on the next floor, towards the front of the building. I'll walk you up."

8
TALES FROM THE EVERGLADES

When he walked through the first floor of the Palm Grove Police Department, Michael noted the curiosity of several of the officers as he walked past, as if he was the answer to all their problems. A few of the secretaries and dispatchers looked up as Berman led him past, gossiping to themselves before resuming their tasks. As they passed through, Michael could feel their eyes burning through his back as they entered the adjacent hallway.

"Sorry," Berman mumbled as they entered the stairwell. "Everyone's just really anxious to have the problem down here resolved. It's got the whole town up in arms, if you couldn't tell."

"No kidding, Jeff. Damn, these killings have really torn the place apart."

They arrived on the second floor, navigated down another short hallway past some police awards, wall decorations, and gun manufacturer artwork, to another room filled with more officers and detectives working at their desks. The size of the small town's police force impressed Michael – for such a small community, there really were a good amount of law enforcement officials.

Berman weaved through the tables to the far end where glass windows covered in blinds ran wall to wall. The word **Sheriff** was printed in gold lettering on the door. Through the blinds, Michael could see a dim lamp light glowing on a tabletop and the silhouetted movements of at least two men moving over some paperwork.

Berman knocked once, and a brief, "come in" was heard inside the room. Twisting the knob, the officer opened the door and courteously let Michael inside.

The sheriff's office seemed cold. The room was large and dark. Two tall shelving units bordered the right wall, covered in paperwork and old books, most of them encyclopedias or documentation binders. A large brown area rug covered most of the hardwood floor, weighed down by two men and a large desk that sat in the center. The men were bent down under an office lamp, staring at papers and glossy images that were scattered over the oak tabletop. Michael immediately recognized them as crime scene photographs taken by a skilled forensic photographer.

Most of the pictures contained graphic imagery of severed body parts and gnawed off limbs that sat neglected in grass and weeds, staining the greenery with a sinister red coating. They were so grisly, he found that he couldn't look away. From the bite marks alone, he identified the killer immediately as a crocodilian.

"Sheriff," Berman introduced, stepping through the doorway. "This is the man you requested. Michael Robinson. He owns and operates the little zoo up in Redland. He knows his stuff about crocodilians."

"Hey, Mike," the bigger man from behind the table said, stepping around to offer a handshake. "I hope you don't mind me calling you Mike. I'm Sheriff Jacob Dawson. This is Officer William Bolasco. We're glad you've come."

"Mike's fine," Michael said, shaking their hands. "It's a pleasure to meet you both. I hope I can be of service."

"Do you need me, sir?" Berman asked, about to leave the room.

"Yeah, Jeff," the sheriff answered. "Why don't you sit in on this meeting. I have a feeling you'll be a key player in the operation we've cooked up, seeing as how you and Michael are already acquainted."

"Okay," Berman replied, closing the door.

Judging by his demeanor, Michael guessed that his ex-friend would rather be anywhere else.

Bolasco gave Michael his seat, pulling another chair out from the corner of the room beside him. The sheriff walked around the table to his own chair. Berman stood in the corner, rigidly watching over the meeting, visibly uncomfortable and yearning for an excuse to leave.

"How was the drive down?" Sheriff Dawson asked, plopping down against the leather.

Sheriff Jacob Dawson reminded Michael of the stereotypical sheriff actors that were cast in old John Wayne western films. He wore a red flannel shirt, despite the grueling heat wave that lingered over Florida. The shirt was tucked in under his braided brown belt, exposing and accentuating his beer gut. A curly gray mustache adorned his upper lip, bouncing like a cartoon character when he spoke. The sheriff's leather boots even resembled a cowboy's, minus the spurs.

"Good and quick," Michael replied. "The protesters kind of freaked me out a little bit, to be honest. They are very passionate people. I think I can still hear them, actually."

"You can," Dawson laughed, pointing over his shoulder. "These windows behind me look down on Main Street. Most of the demonstrators have chosen that area to belly-ache. They should be gone soon, they've been out there an hour already. Kids never stay focused for long. They always get bored and trickle out before too long. Plus, there's no Wi-Fi there."

"School just won't start soon enough," Bolasco laughed, shifting in his chair and resting one leg over a knee.

"So, a crocodile sanctuary?" Dawson smiled. "Pretty neat. Where did that idea come from?"

"It's just something I've always wanted to do," Michael answered, happy that the sheriff had shown an interest in his small wildlife business. "As you know, the American crocodile has come a long way in recent years, making a comeback in Florida after their encounter with regional extinction some fifty years back. When I graduated from college, I had a dream of doing what I could to help them continue their comeback, by offering them a shelter and a place to repopulate. It only seemed natural to include other crocodilians too – alligators and caimans. We're working on getting gharials there too, which are currently listed as critically endangered, so that might be a little difficult."

"Ah, I see," Dawson smiled. "So you raise crocodiles too?"

"Yes," Michael replied. "One of the crocodile pens actually has a small nesting site. It's really spectacular. It's magical when they hatch."

"And you release them into the wild then?"

"Usually," Michael replied. "A few adults are permanent residents. Some of the young we keep behind if we discover they have health issues that require veterinary attention."

"Ever run into any accidents there?" Bolasco asked.

"Accidents? Like what?"

"You know. Wildlife accidents regarding visitors. Like what happened in Pittsburgh a few years back."

It took Michael a moment to remember what the officer was referring to.

In 2012, a young boy fell into an African painted dogs exhibit at the Pittsburgh Zoo where they mauled him to death before help could arrive. The incident resulted in nationwide bad press coverage for the Pittsburgh Zoo as well as the end of the African painted dogs exhibit.

"Well no where near as severe as that," Michael elaborated. "All my exhibits are completely inaccessible to visitors. The Pittsburgh situation was different. That boy fell from an overlook platform. I don't have any overlook platforms – just glass windows and metal fencing. But yeah, minor things will happen. Just today, around the time Jeff arrived, we had a situation with a caiman and one of our employees. When it comes down to it, they are wild animals and can become aggressive. But that's part of the fun."

"What do you mean a 'situation'?" Bolasco asked.

"The caiman was trying to corner her," Michael admitted. "Fortunately, I arrived and distracted the animal so she could run to safety. I'm not blaming her in any regards, but she wasn't careful enough when she entered the pen. Normally, I only send employees into pens if they're empty. I trusted that all the caimans were outside, so I didn't mind. However, one was left inside and I think she may have startled it, triggering its aggression. In the long run though, I'm sure she would've darted past when she had to – she was just really shaken up. Cuvier's dwarf caimans are actually very popular and are kept as pets, did you know? They go for about four hundred a pop when they're just juveniles."

Dawson nodded with a small smile, hidden mostly by the imposing mustache.

"I didn't know that, Michael," he said. "That's actually pretty interesting."

"Isn't it?" Michael said. "I've considered buying one myself, but then again, I deal with them all day long so I'm already getting the experience."

"We know all about aggressive crocodiles," Dawson said, leaning back.

"I've heard," Michael answered. "Another victim, found yesterday if I recall?"

"Dental records should be back sometime in fall," Dawson went on. "Pretty girl in her twenties. Can't get it out of my head. What have you heard so far?"

"Well, that it was the fourth victim," Mike replied. "Most of what I know is just what the reports say on the news. That a large crocodile, or at least they suspect a crocodile, somewhere in the Southern Glades seems to be picking off the Palm Grove residents. To be frank, I haven't heard really anything more. Jeff didn't say much today, just that you need some expertise, and I'm the top pick thus far, of which I'm grateful."

"So far, we've only identified one of the four victims, and we'd like to stop the animal's body count at the fourth. We have pinpointed the purported hunting area to a several mile radius in the Glades. Although, I'm not sure we're dealing with the traditional crocodile here."

"What makes you say that?"

Dawson slipped Michael a few photographs. One of the pictures was the image taken the day before: the size comparison of Bolasco standing beside the large footprint, with his hand hovering over the indentation. Michael studied the image carefully, trying to mentally measure the size of the croc based on the width of the footprint. Whatever had made the print was certainly an apex predator – an animal of record size in Florida, if not worldwide.

"I still can't believe how big that thing was," Bolasco said, pointing over Michael's shoulder at his picture. "Can you imagine how big that sucker is in real life? If that's its feet, shit, what's the body like?"

"So you don't think this is an American crocodile?" Michael asked. "What are you basing that on? The size of the prints alone?"

"Well, we were hoping you could tell us," Dawson told him, pointing at the image. "I'm not a zoologist by any means, but that looks larger than any crocodile I've ever seen. If I didn't know any better, I'd say it was made by a dinosaur, let alone a crocodile."

Bolasco snapped his fingers and pointed at the sheriff, signaling in agreement with a smirk on his face.

"Unlikely," Michael laughed, glancing back at the sheriff and then again at the photo. "But I see your point. The animal is huge, no question about it."

"Well it can't be a typical crocodile?" Bolasco interjected. "No crocodile I know leaves tracks like that."

"An American crocodile is the only thing that I know of in Florida that leaves tracks like that," Michael argued, looking at the photo again. "I see it walked over a muddy bank. It's possible that the ground gave way on the sides, making the track seem larger. I still say it's a crocodile."

"Here is another picture we captured, this one from another area at the same crime scene."

Dawson handed Michael another photograph, this time taken from a professional grade camera. Three large crocodilian tracks stumbled along a sandy shore. In the background, a few police officers were seen rooting through the weeds, presumably looking for evidence. Based on the size of the officers in the photo, Michael confirmed that the tracks were made from the same animal.

"I've been doing some research on crocodilians," Bolasco went on. "Did you know there used to be massive crocodiles here, like back in dinosaur times. I think it was called a sarco-something. I figured that has to be what we're dealing with – as ridiculous as it sounds."

Michael resisted rolling his eyes. The cop wouldn't let the far-fetched child-like dinosaur theory go.

"Sarcosuchus," Michael corrected him. "And that's impossible. Sarcos have been extinct since the Cretaceous period. Also, they were from South America and Africa, not Florida. It's more likely that it'd be a Deinosuchus, since they actually were large prehistoric crocodilians that roamed the coast of Florida. They were apex predators with a bite force that could rival a tyrannosaur. But again, impossible. They've been extinct for millions of years, never crossing paths with mankind."

Michael paused, looking around the room. He realized the detectives were hanging onto his every word, intrigued by his knowledge of crocodiles, even ones that went extinct.

"And you don't think what we're dealing with is a dinosoochoos, do you?" Dawson said, butchering the word. The sheriff was smiling. Michael could tell he didn't really believe it was a prehistoric crocodile, but entertained the idea for comedic purposes.

"Deinosuchus, no," Michael replied, smiling at the sheriff's futile attempt at the word.

"Well what the hell could it be?" Dawson asked. "Some kind of mutated alligator, like from that old 1980's movie?"

"My guess is still an American crocodile," Michael replied, handing the photo back to the sheriff. "Albeit a large one. If captured, it might be the largest one on record."

"So there's no chance it could just be some kind of overgrown alligator?" Berman asked from over Mike's shoulder.

Michael had forgotten that he was back there. He had been quiet, observing without engaging.

"No way," Michael answered. "The largest of the species are the males, which usually top out at fifteen feet. I think the largest ever found was around sixteen feet. This animal is way bigger, maybe twenty-five feet, I'm guessing. Definitely closer in size to an American crocodile, which is the only other crocodilian in the Everglades, that we know of. And this would be a mammoth sized crocodile."

"Regardless of whatever it is, it needs to go," Dawson went on.

"What do you mean, go?" Michael asked.

Bolasco held up his fingers, making a gun shape and cocking the thumb back.

"You can't kill it," Michael said firmly. "If it was an alligator, you could kill it. But American crocodiles are closer to extinction, nearly endangered. Last I checked, they were listed as vulnerable by the Conservation of Nature, thus making the species protected from poaching. I suppose your only option is to find it, tranq it and relocate it."

"I was afraid you'd say that," Bolasco remarked, lowering the finger gun. "This town's gone bat shit crazy over the killings. You see that mob? They're demanding blood."

"Completely off the table," Michael snapped, turning to the deputy. "I certainly won't be a part of it."

He could feel the blood rushing to his head in a rush of adrenaline.

The officer didn't seem to care about the severity of killing vulnerable species. In some cases, the offense would be punishable by prison time and severe fines. And that wasn't taking into account the environmental impact and the ripple effects that could occur after the species was wiped out. Other problems would arise, affecting both the animal kingdom and the human population.

"No one's killing the croc," Dawson assured him, waving a reassuring dismissive hand. "But the attacks really have stirred the pot around here. They started right after the fourth of July and keep coming every week or so."

"Any idea why?" Michael asked, easing back after the sheriff assured that they wouldn't be pursuing lethal force.

"My guess is our added presence in the Southern Glades. We are expanding the Palm Grove residential community at the southern edge of town. A few housing cul-de-sacs have been under construction there for a year, after years in development and bureaucratic hell. Supposedly, the project should be completed by the end of next summer."

"They're calling it Sunset Ridge," Bolasco added. "It's going to be a really beautiful development when complete. A few residents have already moved in."

"And this housing development is near the attack sites?"

"Yes," Dawson replied. "The properties are only a few miles away through the jungle. Also, there's the highway that cuts through nearby, connecting the mainland to the Florida Keys. We figure the animal has a territory that potentially reaches across both areas, adding to our problems."

"But we're assuming it's mainly the housing development," Bolasco added.

"I'd say that's a fair guess," Michael said. "Continuing urbanization may have pushed the animal further into the Glades. It may feel compelled to defend its new territory, given that you've already pushed it to the edge of the state with countless other crocodilians. It probably feels cornered. Now it has other crocodilians to compete with, adding pressure to the natural balance."

"We've shut down any hiking trails and game lands in the region until the situation is resolved," Bolasco said. "We're working on patrolling the waterways too, informing fishermen of the problem. Hopefully, there won't be any more victims until we bag the bastard."

"So it seems the consensus is to tranq it?" Dawson asked.

"It's the only option," Michael said.

"If we can get you to the general vicinity where the attacks happen, can you track the animal?"

"Tracking would be hard, especially in a wetland area like the Everglades," Michael confessed. "Most of the area is underwater and uneven. The best bet would be to take a scouting party out where the attacks occur. If you run into the animal, you might be able to follow it on land and get a clean shot."

"That's what we've settled on just before you arrived," Dawson said. "Tomorrow at noon, we will be heading out to the area with a small fleet. We were hoping you could come with us. Sorry for the short notice, but it needs resolving. I'm already having to talk a few of my guys out of transferring out of Palm Grove. The pressure from the local community is starting to wear on them."

"Well, I'd be glad to, Sheriff," Michael said. "But I'm not sure how much more I can be of service, other than providing you with a few mundane crocodile facts. Honestly, I've never tracked a wild croc before."

"We just feel more confident with someone who knows a few things," Dawson told him. "Already you saved us a few lawsuits from killing the damn thing. And when we find it, and we better find it, we're gonna need somewhere to transport it. What are the odds of us storing it at your sanctuary? I'd ask someone else, but Redland is the closest place that I know of. Consider it a payment for your services – having a record length American crocodile at your zoo. What do you think, Mr. Robinson?"

"I'd love to have it there," Michael said, his voice rising slightly with excitement as he jumped at the opportunity.

The thought of having a record-breaking American crocodile at his facility would be a crowning achievement as a zookeeper. The countless advertising and marketing opportunities that would come along with owning such an animal soared through his mind. The revenue potential would be endless.

"You're sure you'd have room for it there?" Bolasco asked.

"Most certainly," Michael answered automatically. "I suppose I could probably move the caimans from one pen to another, giving the croc the whole pen to itself, assuming throwing him into any of the other pens would be disastrous for my other animals. At least, until I can get the funding to build another pen."

"Okay, so you're onboard?"

"As long as killing the croc is off the table, then I'm on board one hundred percent," Michael said with confidence.

"Fantastic," the sheriff said, extending another courtesy handshake. "Berman here will escort you back to Redland. Berman, please have him here tomorrow no later than 10 a.m. We're going to be heading down to the dock at 11, and I hope to be at the creature's territory by 12. In the meantime, Bolasco, do a weapons check tonight on our tranquilizer guns and nets. Make sure we're all ready to go before you leave tonight."

"Yes, sir," Bolasco said, rising from his chair. "Good to meet you, Mr. Robinson. And welcome aboard."

"You too," Michael replied, shaking his hand again.

Bolasco hurried out of the room, stepping around Berman and shutting the door behind him.

"Well, that concludes the meeting," Dawson announced. "On behalf of Palm Grove, we thank you Mr. Robinson. Have a good night, and see you tomorrow morning. Hopefully, this won't take more than one day of your time and a few mosquito bites."

9
THE NIGHT BEFORE

The streetlights were beginning to blink on when Berman dropped Michael off at the Redland Crocodilian Sanctuary. Most of the lights in the facility were off, except for the exterior security lights which he had mounted near all the corners. All of the employees' cars had vacated the area. Michael checked his phone, showing no calls or texts from Sherry and assumed the rest of the day went smoothly.

He waved goodbye to Berman who zipped past, flying back to the highway responding to another call. After the meeting with Dawson and Bolasco, the two grabbed lunch at a local restaurant in Palm Grove called the *Palm Grove Hot Dog Shoppe*. Michael admitted, Berman had been right about the cuisine. It was a damn good hot dog.

But despite the cordial meeting, Michael still found it difficult to reconnect with the police officer. Most of the lunch dialogue was just like the morning car ride down: one sided comments on Michael's part with short abrupt responses from Berman.

After lunch, Berman was dispatched to a few house calls, prolonging his return to the sanctuary. After he realized that the day was going to be a lot longer than he thought, Michael suggested to Berman that he could just drive himself down. The officer countered, saying that it was the sheriff's orders, and that was that.

Inside he struggled with bringing up their past feud, addressing how it went down or to offer an apology, but decided not to. It was clear that his former friend was still seething about it after all these years. Bringing it up might stir the pot and make matters worse.

After checking to make sure the sanctuary was locked, he decided to quickly go inside and double check all the latch doors in the interior pens. All seemed to be in order, other than the splintering cracked fence near the alligator pens and a patch of black mold he discovered growing on the back of a utility shed. He resolved to fix both problems at a later date.

Michael paused outside of the caiman enclosures, calculating in his head how he was going to move all the caiman to one enclosure to make room for this mysterious titan American crocodile. Thankfully, he didn't have many caimans at the moment, so relocating them all to one pen shouldn't be too difficult.

He debated on moving all the caiman now to get it over with, but decided against it. If something happened while he was alone, no one would be around to help him. Given the morning encounter with Sinclair, he wasn't willing to gamble his life just to save time. Although they were kept as household pets, taking on the chore of moving them all out in one night in his exhausted state would leave plenty of room for disaster.

The new crocodile, if they were lucky enough to rescue it, would take up a good amount of space in the new enclosure. Michael knew the caiman pen would only work as a temporary resolution. A newer, larger pen would be imperative for the creature. He decided if the expedition to the Glades was a success, he would be writing the funding proposal email to the AZA that very day.

He could feel it. The capture and display of this creature would change everything. There would be no more struggling to pay employees or failing to fix bothersome business problems. The croc would bring crowds from all around, maybe even nationwide. Maybe he would even pick a more easy-toremember phone number, which would eliminate any more calls from the Sunglass Store customers.

Finally, he made it back to the car after locking up a second time, turned on the car, and prepared to pull out of the parking lot. Before he shifted into reverse, he looked down at his phone on the passenger seat, noticing the screen had lit up.

1 Missed Call: UNKNOWN
1 New Voicemail

Michael pressed the speaker button and listened to the message. To his surprise, the sultry voice of a beautiful woman began to ease through the speakers. It was a voice he was unfamiliar with. He would've shrugged it off as a prank call if not for his own name that led the message.

"Michael Robinson's number? Hi Michael, my name is Mila Madison from Palm Grove. I operate my own veterinary practice down here. Sheriff Dawson asked me to call you and ask you if you needed anything from me for the expedition tomorrow. I'll be going along as well. Please call me back as soon as you can – sorry it's so late in the evening, but I need to know! P.S. - I've been to your crocodile facility several times since it opened and I think it's a wonderful place. Thank you for helping Palm Grove with this situation. It's long overdue. See you tomorrow!"

The call ended.

Michael smiled, calling the number back as he pulled out of the parking lot and headed for home, unsure of what the morning would bring. He would need a good sleep that night.

10
MILA MADISON

Berman arrived outside Michael's house at 8:30 the next morning. Michael first noticed the squad car sitting outside his house as he ran out of the shower, the sunlight blinding him as it bounced off the hood of the car through the blinds. Michael doubled his pace. He didn't want to keep Berman waiting, figuring it may give the officer more reason to dislike him than he already did.

Most of Michael's gear was packed from the night before. He managed to condense it all into one North Face backpack that he took often on trips to the Everglades or other hiking excursions. Most of the pack was filled with water bottles and spare changes of clothing.

After some mental debate, he figured he should include one of his crocodilian encyclopedias too, assuming it probably wouldn't be of much use. The book was dusty, buried under a stack of books on the cluttered shelf in his closet. Michael hadn't opened it in years. It was a leftover college textbook. He laughed when he saw a large round coffee stain that had dried on the cover years earlier, remembering the incident.

Most of the data in the book was limited to mating, hunting, and biological makeup. There was nothing in the footnotes that explained how to capture a crocodile, especially an enormous croc that was over twenty-five feet long. What he liked about the book was that it covered all crocodilians, even extinct ones from Earth's prehistory. He found those the most interesting. Any additional information could be retrieved through his smartphone, he thought, assuming that there was decent internet service.

As he was about to flee out the front door, Michael realized he hadn't called Sherry to tell her he wouldn't be in again. He left a vague voicemail at the sanctuary, knowing they would have questions when he got back.

Finally, he met up with Berman outside at 8:45, and they fired off to the south.

After a brief meeting at the Palm Grove Police Department about safety procedures in the swamp, they left in a small convoy of police cruisers, heading south to the Glades.

The dock was hidden deep in the wilderness, accessible by a narrow forest gravel road. Michael probably drove past it a dozen times in his visits to Palm Grove, never giving it a moment's thought. The pier was hardly visible from the highway, hidden by rows upon rows of plain willows and pond cypress trees.

When they arrived, the docks had been cleared of civilians, marked off with yellow caution tape. Most of the boats had already been moved from the area by their owners, under order of the Palm Grove Police Department. The dock led out into an area of swamp surrounded by cattails and tall reeds, emptying into a small inlet that continued deeper into the Glades. Michael noticed a few alligators on the cove, swiftly dashing back into the muck when the officers disbanded and began unloading equipment. Moments later, more police cruisers pulled up beside Berman's car. Dawson and Bolasco got out of one, retrieving equipment from the trunk.

"Fine day for an expedition, Mr. Robinson," Dawson said, shaking his hand.

"It is," Michael smiled.

"We're very happy to have you coming with us."

"It's good to be here."

Two other police officers nearly bumped into him as they began yanking out equipment from an adjacent cruiser. Michael noticed large nets and Pelican cases. He assumed they carried additional tranquilizer weapons.

"Whoa, sorry fella," the first officer said. "Are you the guy?"

"The crocodile zookeeper," Michael said with a chuckle. "Yes, it's me."

Dawson stepped forward, unloading another Pelican case before introducing them.

"Michael Robinson, meet Officer Ryan Gray and Officer Clarence Quarles. These two are newer recruits on the force, but they've proven themselves capable. Ryan has a background in the Coast Guard Auxiliary, so he volunteered to operate an airboat if need be."

"Nice to meet you both," Michael greeted.

They were both very young, probably in their early to mid-twenties. Based on their inside jokes and body language, he knew they were best friends, probably recruited around the same time.

"Always nice to know there's an expert on board," the officer named Ryan Gray said. Michael admired his olive complexion and square jaw.

"Well, I'll try to be of assistance when I can."

"You already are," Dawson cut in. "You're helping us get this animal out of here. Who knows. In a few years, there could be kids skipping stones through here if the Sunset Ridge housing plan continues to expand. Last thing they'll want to see is a twenty-five foot gator running at them."

"Well, who knows," Michael joked. "Kids love monsters, after all."

"You may have a point there," the sheriff smiled. "Well, why don't you hang tight while we try to figure some things out. We're still waiting on a few late arrivals. Take in the sights. We'll be leaving soon."

"Yes sir," Michael said, turning and wandering over to the water.

He found himself walking along the edge of the pier, looking out at the wilderness while trying to keep out of the roasting sunlight. The Southern Glades loomed before him like an uncertain, scraggly jungle, comprised of droopy trees and bubbling clouded streams. Somewhere in there, he thought, was an American crocodile like he'd never seen before. One that he hoped to capture and relocate to his zoo, before the crazed Palm Grove residents decided to find the animal for themselves.

The howl of the early winds muted the creaking footsteps of a visitor following him down the docking platform.

"Michael?" came an inquisitive female voice.

He turned around, feeling his heart skip and his face blush like a schoolboy.

It was a beautiful woman in her early thirties. She was dressed in a light green button up that blended in with the swampy backdrop. She had short khaki shorts on, like Michael would expect to see on some wildlife channel, and thick brown boots with high socks. She tussled her curly brown hair, looking back at him from behind her stylish Ray-Bans. The outfit reminded him of a female version of Steve Irwin.

"Yes," Michael replied. "Hello. Miss Madison?"

"Mila Madison, yes" said the woman, extending a friendly handshake. "Good to have you aboard. I can't thank you enough for taking this animal. They asked me to come aboard in case the croc got injured during our expedition."

"Good to be aboard," Michael said, clumsily accepting the handshake.

He found himself engulfed in her beauty, suddenly unaffected by the lush world around him. The way she carried herself, the way she moved. All of it. Her affinity and appreciation for animals and wildlife only added to her allure. He prayed she was single.

"So what do you think?" she asked.

"About what?" he replied, confused by the question.

"The crocodile," she laughed. "You're certain it's a crocodile, and not something else?"

"I'm not sure what else it would be," Michael replied honestly. "The only other thing that remotely matches the description and the photographs I've seen would obviously be an American alligator. And judging by the scale of those footprints that I've seen, there's no way it's a gator. Alligators are nowhere near that size. So yeah, I'd say a crocodile."

"You don't think it could be something else?" she asked.

Something else, he thought.

"Like what?"

"I don't know," she laughed, "You're the expert. The way I see it, that's pretty big for a crocodile track. I've had a few crocodiles in my veterinary hospital, mostly American crocodiles. None of them even come close to the size of this creature. You don't suspect there may be a larger species that you aren't presently aware of?"

"Are you saying there could be another crocodilian present in the Everglades other than the American alligator or the American crocodile? Other than maybe some pet caimans that owners may have dumped when they got too large, I'd have to say no, in my humble professional opinion. We would have found out about it by now."

She shrugged, unconvinced by his logical reasoning.

"All I'm saying, Mr. Robinson, is that the Everglades are an enormous biome, full of unexplored jungles, mangroves and swamps. America has only been here for barely two centuries. And they're always discovering new species of wildlife."

Michael liked that she seemed rooted in her theory, despite how ludicrous and impractical he thought it was.

"Well, I'll concede that it's possible," he replied, trying to stop grinning. "And please, call me Mike."

11
THE FLEET

They waited by the docks for another hour, observing the wildlife while fending off the merciless sunlight. Dawson introduced Michael to a few additional police officers that arrived, before he found Mila near the dock's edge, striking up a conversation to pass time. Behind him near his police car, he could hear Dawson complaining about the rising heat, unbuttoning his flannel shirt, exposing thousands of curly gray chest hairs.

"Jeez, this heat is becoming intolerable," he lamented, trying to stop the beads of sweat from rolling down his sideburns. He padded his skin incessantly with a handkerchief.

"We may be getting relief tomorrow," Bolasco remarked. "The weather report was calling for some afternoon and evening showers. Might even be a pretty serious storm, they're speculating."

"Well it's about time," Dawson groaned.

Michael could feel Mila leaning into his ear.

"You know, if he wore something other than that lumberjack flannel shirt, he might not be so warm," Mila whispered, fanning herself with a wrinkled magazine she had been reading before Michael arrived.

"I was thinking the same thing," Michael added, checking his watch.

The sheriff's impatience was about to reach a boiling point when a large motor sound began to creap through the cattails.

"Finally," Dawson whined. "Here they come!"

From around the bend, a pair of motor boats began to materialize together through the palm fronds. As they rounded the bend, Michael was surprised to recognize them as Coast Guard patrol boats. He saw them often in various ports near Miami Beach, doing routine treks around the shores for safety inspections.

The boats pulled up to the dock on either side. Seamen jumped onto the pier and secured the ships before the engines shut off.

"Jeez, Graham," the sheriff complained, walking down the dock. "What took so long?"

"Sorry," the officer named Graham replied, stepping off the first patrol boat. "I underestimated the amount of time it would take to get these ships from the base all the way up here. It's a lot of swamp land, you know?"

"Yeah, yeah," Dawson said, dismissing his excuses. "Let's kick this thing off here. Bolasco, Berman, Gray – start loading up."

The dock became alive with the shuffle of police officers transporting various supplies onto the boats. Michael and Mila stood behind, trying to stay out of the way and observing from afar. The boats rocked back and forth in front of them, wading gently in the murky waves as the officer stepped on and off, loading the worn out Pelican cases.

Each boat had three additional Coast Guard seamen, manning various tasks like weapon checks and operating radio equipment. Bolasco and Berman began loading the equipment onto the boats, helped by Graham, Gray and Quarles and other Palm Grove officers that remained on the bank. Michael noticed the firearm symbols engraved in the Pelican cases, assumed they were weapons and felt compelled to discuss it with Dawson.

"Just a precaution," the sheriff assured him.

"You don't have your own boats, Sheriff?" she asked, eyeing the Coast Guard cutters.

"We do," Dawson replied. "But they're all assigned to keeping other boaters out of the area for now. So we're partnering with the Coast Guard for help throughout this operation. They have additional resources that we as a small town police department don't have access to. Seriously, you'll feel a lot safer on one of these than our dinky little patrol boats. If it becomes too hard to handle, we'll be calling in our airboats for support."

"Don't worry about me," Mila laughed. "Hell, I've been swimming in the Glades before! I'll be fine, Sheriff."

"Okay, you two," Bolasco said, waving them aboard. "Time to go! All aboard. We're about to get underway. Let's go hunt some dinosaurs!"

"Dinosaurs?" Mila asked with humorous skepticism.

Michael followed Mila onto the boat, setting his pack down on a small table near the cabin.

The cutter was small, maybe thirty feet in length, surrounded by a dark orange base and a tiny metallic cabin that seemed to amplify the sunlight. Radio equipment and antennas dotted the roof of the cabin, jutting upward like porcupine quills. A machine gun bay was mounted near the bow. Michael was grateful that there wasn't a weapon mounted on the top.

Dawson, Bolasco, and Berman followed them onto the craft, carrying additional nets and Pelican cases before setting them down gently on the cutter floor. Graham and three other officers prepared to board the other boat, untying the ropes of both vessels on the docks.

With a load roar, the engine came to life on board Michael's cutter. The other boat began to reverse into the swamp, sending fierce waves flying over to the beach. A minute later, Michael felt his boat do the same, following the first cutter's churning waves into the bog.

On the beach, the officers waved goodbye before piling into their squad cars and departing to other assignments. Slowly, the overgrown dock began to slip away in the foliage. Soon they were alone in the Everglades, drifting carefully around the pockets of land down the channel into the unknown.

Michael found himself looking out the back of the boat as they traveled farther away from civilization. Over the imposing fortress of cypress trees, rooftops of distant houses could be seen far off, presumably from the Sunset Ridge development or a neighboring community. In the water beneath, occasionally he would notice a flicker of an alligator tail snaking through the seaweed, but nothing that looked like a massive, murderous crocodile as long as the cutter.

"Don't worry," Mila said sarcastically, coming up behind him. "I'll watch your back out here."

"What makes you think I need someone watching my back," Michael replied, pursing his lips in fake irritation. He detected a hint of flirtation in her voice.

"You manage crocodiles and alligators in captivity, Mike," she replied. "But this is their territory. You'll need someone who knows this area well enough to make sure you don't wander into a crocodile nest."

Michael laughed, turning back to the swamp.

"I think I know what a crocodile nest looks like. We actually have one at the sanctuary."

"Really? That's really interesting! I'll have to come up to Redland and see it. Is it new?"

"Fairly new," Michael replied. "A croc built it a few weeks ago."

He recalled to her the story of how he came into work sometime in mid July, to find a mound of scraggly twigs and brush pushed to the middle of the enclosure. In the center of the mound was a ring of beautiful white ovals and an irritated mother protecting her unborn family. It was really a beautiful thing to see.

"How long will they take to hatch?" Mila asked.

"Well, it will still take some time," Michael said. "Sometime in the next few months. Normally it takes eighty-ish days for the hatchlings to pop out, give or take some."

"That's fantastic," Mila remarked.

"So, you seem very familiar with the Southern Glades," he said, turning towards her.

"I am. We used to hike through here when I was a kid. All the days spent down here with my father, observing the wildlife, bird watching, boating – it's what made me want to become a veterinarian. My whole childhood can be traced here. You haven't traveled through here before, no?"

"A handful of times," he replied. "I've hiked in a few areas one time or another. Bird watched occasionally. I've never been in this area though."

"A crocodile zookeeper in Florida who hasn't thoroughly explored the Everglades," Mila smiled. "Seems a tad unlikely."

"More like a crocodile zookeeper who's trying to run a successful business," Michael corrected her playfully.

"I've been all around here," she bragged. "It's a beautiful mess of nature, isn't it?"

"And you've been to the area where the bodies have been found?"

"Well, I've crossed through there a few times over the years, so yes. The area isn't exactly easily accessible by hiking. Most of the land patches are isolated little islands. I've boated through the area before, but not long enough to know anything about this particular crocodile, other than what the news reports and the police have said."

"How long ago was your last visit through the area?"

"Maybe two years ago," she replied, thinking for a moment.

"Well consider yourself lucky," Michael replied. "Maybe the animal wasn't in this area at the time. It sounds like it has a zero-tolerance policy against humans."

"It definitely wasn't in the area," Mila assured him. "I'm quite convinced the Sunset Ridge development shuffled around the crocodilian territories in the area. Now, new territory lines have been drawn in the sand for these animals. It's the only reason I can think of for this creature's sudden appearance in this stretch of swamp."

"So all these years, you've never seen a big crocodile like the one that made those prints in the photos?"

"Oh, I've seen big crocs," Mila laughed. "Obviously, not as often as the gators. But have I seen anything like the one that made those footprints from Bolasco's photo? I must confess, I've never seen anything that big. But that doesn't mean I don't believe it exists. Like I said, it's a big biome. But I understand your skepticism. My first thought was that the tracks were a hoax."

"Well it's certainly not a hoax," Berman said, stepping up on the other side of Mila. He was chewing a stick of bubble gum at an obnoxiously loud volume, cracking it with his molars, staring out at the swamp through black aviators.

"Well I'm not saying it is," Mila shot back at Berman. "Just that it was my first thought when I saw the images. Obviously, the footprints are real."

"There's something big out there," Berman assured her. "And we've gotta get it the hell out of Palm Grove. The thing's a menace, right Mikey?"

"Right, Jeff."

Berman turned and stared out at the swamp again, scanning over the water as if he were Captain Ahab looking for Moby Dick, trying to appear mysterious and unafraid. Michael thought it made him look like a prick. With a quick turn, he looked Mila over before walking away to the other end of the ship, retrieving binoculars, and scouting the surface of the oncoming swamp.

Michael could sense there might be an old rivalry forming over the kind, well-mannered veterinarian. He could tell by the look Berman shot him that the officer was already interested in Mila.

"What a douche," she said bluntly after Berman walked off.

Michael couldn't help but choke back a laugh. The statement seemed too random and sophomoric for such an established, polished woman like Mila Madison.

Suddenly, a glitching blaring whine erupted on the cutter. The radio started going off in the ship's cabin. Several of the soldiers were fumbling with the equipment, trying to fight through the static to get a better reception. A sputtering voice muttered something over the airwaves. It sounded urgent.

Dawson was rambling something over the radio, trying to relay instructions to other officers. The sheriff was sweating again, padding himself down with the handkerchief.

"What's going on?" Michael asked as they ran into the cabin.

"Son of a bitch!" Dawson yelled. "We're gonna have to take a detour and do some damage control. Somehow, a civilian boat weaved its way through our patrol ships into the Glades. Our animal found it. There's been another attack!"

12
THE FIFTH VICTIM

The Coast Guard cutters were given the new coordinates of where the attack occurred earlier that morning, rerouting their path to the new location and accelerating to arrive promptly. Michael spent most of the time on the back of the boat in a state of shock. He had witnessed the order and calmness of the operation collapse, giving way to panic and urgency. The crocodile search had turned into a surprise rendezvous with a forensics unit somewhere in the Everglades, halting their progress and undoubtedly delaying the apprehension of the croc.

Berman and Bolasco attempted to calm Dawson down, who had been sputtering off rampant profanity since the news broke through the transmitter ten minutes ago.

"They're gonna fry us for this back in town!" Dawson raged. "Those townies will fry us, you realize this? How could they let another civilian boat into the swamp? I thought we shut down all the canals."

"We may need more help with this operation," Bolasco advised. "It's a pretty big area down here, Sheriff. We have a big force for a small town, but not enough manpower to patrol every entrance all the time. And this thing's on a killing spree!"

"We need to do a better job of informing people of the situation," Dawson said. "We need to make it more incriminating. Everyone crossing through the Everglades near Sunset Ridge should be charged with interfering with a police investigation. It's for their own safety."

"I couldn't agree more, sir," Berman suggested.

"Damnit, it's all gone to hell," the sheriff whined, slamming his fist down on the cutter's dashboard. "What are we gonna do, Willie? Call in the whole Florida National Guard just to find one piece of shit crocodile? We'll be the laughing stock of the whole state."

The emotion in his voice impacted everyone on the ship. He had transitioned from a fearless sheriff to a frustrated man, burdened by the pressure of the investigation coupled with the growing unrest in Palm Grove.

Details about what had happened earlier in the day eventually filtered through the airwaves on the cutter. According to the police on the other end, a father and son, whose names were distorted over the radio static, had slipped past the police patrol boats to the north, entering the swamp from somewhere just south of the town, near the backwater inlets near Sunset Ridge. Through some morbid twist of fate, they wandered into the area that the crocodile attacks had occurred. From what Michael overheard through the white noise, it sounded like other law enforcement units were already en route, policing the killing zone.

"We are almost at the scene, over," said one of the coast guard seamen over the radio, taking over while Bolasco and Berman tried to reason with Dawson.

"At least the press won't be there," Michael heard Berman mumble. "Too remote."

"It's amazing, isn't it," Mila said.

She was still standing with Michael near the front of the boat, who was still in awe over what had happened and what they were about to drive into. He had never seen a dead body before, except at a few funerals in his youth, which he didn't count.

"What's amazing?" he asked, snapping from his stupor.

"All of this," she replied. "These random attacks in the swamp, all of a sudden. They just started out of nowhere. A large crocodilian, unseen before by any of the locals and undocumented by science. It makes me wonder what else is out here."

"Did you hear them over the radio? They think the fishermen may have slipped into the swamp near Sunset Ridge, which backs up our theory that urbanization in Palm Grove may have contributed to the creature's sudden appearance and aggression. Given all the human boating and hiking activity in the area from the new housing plan, I'm starting to believe the animal now feels compelled to defend the entire swath of swamp just south of the town."

"It was in the Everglades all along," she added. "Right under our nose, and so close to Palm Grove! It's a miracle no one encountered this thing until now."

"This new victim situation has me thinking."

"About what?" she asked.

"Well, think about it. This is the fifth victim. This creature has killed five humans, Mila. I don't know the statistics, but this has to outnumber any record of human-crocodilian related deaths attributed to a single specimen."

"Not true," she informed him. "Ever hear the story of Gustave? They made a film about him in 2007 called *Primeval,* starring Dominic

Purcell – one of my favorite actors! I fell in love with him after *Prison Break*. Anyway, Gustave is a man-eating Nile crocodile said to have killed over hundreds of people in the Republic of Burundi. To this day, he remains uncaptured. Our specimen's only killed a fraction compared to Gustave."

"Never heard of him," Michael said, impressed by Mila's history lesson. "Even so, what kind of vengeful man-eater are we dealing with?"

"I think we're about to find out," Mila said, peering over his shoulder.

He turned, seeing the shapes of boats and forensics teams beginning to appear around the oncoming bend. Through the grass ahead, red and blue police lights crept slowly out in between the slender leaves, marking the location of the animal's newest killing site.

"Hey, Sheriff Dawson," one of the seamen called out. "We're here, sir."

The cutter glided through the reeds, approaching an overturned fishing boat in the center of the water. Streaks of reptilian claw impressions engraved the wood, foretelling the viciousness of the attack. Twenty yards away, officers on foot combed through the vegetation on the shoreline, looking for unseen signs of evidence among the grass.

In the center of the cove, a young boy was draped in a blanket while officers questioned him. The child looked pale, staring past the police officers into the emptiness of the lagoon where the overturned rowboat drifted, slowly slipping under the surface.

A shade of red coated the surface of the swamp, wreaking of diluted human blood.

The seamen pulled the cutters as close as they could to the beach, dispersing the traces of blood throughout the waves. Dawson jumped out, splashing into the shallows and raced to shore, followed by Michael, Mila and the other officers. The seamen stayed behind to operate the ships, studying the ominous body of water that surrounded them, searching for the fabled killer crocodile that supposedly lingered nearby.

"He's not telling us anything, Sheriff," one of the officers said as Dawson arrived near the boy. "I think he's in shock."

"Okay, Devin. I'll take it from here. Go search the shore with the others. Ryan, Clarence – go with him."

"Yes, sir," Ryan replied, hustling down to the water with Clarence and the officer named Devin.

Dawson approached the young child gently like a caring parent, kneeling down beside him. Michael and the others watched from a distance, staying clear of the first responders who picked through the vegetation around them. To Michael's surprise, the sheriff seemed to master an artful parenting style of communicating with children.

"Hey son," he started. "I'm Sheriff Jacob Dawson with the Palm Grove Police Department, but you can call me whatever you want. Even Jake's fine, all right?"

The child was quiet, shivering in his towel despite the glorious heat that the sun was burning down onto the muddy bank. He looked to be about nine or ten years old, hidden by thick rimmed glasses and a perfect bowl haircut. In his right hand, he clutched a small outdated PlayStation Portable device with a cracked screen, covered in sand and mud. In the other hand he held a smartphone with a black screen, presumably what he called for help on.

"Okay," the boy managed finally. His voice was faltering and his eyes were still elsewhere, hypnotized by the bog.

"What's your name?" Dawson asked.

"Owen."

"Owen, I always liked that name," Dawson smiled. "Can you tell us what happened? Anything at all that might help us catch this thing? Where it went?"

The boy shook his head slowly.

"His call from the station told us enough about what happened," a female officer with a Palm Grove badge answered.

She had been quietly standing beside the boy since the beginning, watching over him while her colleagues rooted through the thicket. Her hair was tied tightly behind her head in a long brown ponytail that ran halfway down her back. She had a friendly welcoming face, Michael noticed, as well as a toned physique that could kick his ass.

"What did the call say?" Dawson asked.

"The attack happened about a half an hour ago," she answered. "The boy and his father wandered through here to do a little fishing and sightseeing. Right in this stretch here, something hit the boat from underwater. Then the boat got bumped again, this time rising up and flipping over. Owen made it to shore, but the father..."

She stopped herself before divulging the fate of the father, knowing Owen was listening just a few feet away.

"The father what, Adrienne?" Dawson asked. "What happened?"

Adrienne pulled Dawson aside, over near Michael and Mila.

"He says a big alligator came out of the water and took his father. He saw his dad die, Jake. The whole thing is totally screwed up! This gator business is getting insane."

"An alligator?" Michael asked, butting into the conversation.

"Yeah. Why?"

"If this is the same creature that's been picking off the locals for the past month, it's not possible. American alligators top out at sixteen feet, and that's at the very top. Most won't reach anywhere near that length, even the males. The track in the photographs from the last crime scene was made by something much bigger. It has to be an American crocodile. An enormous one, but a crocodile, nonetheless."

Dawson stared blankly at him, wiping sweat off his forehead. Michael immediately knew that it might not have been the best time for a crocodilian factual lecture, instantly regretting his comments.

"Well whatever the hell it is, it's big," Adrienne said, annoyed with his comment.

"Michael Robinson, this is Adrienne Hulme," Dawson said, introducing the two of them. "Mr. Robinson has agreed to help with this case. He is also volunteering his wildlife sanctuary as a home for this animal once we manage to obtain it. Adrienne wasn't at the preliminary meeting this morning. She was dispatched out at the time, but she'll be involved from this point on."

"How do you do?" Michael said with a firm handshake. "Sorry, didn't mean to come off as a know-it-all."

"You didn't," Adrienne replied. "Just a nerd with too much time on his hands to know so much about this stuff."

Michael shrugged, knowing she was busting his balls.

"I guess it comes with the job," he managed, unsure of how to comeback.

"Hey, Sheriff," Bolasco shouted. "Hey, the kid has something to show you. He took it on his phone, just after the encounter. You have to see this!"

They gathered around the boy, who swiped through the smartphone to the photo app, opening the video option. He tried to recollect himself, trying to appear confident to the adults as he navigated to the file. A watery thumbnail scaled up until it filled the full frame. Owen pressed a button, starting the video at the beginning of the timeline.

At first, they saw nothing, only the swirling violent ocean of swamp water and distant cypress trees. When the video was recorded, Owen was in a state of panic, waving the phone around until it struck the sand, burying the lens under the tan grains. Suddenly it snapped back into the air, pointing at the swamp water again. He fixed the camera on the ruins of the boat, centering the wreck in the frame. In the audio, his sobbing could be heard over the sloshing waves.

"Are you seeing something I'm not, Willie?" Dawson asked impatiently. "I know my vision sucks, but I'm really not seeing anything."

"Just wait," Bolasco said.

In the video, Owen seemed to calm himself, not shaking the camera as much as he did in the earlier frames. He zoomed the camera forward, sacrificing video quality for a better shot.

Suddenly, towards the middle of the clip, the wreck of the boat shifted with a jolt, struck by something heavy just underneath the waves. The boat turned once, drifting to the left. Then, for a few fleeting seconds, something rose out from the water, heading off frame through the current.

"Whoa!" Dawson screeched.

He leaned away from the phone as if he was caught off guard from a jump scare in a horror film.

"Holy shit, Bolasco! Go back, give me a replay of that, will you Owen? Thank you, son."

The boy scrubbed back on the timeline and replayed the portion of interest. Michael's eyes widened with amazement as the breathtaking action repeated itself.

Near the front of the wreckage, a colossal crocodilian head rose out from the waves. The coloring on the scales were hard to decipher from the exposure, but Michael thought it looked like a dark green with yellow stripes. Two gold reptilian eyes burned through the brown water, locking eyes with the camera as the crocodilian headed for Owen.

Michael instantly knew by the odd coloration that the animal wasn't an American Crocodile like he suspected earlier.

The camera started shaking again, before the boy let the phone slip from his hand. When the phone landed on the sand with a muted thud, the monster was seen briefly diverting its trajectory, fleeing back into the mangroves. The auto-focus feature on the camera focused first on the grains of sand in the foreground, before locking onto the crocodilian again, this time capturing the end of the bumpy tail as it slipped back into the depths.

The video jumped back to a play icon screen, indicating the clip had ended. For a second, the viewers were speechless. The reports and speculation surrounding the case had been confirmed. The creature was of legendary size.

"Did you see that thing?" Bolasco pointed. "The head was as big as the boat! If that's not a dinosaur, I don't know what is."

"I've seen enough," Dawson said, letting the boy take the phone away. "Adrienne, take the kid to the hospital to check for injuries. Report back when you can. Make sure you get a hold of the family. You'll be okay, son."

"You got it," Adrienne replied. "Come on, Owen. Let's get out of here."

She took the boy through the grass, starting a long trek back to the main road where her squad car was parked. Owen picked up his broken PlayStation and lumbered after her, towards the flashing police lights deep through the thicket.

"Is this the same area that the other attacks took place, Sheriff?" Michael asked.

"No, that's what's strange," Dawson replied. "The first four attacks took place deeper in the Glades. This happened just a stones throw away from the housing developments. The construction site is just a few miles inland. Look, you can even see the rooftops of Sunset Ridge over those hills. Shit, it's moving back into the Palm Grove city limits. Not good."

"Do you think it's still in the area?" Graham asked, looking out at the water.

"I doubt it, Graham," Michael replied. "At least, not in this vicinity."

"How can you possibly know that?" the sheriff asked.

Michael pointed over to the coast guard boats, wading nearby on the sandy cove.

"Because the boats are still afloat."

13
EXTENDED OPERATIONS

Michael stood in the shower of his Redland ranch, letting the warm pressurized water spray over his face, washing over the sweat and grime of the swamp adventure. He held onto the wall with both hands, exhausted from the day's events that left him second-guessing what he knew about crocodilians. He scrubbed meticulously with body wash, expecting to find some parasite or tick on him from the excursion through the Southern Glades, but found none. The mosquitoes had left a mess of red bumps on his arms.

The video from Owen's smartphone looped endlessly in his head. He kept fixating on the strength through which the animal pushed the boat aside, like it was a plastic toy. And the eyes – beautiful golden eyes like a pair of amber artifacts from ancient Egypt. They were infinite and welcoming – alluring, but deadly.

What the hell was that thing?

He had acknowledged his wrongful assessment of the American crocodile as the culprit, struggling to come up with the true identity of the animal in the video. It was a crocodilian, sure, but what kind?

Was there another crocodilian in the Everglades that he had forgotten about? No. He shook the idea out of his head.

Michael turned the shower knob, cutting off the water. He pulled a fresh towel off the rack, stepped out of the bathroom and turned on his desktop computer in his bedroom. Research was the last thing he wanted to do after the hectic, fast-paced day that he endured, but if we were going to be of any help at all, some effort on Google would be required.

Sheriff Dawson had called the hunt off shortly after they left the scene of attack, reassessing his resources and manpower. Berman informed Michael that an official press release would be airing in Miami the following morning, telling all residents that traveling in the Southern Glades near Palm Grove was off limits, punishable by fines until the situation was resolved.

With the fifth victim, later identified by Owen as his father, John

Sanders, the operation was now full-speed ahead, spearheaded by a joint partnership between the local Coast Guard and the Palm Grove Police Department. Dawson sent Michael home after they left the scene of the attack. Berman drove him home again, quieted by the disturbing video that Owen recorded.

Michael told Berman that he would be fine driving down to Palm Grove by himself the following morning, but appreciated the gratitude on behalf of the police department. This time Berman was forced to comply, as the sheriff didn't specify whether Michael should be picked up or not.

The next day, a newly organized expedition into the swamp would be taking place, taking up to a week if necessary. The operation would demand larger nets, more patrol boats, and most importantly, more powerful tranquilizers.

Dawson was insistent that Michael come along again, this time giving the zookeeper some homework. Michael's self-assigned task in the mission, for the moment, would be simple: identify what the hell kind of creature they were dealing with.

So far, he was sure of one thing. It was no American crocodile. Mila was right after all.

Could it have been a crocodile from another part of the world, imported by someone overseas and dumped there when it got too big for the owner's enclosure? Michael decided against it. No crocodilian in the world looked and moved like this creature.

From what he knew, only two crocodilians inhabited the Everglades: the American alligator and the American crocodile. The monster was too large to be either. In fact, the monster looked to be larger than any crocodilian he had ever seen, even bigger than a Nile crocodile. Additionally, the coloration was off. Owen's camera was operating at a blown-out exposure, making everything seem washed out and bright. But even in the glowing background, he could see that the scales featured golden stripes that descended all the way to the creature's tail.

He made himself a cup of tea, blowing on it on his way back to the computer, which by now had booted up to the internet browser.

He searched a term on Google, typing in "Everglades crocodiles".

Immediately, a flurry of news reports surfaced from the recent attacks in Palm Grove, but nothing that answered his question or provided information that he didn't already know. He was surprised that there were no news descriptions of Owen's video or what the animal looked like.

Michael figured that Dawson must be keeping the information confidential. Although he didn't take Owen's phone or tell him not to share the video. The world would surely know soon enough about the new tenant in the Everglades, if the video was released, which made Michael fret about rogue poaching parties that may try to breach the swamp, adding to the urgency of the already delicate situation.

On a whim, he searched "crocodilian with yellow stripes".

A few cartoons popped up, most of them stock images or clip art. There were no photo realistic animals. Even the paleoart and wildlife illustrations didn't show him anything.

He stared blankly at the screen, unsure of what to type that might lead him in the right direction.

What kind of crocodilian is that long, that big? With yellow stripes?

Nothing that he knew of.

There was no more information on the internet provided for this creature. He found himself on the tenth page of Google, still showing no leads for the mystery crocodile.

He sat back, taking a sip of his tea as he mindlessly stared at the screen, faced with the only possibility he could come up with. This was an undiscovered species, and probably critically endangered if it had never been documented before. And it was right there, a half an hour south, waiting to be saved from extinction in the Everglades. Capture of this animal was now imperative to ensure it didn't get picked off in the wild.

Michael picked up his smartphone that was charging on the desk in front of him, and dialed the number for his crocodile sanctuary. An automated message greeted him that business hours were closed, before redirecting him to Sherry's voicemail.

"Sherry, hi – it's Michael. Hopefully when you get this message, I'll already be talking to you in person. Tomorrow I'm gonna be coming in for an hour to show Sandra and Charlie how to properly move the animals. This situation down in the Everglades is heating up, and we may be on the verge of not only discovering a new species of crocodilian, but bringing the creature to Redland. All of the caimans have to be moved into one pen to make room for this new animal. I may be gone for up to a week helping the police and the Coast Guard track the animal down. We will hold off on cleaning the pens until I come back. Talk soon, thanks Sherry."

He hung up the phone and opened the text message app. He entered Mila's name in the app screen and started typing his message.

You were right. It's a new species – has to be! Sorry I doubted you. Forgive me? - Michael

Then he crashed on his mattress and was fast asleep, his thoughts elsewhere to the south.

14

IMPROMPTU TRAINING

"What the hell is going on down there, Mike?" Charlie asked, leaning on the lobby reception desk. "I just saw the newscast this morning. Another victim?"

Michael was beginning to tire of Charlie's lack of respect.

The doors to the sanctuary were locked, despite the fact that the zoo had been technically open for fifteen minutes. Michael didn't want any visitors walking in and hearing the conversation.

He stood on one side of the reception desk. Sherry was sitting in her chair in front of him, while Charlie and Sandra listened eagerly from the other side of the desk. The remaining employees that couldn't make the meeting would have to be briefed at a later time.

"That's only the half of it, Charlie," Michael told him. "There was a video taken shortly after the attack. The victim's son, Owen, was filming the aftermath on his smartphone. They're probably gonna push not to have the footage released because of the sensitive content surrounding the video. Whatever the thing is, it's huge, bigger than any crocodilian on record."

"Even bigger than a saltwater crocodile?" Sandra asked.

"Way bigger," Michael smiled, surprised that she knew the largest known crocodile.

"So what, this thing's like a new species?" Charlie asked. Michael could hear the doubt in his voice.

"Yes, Charlie. I'm expecting that it is a new species. It hasn't been documented anywhere on Earth."

"Did you see it?" Sandra asked. "In the video, I mean."

"Just a little bit," Michael admitted. "The video quality wasn't very good."

"So, that's where you went yesterday," Sherry said. "I was gonna ask. Your voicemail you left me sounded a little brusque."

"Sorry about that," Michael laughed. "I was literally running out the door at the time."

"Do you think you're gonna see it again?" Sandra said.

"I'm hoping to. That's why I called this impromptu meeting. There's an expedition, leaving today, and they want me there to help. If we capture the animal, it will be coming here. Which is why I need the three of you to sign these papers."

He handed them some printed forms that he ran off at home, typing them up the night before after researching similar sample templates online.

"What are these?" Charlie asked.

"Confidentiality agreements," Michael explained. "I'm asking you to not disclose anything about the animal, including emails, texts, social media posts, videos, photographs – nothing – until I give the go ahead. This animal could change this company's future if we capture it, so I don't want any information leaking out before we're ready to have it on display. This could be a game changer for our zoo. I'm talking raises for everyone."

Sandra's eyes perked up. Charlie remained deadpan.

"Sherry, please distribute these to the other employees and have them sign off in my absence."

"How cool," Sherry said, looking over the forms and handing them to Sandra and Charlie. "A new species of crocodile, right here at our facility!"

"If it's a crocodile," Michael said. "It could be another species of alligator for all we know. The only species of alligator left are the –"

"We know, we know," Charlie rudely interrupted. "The American alligator and the Chinese alligator. So, is that where you went the other day?"

"Yes, Charlie," Michael said, quietly considering using the teenager's arrogant attitude as a way to screw him out of the wage increase.

"Why are you just telling us now?" Charlie asked, looking over the agreement.

"Well, to be honest, I didn't think that the creature was as big as it really is. I figured that if I brought it back, we could throw it in with the other crocodiles and then I could clear a pen later. But after seeing how big the damn thing is, we'll need to move out a pen as soon as possible. I don't want it in with the other animals, at least until we know more about it. We already know how aggressive it is."

"So what are you saying?" Charlie said.

"I'm saying I might be gone for at least a week, Charlie," Michael went on. "But I'm hoping it doesn't take nearly that long. I'll be leaving here for Palm Grove within the hour. Before I pull out, I'll be showing you and Sandra how to move the caimans. We need to clear one of the pens completely out for this new addition to our habitat."

"You want us to move the caimans by ourselves?" Sandra said with a concerned tone. "I don't know, Mike. After what happened the other day with Sinclair..."

"That won't happen again," Michael assured her. "First of all, I'll be moving Sinclair out myself, to show you the process and everything involved. Second, the two of you will always be together throughout the process. If you're not sure about a particular caiman, come back to it later and move onto another. Regardless, I need them all moved by the end of the day. Who knows? I might be back tonight with the creature and a police escort, and the last thing I want to see in the pen is a stowaway caiman. Do you understand, Charlie?"

"Yeah I guess," said the teenager with a snarky tone.

"Obviously I wish I had more time to teach you two this training, but given the time constraints, I don't see any other option. Besides, I know you both have seen me move them out a million times. Sandra, are you able to help me with this?"

"I think so," she said. "As long as Charlie or someone else is always with me."

"He will be," Michael assured her.

"Then yeah, let's go do this!" Sandra said enthusiastically.

Michael smiled. He could always count on her to be brave and attempt to learn new things.

"Then let's hurry and I'll show you how to move Sinclair," Michael said, leading them down the hall to the zoo enclosures. "I'm already running late as it is. The important things to remember are to be observant and patient. And most importantly, don't underestimate an irritated crocodilian."

15
FIREARMS AND TRANQUILIZERS

Flooring his Taurus onto the highway, Michael swerved through the on ramp and accelerated south towards Palm Grove.

He checked his watch occasionally, forgetting that there was a clock right in front of him on the car's dashboard. He laughed, knowing that his mind was still reeling and he wasn't thinking logically. The idea of an expedition into the Glades excited him. It was a mix of an adventure and the unknown.

His heart was racing. He yearned to get down there and start learning more about the animal.

Owen's video from the day before confirmed the danger they were up against. A super predator of the Everglades, undiscovered by mankind until now – truly a miracle in modern America. And an animal that had no problem picking off humans.

The Taurus rocketed through to Palm Grove, through Main Street where more protests were being held with the news of the latest victim, John Sanders. Several rebellious teens tried to wave signs in his face as he passed by the police station.

He didn't dare look at them, continuing his journey through the town and farther south to where the jungle began to creep up on the town. The drive from the day before seemed like a blur, and he struggled to remember the exact turn that Berman had taken to the docks.

Eventually, a sign that read, Southern Glades Dock B, appeared in front of him. Through the fronds, he could vaguely make out the distinct shape of police cars parked through the vegetation.

That looks right, he thought.

He hooked a sharp right turn and ripped the car into the forested trail that emptied out into the hidden cove where the docks sat. As he pushed through the last set of branches that bordered the trail, Michael noticed that the beach looked a lot different today.

Squad cars filled the parking area, some from neighboring police departments, and a handful from Palm Grove. Most of the officers were walking near the water, talking among themselves and making jokes that Killer Croc from Batman was waiting for them just beneath the waves. Officers Ryan Gray and Clarence Quarles saw him pulling in and offered a friendly wave as he navigated to a parking spot.

An additional large white cutter was stationed at the dock, accompanied by the two smaller boats from the day before. It was an imposing craft that looked more like a naval battleship than a Coast Guard rescue ship. Metal fencing lined the massive deck, surrounding a tall communication spire at the top of the cabin. Michael had doubts that the ship would fit through the narrow swamp trails of the Glades.

Two Palm Grove police airboats were docked beside the flagship cutter to serve as scouts and additional manpower. No civilian boats remained in the water. Michael guessed they had all been offloaded and driven away, under fear of penalties.

He rummaged through his trunk, making sure he had everything he needed in his suitcase. When he paused to check his phone for any new texts, a familiar pleasant voice called out behind him.

"Don't even bother with that thing," Mila laughed, crunching up the gravel towards him. "Cell phone service sucks out here. Mine keeps going in and out. I forgot my charger anyway, so I'm thinking about just leaving it off until we're done to conserve the battery. Plus, no Wi-Fi."

Michael frowned. The lack of communication with society would come to bug him. He looked at the phone screen and saw that his service level barely had one bar before shoving the device back into his pants pocket, defeated. Hopefully, nothing terrible happened at the sanctuary while he was gone.

"I take it there isn't a Verizon or Apple store in there," Michael joked.

"I see you weren't scared off from yesterday," Mila observed, ignoring his humor. "Good to have you with us again, Mike. I got your text message. Thank you for admitting defeat!"

Her hard-to-get charisma made him laugh.

"Well, don't get used to it," he replied, shouldering the backpack. "It's not something I admit often."

"Well when you're around me, it's something you'll have to learn to adapt to," she said, brushing past him. "Walk with me."

He double checked to make sure he had everything and began walking with her towards the pier.

"Dawson wants us on the main cutter for added safety," she went on. "The fleet should be departing in twenty or so minutes. So, any idea what this thing is that we're about to try and locate?"

"No clue," Michael said, locking his car and continuing down the sandy cove after her. "I was up late last night doing research, and I got nowhere. Mila, this is unlike any crocodilian that the world has ever seen. It really is a one in a million that we've stumbled onto it, and so close to civilization."

"Do you think there may be more of them in there?" she asked.

"I don't know, but after yesterday, I'm willing to admit anything's possible."

"Have you looked into extinct possibilities?" she asked.

"Like what?" Michael asked, wiping sweat from his forehead. It was bound to be another hot day.

"Well, take the giant squid for instance," she began. "Experts have argued for years that they have disappeared from the oceans, presumed to be extinct. Now, in the past twenty years or so, they've started showing up again. If I remember correctly, one was even captured on video in 2006."

"Well the difference between the giant squid and whatever is waiting for us in the Everglades is a little different, from an environmental standpoint," Michael explained. "For one, it's very difficult to determine extinct marine animals. The oceans are just so vast and deep. Also, I'm not sure that the giant squid was ever thought to be extinct, but rather incredibly elusive."

"Is this you trying to show off while getting me back for yesterday?" she asked. "You just can't stand that I was right!"

"I'll tell you what," Michael said, stopping and turning towards her at the foot of the docks. "If we make it out of this, alive, I'll give you a personal tour of my facility, free of charge. Just to show you I'm not a total jerk like you make me out to be."

"Is that a promise?" she asked flirtatiously.

"You betcha," Michael replied, immediately regretting the cheesy line. But when Mila laughed at the comment, he decided maybe cheesiness was a potential way to win her over.

But before he could come up with another, romantic comment, his eyes caught something wrong with the cutter – Berman.

Berman with an assault rifle.

The officer was standing on board the main cutter, talking with one of the Coast Guard seamen who was admiring the weapon. He turned, saw Michael and Mila approaching, and offered a brief wave.

"Uh, Jeff," Michael said. "What the hell is that?"

"It's an M4," Berman replied bluntly. "What about it?"

"I thought that we agreed with Dawson the other day that firearms were off the table," Michael said, as one of the seamen helped him and

Mila board the cutter. Berman turned and shot him a nasty stare, holding the rifle with the barrel pointed in the air.

"Relax, Mikey," he said. "Dawson ordered all of us to bring assault rifles just in case we run into additional problems. What if there are more of these things and they try to swamp us? Then they wouldn't be endangered any more, now would they? Shit, we already know they can take down a boat."

"Well that was a small fishing boat, not a naval ship," Michael shot back. "And yes, they would still be considered endangered. Probably even critically endangered."

"Whoa, hey, what's going on over here?" Sheriff Dawson said, coming around the bend of the cutter's cabin. "Michael, are you ready to become Florida-famous for this animal?"

"I thought that we weren't using lethal force," Michael said, ignoring the question. "What's up with all these machine guns?"

"Just a safety precaution, Mr. Robinson," Dawson replied. "Suppose we have to go into a gator nest to get to this thing. Well, like you said, gators aren't endangered at all. If they try to swarm us, I want to be ready. Trust us, Michael. We have plenty of tranquilizer guns. Berman, why don't you put that thing away for a while? We have a little ways to go before we reach the creature's territory, anyway."

Berman shrugged and agreed, turning down one of the ship's corridors to retrieve a tranquilizer gun. Dawson walked away with the seaman, discussing maritime safety techniques and matters that didn't concern the mission.

"Do you two know each other?" Mila asked.

"Dawson and I? Not exactly."

"No, not the sheriff. The other guy? The guy from yesterday, whom I got easily annoyed by?"

"Oh, Jeffrey Berman. Yeah, we were friends in a past life. Now I'm not really sure what we are. Just two former acquaintances that have been thrown into a maelstrom together."

16
LEAVING THE DOCKS

Michael was informed by one of the seamen that the largest cutter, and the cutter he would be bunking on, was known as a Coast Guard Marine Protector. The ship was named *Anglerfin*, stretching out to 87 feet long and coated in the traditional Coast Guard white paint with the red stripe insignia near the bow. On the back deck near the stern, the boat was separated down the middle, where a small landing boat was parked, ready to deploy. Despite the ship's size, Michael wondered if there would actually be room for him on board below deck.

The soldier, who introduced himself as Sam Sheraton, elaborated on the *Anglerfin* and its purpose on the mission.

"Yes sir, me and the boys jumped at an opportunity to aid the police department with the issue down here," Sheraton went on, showing Michael and Mila around the deck. He was a younger recruit. Michael guessed the man just graduated out of Cape May a year or so earlier.

"I bet," Mila said. "It's been a hell of an adventure so far."

"I wouldn't know," Sheraton said. "When Sheriff Dawson told my superior officers back at the base about what happened yesterday, you know with the new victim and all, they sent us down with *Anglerfin* for added comfort. All of us on board are glad to get away from the usual Miami boating patrols. Personally, I think having *Anglerfin* here might be a bit of overkill. I think the other boats will do fine against a croc, but it's nice to have a safe peace of mind. The only drawback is the ship can only go so far into the Glades, because the streams will get progressively narrower. Even getting it into this little cove to dock was a nightmare."

"So, they're talking about the crocodilian up in Miami?" Michael asked, stepping around an industrial looking pipe that protruded up on the deck.

"Are you kidding?" Sheraton laughed. "It's all they talk about!"

They continued to walk around the deck, nearing the tower cabin. Sheraton explained more terminology, happy to hand over some Coast Guard wisdom to the civilians.

The other two cutters, one of which Michael rode on the other day, were known as RB-S, which stood for Response Boat-Small. They were 25 feet long, encompassed by a chrome outer plating with an orange trim around the top, operated by only two seamen. The two airboats were manned by police troopers.

"Mr. Robinson, Ms. Madison," Bolasco said, walking up to them. "We're ready to ship off, no pun intended. Is there anything else you need from your vehicles?"

"Other than a Wi-Fi hotspot?" Michael answered with a smirk.

"I'm afraid not," Bolasco laughed. "I know. I'm gonna have a hard time without Facebook. But that's just how it goes."

"Then I'm all set," Michael assured him. "Mila, is there anything I can get for you?"

"Thank you for asking, but I have everything," she said, patting his back.

"Are you sure?" he asked.

"You betcha," she said, making fun of his recent joke.

"Can I show you around the cabin?" Bolasco asked. "This ship isn't exactly built for crocodile hunting expeditions, so your sleeping arrangements might be a little crammed. Dawson, Berman myself, you two, and three other Coast Guard seamen will be on this ship. Adrienne, Graham, Ryan and Clarence are taking shifts on the airboats and might be switching off intermittently, so it'll just get more crammed."

"I figured as much," Michael said as Bolasco and Sheraton led them up the stairwell to the cabin.

Dawson was there, with another two seamen, looking out over the swamp. It was the bridge, filled with complex driving levers and gauges. Windows looked out onto the swampland ahead, facing the endless greenery that saturated the numerous islands. From this elevation, the room looked out over much of the treetops.

"All right, Willie," the sheriff asked, "are our guests all ready? We're about to set course for the wilderness."

"We're all good," Bolasco replied as they walked into the cabin and shook hands with the other Coast Guard seamen, who introduced themselves as Nico and Matty.

"Okay, gentlemen," Dawson said. "We're good to depart. Let's head out. Nico, can you send a radio call to Ryan, Adrienne and the others. They can begin to move ahead in the airboats."

"Aye, sir," the seaman called Nico said, starting the cutter by various controls on the console. "All units clear to depart. Airboats first. Try not to get too far ahead. Weather will be getting worse throughout the day. Over."

The other boats in the fleet started to pull away from the docks, backing out over the waves. The two RB-S boats followed the airboats into the cattails, darting down the inlet. Michael grabbed a hold of the wall as the *Anglerfin* slowly eased out of the dock, surprised by the power behind the ship. To his front, he could see some of the police officers waving goodbye to the ship as the cutter turned slowly. Soon the vessel was facing the other direction, following the other boats slowly from a distance into the Southern Glades.

"How long until we reach the place where the attacks have been occurring?" Mila asked.

"Should be about half an hour," Dawson said. "We'll be moving slower than the other ships. The swamp's a little tight in here. It's a big ship for the Everglades."

"We'll have to move pretty slow," Nico stated from the controls. "Plus, the storm coming later will definitely complicate things. The trek will get progressively worse."

"Storm?" Mila asked.

"Yeah," Sheraton cut in. "It's supposed to be a nasty one, too! Sure picked a good time to go hunting a crocodile, huh. Oh well, you're always in good hands on a Coast Guard Marine Protector."

"It's a miracle the Coast Guard lent us this ship for the operation," Dawson said. "On behalf of all Palm Grove, we thank you gentlemen."

Berman and Bolasco nodded in agreement.

"I was gonna ask," Michael said. "How did you manage this, Sheriff? Sam was just telling us how excited he was to go on this excursion."

"I just wanted to feel a little safer than I did yesterday," Dawson smiled. "After seeing that video that Owen took, I knew we needed something bigger as a base of operations. The Coast Guard was happy to offer this to us for the duration of the expedition, provided the *Anglerfin* doesn't go too far into the Everglades where damage to the hull might happen."

"I hope you aren't expecting to put that animal on this ship," Michael said. "Judging by the length in the video, I think it will barely fit on the back deck, even when it's tranquilized."

"You don't suppose it will fit on the back?" Dawson asked, jokingly. "No, of course not. I wouldn't feel comfortable putting it on the ship anyway. I don't see any possible way we could lift it up here anyway. When we find it, we'll send out coordinates to one of the Coast Guard choppers and we'll airlift the animal to the dock, where a truck will be waiting to take it to Redland. Relax, Mr. Robinson, I've already worked out all the little details."

"Sounds like a lot of moving parts," Michael observed. "But it sounds like you've got the logistics covered. I'm impressed. I wouldn't have thought of an airlift. You sure a helicopter can get in here during a storm?"

"Easily," Matty, the other seaman assured him. "Coast Guard Jayhawks fly in bad storms all the time. Those birds are used to it."

"It's our only option," Dawson added. "There's no way we could get a truck or a forklift back here. Sure there are a few back roads that wind through the area, but even the closest attack was a mile from any road. Anyways, Willie, can you show them where they're sleeping and where to store their packs?"

"Right this way," Bolasco said, leading them down an interior stairwell towards the rear of the bridge that fed below the ship.

The area below in the hull was very tight. Everything was a mundane gray and industrial looking, with weird entrances and exits that reminded Michael of a tightly crammed submarine. Above, harsh fluorescent lighting lit up the corridor like a nuclear fallout bunker. Beside a series of pipes and ducts were two small rounded openings that entered into crammed bedded nooks wedged into the wall.

"You'll have to sleep here," Bolasco said, pointing to the nooks with an apologetic tone. "Sorry. I hope neither of you are claustrophobic."

"It's fine, Willie," she said. "None of us are treating this like a vacation in a five star hotel. Besides, it's kind of fun bunking out on a Coast Guard cutter. One more item off my bucket list."

"Very funny," Bolasco grinned. "But, I'm glad you understand. We should be in range of the croc's territory in a half-hour. Dawson's hoping we'll encounter the thing in the first hour and get this over and done with on day one. The rest of us aren't as hopeful, but we'll see. By the way, you can get back out to the deck by going through that hatch. Is there anything else you need from me for now?"

"No, I think we're good," Michael said.

"Okay, call up if you need me. Dawson wants to go over a press release for when we brief the town on the situation, and he wants my help to brainstorm how to write it. It's my fault for being an English major for one semester. Oh, happy days! See you both in a bit!"

Bolasco vanished back up the stairs, leaving them to settle in.

"Well, I'm going to go out to the deck and do some wildlife photography until we reach our destination," Mila said.

"I didn't know you did photography?"

"Oh, yeah. With my Nikon D850. It's my second passion after animals. Do you want to come along? You can be in the pictures, too! I'm still messing around with my new prime lens. They call it a nifty 50, because it's a fifty-millimeter lens and very compact. Cute, right?"

"I might be along in a little while," Michael said. "I want to do some research first in my crocodilian book that I've brought along, just to double check for sure if this really is a new species. I'd hate to be wrong about this, just because I missed a chapter. I need to prove my worth somehow."

"Suit yourself," she said, flashing a smile before opening the hatch and melting into the fading sunlight.

Michael cracked open the ancient college book he had brought from his suitcase, sitting down on the Coast Guard couch in the break area, opening the cover under the bright overhead light.

The book was titled: **Crocodilians – The Complete Overview**.

He thumbed through the book from cover to cover in five minutes, but nothing jumped out at him as anything resembling the man-eater from the day before. So far, the theory was holding up. There was a new crocodilian species alive in the Everglades.

Before he packed the book away, he decided to skip back to a chapter he paid little attention to.

Prehistoric Wildlife of North America – Dinosaurs, Mammals, and Beyond.

It was worth a shot, he figured, skipping through until he found a section about ancient coastal North American predators.

17
CHARLIE AND SANDRA

"Watch out for his jaws!" Charlie shouted, grabbing Natalie by the tail and dragging her kicking and thrashing out into the enclosure hallway. Sandra narrowly avoided the jagged teeth as they snapped closed, inches away from her hand. The violent hiss of the crocodilian rang out through the corridor.

"Sorry," she said, stepping around the caiman and running past Charlie as he lugged the five foot long reptile out of the pen. Natalie was the final caiman that needed relocating, rendering the entire pen free of reptiles.

Sandra ran down the hall to Pen 6, peering through the bars. All of the other caimans that were already transferred had lumbered away from the door. Most of them had already exited the interior enclosure, heading for the outside savanna exhibit to bask in the afternoon sun. For the most part, they commingled without any aggressive behavior and paid no attention to the employees.

"Is the doorway clear?" Charlie asked, laboriously pulling Natalie down the hall. She ceased her thrashing, now confused and infatuated by the change of scenery of the dark tunnel.

"Yeah, they're all away from the door. Wait, let me double check. Okay, yeah, it's all clear!"

"Okay, open it up. I'll be quick about this and we can finally get to lunch. Hurry up!"

Sandra yanked back the locking mechanism and twisted the lever, flinging the door wide open. The caimans on the inside turned and watched, stirring from the loud clang of the iron door but making no attempt to escape back into the hall. A few hissed angrily, but moved away as Charlie lumbered inside, hauling with him the final caiman.

Once he made sure Natalie was at least five feet inside, he ran around the reptile and back into the hall. Sandra shut the door behind him, locking it up securely before she took her hand off the handle.

Sandra watched through the glass window pane in the door as Natalie hissed once at her new surroundings before trotting off into the outside enclosure. The other caimans in the interior room turned to follow her.

"Wow, what a rush," Charlie commented. "Glad that's over. That took all morning!"

"Yeah, it helped that Michael already moved Sinclair this morning. After that one day, I've pretty much decided I won't be handling him anymore."

"I'm just happy Mike finally trusts us to do this stuff," Charlie said. "I feel like I actually learned something from this lame place."

He stretched in his high Judas Priest shirt, trying to flex his minuscule muscles for her. With his greasy ratty hair and phony tough-guy behavior, Sandra could feel herself growing more repulsed by everything he did. She resisted the urge to comment on the large ketchup stain on his jeans that had been there since last week.

"What do you mean?" Sandra asked. "I'm always learning something new here."

"Well, you know, he never lets us do anything with the animals," Charlie argued. "Other than clean the pens and give lessons to the visitors, which are just bull shit facts that don't mean anything. No one ever listens to our speeches. They just wanna see the crocs!"

Sandra smirked. She could feel her sanity beginning to collapse under his annoying commentary and disinterest for the zoo.

"Why would he let us handle the animals, Charlie? If anything were to happen, he and the sanctuary would be liable. I think he's smart not to involve us with his wildlife. Michael's just looking out for his business – and us. You should really be more appreciative, Charlie! This zoo is an awesome job and a really great place to make a difference. After all, isn't that what it's all about?"

"Yeah, yeah," Charlie muttered, pulling out his phone and ignoring her question.

Sandra shrugged him off. She was beginning to tire of his pathetic attempts to be a rebel. The way she saw it, Charlie was the most immature nineteen-year-old she knew. When was he going to grow out of the "bad-boy" phase? His attitude was repugnant and his personal hygiene was deplorable.

She started out of the security tunnel and back to the exterior visitor trail, when Charlie called back to her.

"Hey, Castillo!" his pubescent voice echoed down the passageway.

She stopped, rolling her eyes before finally turning back to him. She wanted desperately to avoid him for the rest of the day.

"Yeah?" she asked, visibly annoyed with her colleague.

"Hey, what are you up to this Saturday night?"

"Why?" She tried to feign interest, but didn't really care what he was inviting her to.

"Nothing. Just that a few of my friends are going out for drinks, I was wondering if you'd like to go with us? We'll probably be heading up to Miami, probably to South Beach, if you're interested."

"Charlie, aren't you only twenty?"

"Yeah, so?"

"How are you planning on getting into any of those clubs? And getting drinks?"

"My cousin works at one of them. He'll let me in. Trust me, he's cool. As for the rest of my friends, they're on their own. But I know my cousin will make an exception for me if you're there."

She couldn't decide what that meant, but it aggravated her further.

"I don't know," Sandra said finally, searching desperately for an excuse. "It's supposed to be kind of shitty throughout the week. I think the heat wave is about to end. It's gonna be rainy on and off – too rainy for South Beach, don't you think?"

"No way. It'll be great, we'll just stay at the one club. I'll buy all the drinks. You in? Or do you have a more important night of Netflix and ice cream planned?"

She was unsure how to respond to the comment.

Sandra thought for a second, temporarily seduced by the offer. She was twenty-one and hadn't had a decent night out in months. But her distaste for her co-worker outweighed the possibility of a good time. Thankfully, she remembered a potential prior commitment.

"Sorry," she said. "I forgot, Michael asked me to be on call all week for overtime help at night. If he comes back with his new crocodilian, he wanted me here to assist in health setup and documentation. And if he doesn't need my help, I was planning on finishing my term paper on Saturday night."

"You're in school?" Charlie asked in disbelief.

"I'm in accelerated curriculum track, yes," Sandra shot back, offended. "I swear I've mentioned this to you before. If I take an additional class each summer, I'll get my degree faster. Millions of students do this, Charlie. But have fun – tell me how it is!"

"Okay, but –"

Sandra shut the door behind her, sealing her immature teammate back in the corridor before continuing out into the mulch trail, waving hello to a family of visitors who were reading a brochure on the bench near the alligator pen.

The twin four-year-old boys raced away from their parents, eagerly pointing through the glass at Buck who slipped into a pool near a waterfall feature. Their innocence made her temporarily forget her loathsome co-worker.

She went to the employee lounge up near the welcome building, reached into the refrigerator and pulled out her half-eaten hoagie. As she sat down to finish it, Sandra decided to go for a drive instead. Odds were that Charlie would be coming up to the break room for his leftovers from yesterday. The less time she had to spend around Charlie, the better.

That attitude of his is going to get him in trouble, she thought as she brushed through the lobby doors and into the sunny parking lot.

He was really starting to piss her off.

18
THE VOYAGE

"Graham, any sign of anything up there? If any of you candy-asses see anything, you better believe I want to be the first to know. We're using up a lot of the Coast Guard's resources in doing this. I wanna have these boys back at their usual duties in no time. Over."

He turned and nodded to Nico, who remained expressionless at the wheel.

Michael had gravitated up to the top cabin where Dawson was communicating with Graham over the radio. Bolasco and the other seamen were there. Nico was driving the ship, Sheraton was operating controls on the console, and Matty was at the window, scanning over the swamps through binoculars. Berman was somewhere below deck. His absence made the bridge more approachable.

He found it hard to read through his book with all the commotion, but the clear lighting from the windows made it easier to read.

"*Graham here*," Graham's voice replied over the radio system. Graham was riding ahead in the first police airboat, accompanied by the two RB-S boats. Through the windows, Michael could see that the other boats were far ahead, weaving in and out between swamp land patches. The *Anglerfin* had to move slower. Nico commented that the ship wasn't built to traverse such tight corners, which made Michael anxious.

As the journey continued to progress, the island and swamp pockets became tighter together and the bends sharper, which slowed the momentum of the *Anglerfin*. Several times, the RB-S boats circled back to check on the flagship, doing arcs around the rear of the ship before continuing ahead again.

"Well, anything yet? Over," Dawson asked impatiently, looking out the front windows.

"*Nothing yet, sir,*" Graham said over the radio. His voice was hard to hear over the buzzing of the airboat fan. Adrienne could be heard in the background, mumbling something about the burning temperatures.

"There's a few normal gators on the shore. No crocodiles. Definitely not any crazy dinosaur killer crocodiles like we saw on that little boy's video. Have you heard anything about that, by the way? How's the kid doing? By the way, you can tell Adrienne that storms will be blanketing the area later this evening, so she'll get some relief from the sun. Over."

"The boy's grandmother is coming down from Georgia," Dawson replied. "There will be a memorial tomorrow in Miami for John. Unfortunately, Owen's parents were divorced. They're having a hard time getting in contact with Owen's mother. Over."

"What a shitty situation," Graham replied. *"Well they sure as shit better get a hold of her. That boy needs his mother, now more than ever. I don't know how their ship made it through the swamp without the patrols catching it. It's a real tragedy – a terrible twist of fate."*

Owen's father's death interrupted Michael's studying as he continued to scan the prehistoric section. The scene from yesterday was still fresh in his mind. He would never forget the lifeless expression on Owen's face when they saw him first, before Adrienne took him away for medical attention. The capture of this creature was imperative, before more boats went under and more children were orphaned.

"Hey, how close are we to the croc's territory? Over."

"The GPS says less than two minutes," Dawson answered. "That's probably two minutes for you, but five for us, at the rate we're going. Over and out."

The sheriff turned to one of the seamen.

"Can't you make it go any faster?" he asked.

"It's pretty tight in here, Sheriff," Nico replied, slowly turning the wheel. "Any faster and we may risk scuffing the swamp floor. The Everglades isn't that deep, you know."

"How deep are the Everglades?" Michael blurted out. He was surprised he didn't know the answer himself.

"Nine feet-ish," Matty answered, refusing to look away from the binoculars. "Maybe deeper in certain scenarios."

"Wow. And this ship can fit in here?"

"Barely," Nico remarked. "I'm keeping an eye on things carefully through the sonar systems. There may come a time where we have to stop altogether. When that happens, we'll just have to rely on the RB-S boats and the airboats."

"Damn," Dawson said. "Sorry, I just want to get this over with. I hope it doesn't take all day."

"I understand, sir," the soldier replied. "Please know that we are going as fast as we can."

Michael could sense the tension growing in the cabin, closing his book and stepping into the conversation.

"Exactly how big is the hunting territory, Sheriff?" Michael asked. "How far apart between all the killings?"

"This son of a bitch has a range on him, that's for sure," Dawson replied, pressing his binoculars against the window, stepping beside Matty. "To answer your question, between Jonah Levine's scene and where we found Owen's father's boat, it was about five miles."

"Five miles?" Michael was shocked. "That's a hell of a territory, Dawson. You think we'll be able to traverse through that in a week?"

"We'll need to do more than that, Michael," the sheriff laughed. "Of course, assuming *Anglerfin* can take us in that far. And that's not counting the distance from Owen's attack scene to the cove where the first attack occurred a month ago. That victim is still unidentified. That's probably a distance of eight miles."

"Eight miles?"

"If I had to guess," Dawson shrugged. "Just pray that the animal shows."

"Oh, it'll show," Michael said. "I'm not sure if it will be in our first week, but he'll show up eventually."

"You sound pretty confident about that," Dawson stated. "I hope you're right."

"I figure the animal might be drawn to motorboats," Michael explained. "They would be easy to spot driving up through the surface if the crocodilian was waiting from below. I could imagine the animal waiting until the boat stopped, and then attacking from below the surface. Were any of the victims found near damaged boats like the one we saw yesterday?"

"Nice theory," Dawson said, impressed by the biologist's speculation. "But no, there were no other boats present, other than the one from the Sanders killing. Bolasco, how close are we now?"

"We are officially within range of the suspected creature's habitat," Bolasco replied. "Levine's body was found just a few hundred yards north, in an adjacent tributary. The airboats are already scouting ahead there now."

"Okay, the hunt is on!" Dawson smiled, peering back through the binoculars.

Michael followed the direction that he thought Dawson was staring, tracing the angle down to the bow of the boat, just below the cabin. The sheriff was watching Mila, who leaned towards the front railing like Rose and Jack from Titanic, bending over to look across the lake.

The lack of subtlety on the sheriff's part made Michael smirk.

Mila turned and saw them up in the cabin, waving him down to meet her. She was moving her hand quickly, as if she had seen something that demanded immediate inspection. Her hand kept pointing to the right, over to the thicket twenty yards away.

"I think she might have something," Michael said, leaving the cabin and racing down the stairwell, his heart racing and ready to burst out of his chest in excitement.

19
FIRST SIGHTING

The scorching sun blinded Michael as he fumbled down the cutter stairwell to the bow of the *Anglerfin*. The mid-day heat of the Everglades was becoming unbearable, and the expedition was not even an hour underway.

"Hey, I think I see something over on that beach there!" Mila called to Michael as the wind rustled through her semi-curly hair.

The veterinarian pointed over to a small sandy cove, surrounded on all sides by palms and exotic plants. There did appear to be something on the bank, but he couldn't immediately make it out from their distance. On first glance, it looked like an elongated crater.

"Can you see it?" she asked.

"Yeah, but not well enough to identify what it is. But you're right – it shouldn't be there. And it's big."

"What's going on?" Dawson said, racing out to the bow with Bolasco and Berman seconds behind him.

"Give me those binoculars," Michael requested.

Dawson handed them over and Michael threw them over his eyes, looking out over the marshes. After focusing the lens, he finally found the spot that Mila had seen. She had successfully discovered a large crocodilian trackway running from the water's edge up into the greenery, slipping into the jungle under the branches. Whatever animal had made the tracks was not on the beach. But the tracks seemed fresh.

"What is it, Michael?" Bolasco asked, squinting at the dunes.

"Tracks," Michael replied, handing the binoculars back to Dawson. "Large ones, by the looks of it. They're fresh but they go off into the jungle. Good find, Mila."

"Can you tell how big they are?" Mila asked.

"Not from this distance, but they're definitely from an adult."

"Could they be from our croc?" Berman asked, squinting through the aviators.

"It's possible," Michael admitted.

"I'll get Graham on the radio to stop the fleet," Bolasco suggested. "We can get a scouting party on foot to go in the jungle. With any luck, he'll be right in those trees, and the mission will be wrapped up in no time."

"Good thinking," Dawson praised his deputy. "Let's head to shore and see what we can find."

"You're sure it's safe?" Michael asked. "It looks pretty tight in there. From what I see, there's only a thin dirt path that goes into the jungle. We'll be easy targets if our crocodilian is in there."

"We'll be fine, Mr. Robinson," Dawson said. "If it gets too thick, we can cut through with machetes. Berman, tell the seamen to get the boat ready to take us ashore."

"Yes sir."

Within a minute, the *Anglerfin* stopped moving forward. The airboats and RB-S boats circled back and regrouped with the flagship, patrolling around the water. Michael and Mila were escorted by Sheraton to the rear of the deck. Back there, the floor was manufactured with a divide in the middle, where a small motorboat was waiting to depart from the flagship and drive to shore.

Berman, Bolasco and Dawson were already there. The sheriff and Bolasco both had tranquilizer rifles with them. Much to Michael's chagrin, Berman had retrieved his M4 again.

"Here, throw these on," Sheraton said, handing them life vests. "The water isn't that deep, but still. Good to have."

After Michael and Mila got into the boat and draped the life vests around them, Sheraton opened the rear access panel, stepped into the boat, started the motor, and they glided out to the murky water. The dark waves washed around them, and with them, the uncertainty of what was lying beneath.

"There's no way he's down there," Bolasco shouted over the motor. "Our fleet probably scared all the crocodiles away within a one-mile radius."

"I wouldn't count on it," Michael replied loudly, recounting his theory on the animal's potential attraction to boating traffic.

"I bet he's watching us right now," Berman said ominously.

"You better not intend to use that on a crocodile," Mila urged him. "They're endangered."

Berman looked at her for a moment, then turned away. The comment appeared to bounce off him effortlessly. Michael assumed by now that Jeff was just being an asshole, holding the weapon for the sheer joy of pissing them off.

"Any potential leads from your book?" Mila asked, angrily turning away from Jeff.

"Not yet," Michael laughed. "Honestly, I'm hoping I don't find anything. It'd be great to officially label this as a new species, which I'm still thinking it is."

The boat ripped over the cove in no time. They braced themselves as the craft beached itself against the sand bar, coming to a halt with a muted boom. Sheraton jumped out and secured the boat, pulling it onto the bank and motioned for them to follow.

20
THE TRACKWAY

All around the cove, the jungle rose out, shooting out from the dunes like invasive weeds. Behind them, Michael could hear the other RB-S boats patrolling the water's edge, looking for anything peculiar under the cloudy surface.

He kneeled down on the sand, studying the tracks with Mila, while the three policemen secured the area, poking their tranquilizers into the leafy fronds that bordered the embankment. So far, the area seemed free from danger, but behind the hedge of vegetation, safety was uncertain.

"Well, Michael?" Dawson grumbled, wading around in the shallows just behind him. "Are they from our animal?"

"Hard to say, Sheriff," Michael said, placing his hand in the footprints.

"Why's that?"

"The tracks are too ruffled up in the sand."

The problem with the trackway was that it was falling apart, imploding on itself. What footprints that remained were partially caved in when the sand around the edges crumbled. The tail was considerably wider, an unfortunate trait of the animal that helped distort the footprints as it was dragged along.

"Damn. How'd that happen?" Bolasco asked, poking his barrel into the brush.

"The sand bar here isn't very strong," Michael explained. "It's practically mud. Something could have walked through here and have been half as large as our specimen and we would never know it. Look where we've walked already. The whole beach is already sunken in because we've trampled through it."

Even as he spoke, Dawson began to sink in the sandbar, stepping hastily out of the mud and onto the ground where the beach met soil.

"In other words, it could be our monster crocodile. But also, it could just be a normal fat-ass alligator," Mila noted.

"Right," Michael laughed, again surprised by her word choice. "It's virtually impossible for me to say yay or nay, without finding the actual animal to compare."

"Well, what are we waiting for?" Berman asked, who'd remained silent since Mila criticized him on the boat for having his rifle. The officer was crunching down on the sandbar near the foliage, following the trackway until the footprints slipped behind the jungle wall.

"You said it yourself that the tracks are fresh, Mikey," Berman said. "It's probably just through the brush here. We can just follow the tracks until they take us right to him."

"I don't know Jeff," Michael said. "It looks pretty thick in there. Maybe instead –"

Berman pushed aside one of the palm fronds with his rifle, slipping into the corner. The jungle overtook him instantly, and he was gone.

Dawson stepped up to the edge of the plants, shaking off mud from his boots.

"Hey Jeff?" the sheriff called out. "Jeff Berman!"

There was no answer.

"Okay, we're going in," Dawson said. "He may be onto something. Bolasco, hold up the rear and let's let these two go in between us. It looks fairly complex through here, so stay tight. I'd hate to run into an anaconda when we're all separated. Sheraton, would you mind staying with the boat?"

"I'll stay, sir," the seaman answered eagerly.

"Good. We shouldn't be long."

The land behind the jungle border was dense and difficult to predict. The ground rose and fell uneasily, morphed by thousands of years of evolving swampland. Weeds and rocks protruded out sporadically. Thorny bristle bushes often blocked the trackway, causing the group to circle around and relocate the trail.

"I tell you for all the shit we're going through to find this son of a bitch, these better be the right tracks," Bolasco complained, swatting at a brave dragonfly that whizzed past his brow.

The heat of the day amplified under the leafy canopy of the Everglades jungle.

Michael could feel the sweat stinging his eyes as he wiped his forehead with his shirt, leaving an unflattering golden stain soaking into the collar. Mila was fanning herself against a thick dead tree trunk beside the trail. For the moment, the group had paused the journey. They had lost the trackway through the jungle, and could barely see the *Anglerfin* through the greenery. Jeffrey Berman was nowhere to be seen.

"Hey, Berman!" Dawson shouted through the jungle. "Where are you? Let's head back and regroup at the beach."

No answer, other than a few calls from exotic birds. Michael swatted angrily at a mosquito, missing.

"Hey, Berman!" Bolasco called, his voice echoing through the forest. "Let's get the hell out of here, man!"

Still no answer.

"Where is he?" Dawson asked.

"I don't know," Bolasco grunted. "You know how he does this shit sometimes."

The wilderness engulfed them from all sides, rising up until the trunks met with the green umbrella of canopy. Michael couldn't see more than a few feet away to his front, and could barely make out the cove behind him through the leaves. The white form of the *Anglerfin* hovered in between two fronds, far off to the rear.

He noticed Mila coming close to him. The jungle was making her nervous. Far above, a crane swooped over the trees, casting a shadow over the path before it vanished over the palms. Clouds above momentarily blocked out the sun, covering the wetland in shadow.

"This place is starting to freak me out," Bolasco remarked.

"Hey, Berman!" Michael yelled, cupping his hands over his mouth. "Jeff! Where are you?"

"He better not be screwing around," Dawson said. "Where in the hell has that bastard got to? I ought to demote his ass."

Suddenly, a burst of gunfire rang out through the jungle. Birds jumped from their branches, crashing through pockets of fronds and taking to the sky, soaring over the heads of the explorers. The weapon's discharge sounded close, maybe a few hundred feet into the foliage.

"Is everyone all right in there?" yelled Sheraton, calling far away at the beach. Through the dense leaves, they could see the RB-S boats swerving from their positions and heading towards the beach, regrouping towards the sound of weapon discharge. The gunfire rang out again, this time in more frantic bursts.

"That's his gun!" Bolasco yelled.

"He might be in trouble!" Dawson cried, crunching through the path towards the blasts.

21
THE OTHER SIDE OF THE ISLAND

The gunfire rattled off again. From far away, it sounded like the rounds were ricocheting off similar rocks and trees, coming in controlled bursts before ceasing and restarting intermittently. More birds continued to flee to the skies, shaking the leaves overhead.

"It's definitely his M4!" Bolasco said as they sprinted up a path that snaked through the ferns.

The crocodilian trackway appeared again in random areas, vanishing when the mud transitioned to grass. Berman's boot marks were visible now as well, walking alongside the edge of the crocodile foot impressions. Michael struggled to keep up, blowing through vines and wide leaves that smacked off his face.

The vegetation ahead began to slope downward. Ahead, through the reeds, another body of water began to appear. They were nearing the other side of the micro wetland island. The sounds of the M4 drew near, louder with each passing step.

Berman had to be close.

"He's down there!" Bolasco guessed, pointing to the new beach that would undoubtedly be on the other side of the next round of trees.

"Jeez," Mila yelled over the rifle fire. "What the hell is he shooting at?"

The beach on the other side of the wetland island was larger, more expansive. They stumbled onto it by accident, falling five feet from a small, hidden cliff onto the brown dunes beneath. Michael face-planted first into a puddle of seaweed, regaining himself quickly enough to catch Mila as she spiraled off the ledge, saving her from touching the slosh. Dawson and Bolasco tumbled just a few feet away onto a spongy grass bed with a dull thud, their tranquilizer guns falling in the earth beside them.

"Are you okay?" he asked her.

"Yeah," she replied. "Thanks for the catch. That would've been bad!"

Michael set Mila down, looking around cautiously for fear of some unseen predator that may be waiting nearby under the mud. He relaxed when there were no alligators around him.

Before he could figure out where he was or what had happened that caused them all to fall, the figure of Berman filled his vision.

"Berman," Michael started. "What the fu –"

The M4 rang out again, this time over the water. Berman was standing on a large boulder that sat half submerged in the murky swamp. Surrounded by cypress trees that rose up like a cage, he scanned the water around him, barrel pointed at the waves. Berman's target was unseen, but swimming somewhere, presumably near the rock. Finally, the officer's rifle stopped firing. Berman ejected the magazine carelessly, letting the clip plop below the surface of the water before he hopped down on the dunes, facing Michael triumphantly with a smug look.

"Oh, hey Mikey," he smiled. "I was waiting for you to show up."

"Jeff, don't ever run off like that again!" Dawson commanded, coming up behind Michael with Bolasco, who was trying to clean the clumpy sand from inside his boots. "Why the hell didn't you answer me when I was calling for you?"

"Sorry, Sheriff," Berman replied in a calm, cocky voice, inserting anther clip into the M4. "Guess I got kind of carried away in the hunt. I followed the tracks to this side of the island. Shit, by the time I got over here, the damn thing got the jump on me. Popped out of a small pool just beside the cliff you just dropped off. I don't think it was the one we were looking for, but it sure was a big guy. By the time I was finished with it, a few other gators came over. They must've been attracted to the M4 rounds. Sorry, Mikey. I know you told me not to, but it gave me no choice."

Berman gestured over to a large dark green lump that sat rigidly on the coast, just a few yards from the jungle. It was a slaughtered male American crocodile, dead from many gunshot wounds to the head and body. Blood slopped out from the red dots, collecting in thick concentrations under the corpse that coated the sand red. The eyes had glazed over, staring back at Michael with a haunting tale of the creature's final moments of life.

To make it worse, the size and coloration of the carcass indicated it wasn't the monster from Owen's smartphone video.

Rage overwhelmed him. He couldn't believe what Berman had done.

"Jeff! I told you that the American crocodiles are endangered!" Michael yelled in an angry fit, whirling back to face the officer. "I told you all that back at the station, during the first meeting. Why would you do this?"

"Look, Mike," Berman started, trying to sound calm, "I told you the thing almost –"

PTTT!

Berman's jaw swung to the side as Michael's fist connected with the officer's face in a quick right-handed hook. Berman tripped backwards, dropping the M4 onto the sand, but remaining on his feet.

Dawson and Bolasco watched, their faces frozen in disbelief. Mila muttered a gasp, taking a step back out of the fray. Michael retracted his fist, immediately remorseful of his actions. He knew that Berman would be on his feet in an instant, ready to hand over an ass-whooping.

"Look, Jeff, I'm sorry. That was out of line," Michael said, taking a step back, hoping his attack wouldn't be avenged.

"You bet it was," Bolasco shouted from the sidelines. "Assaulting an officer. That's at least a year in prison. And you've got three witnesses here."

"Willie, forget about it," Berman said, rising up to his feet. He picked up the M4 and dusted it off. "Mike just got a little carried away, didn't you Mikey?"

"Are you kidding me, Jeff," Willie started. "This guy just –"

"It's okay, Willie," Berman repeated himself.

He stared coldly at Michael, his eyes like ice.

"Yeah," Michael said, confused at why Berman wasn't smashing his skull into the sand. "Sorry, Jeff. I guess I don't know the events leading up to the crocodile's death. I believe you. Next time, could you just try to use the tranquilizer? I promise, it will be every bit as effective."

Berman wiped a drop of blood that crawled down his lip, refusing to answer. His hair was a mess, speckled with grains of sand, and his eyes lit like torches. He was angry. Michael could sense it, but yet, refused to attack. Berman had outsmarted him – and he knew it.

"You hit like a pussy, Mike," Berman said, ruffling his hair. "Okay, Sheriff. Let's head back to the ship. Sorry for the confusion on my part, was just trying to get this wrapped up quickly. I won't wander off again."

Dawson said nothing for a moment, trying to recollect his thoughts from everything that had just played out before him.

"Well, all right. I think the path was somewhere up there. The Coast Guard is probably wondering what's going on. Don't wander off again, Jeff. There's a crocodile titan out here, after all. And Mr. Robinson, please refrain from striking my men. I understand you're very passionate about your line of work. But punching an officer is a criminal offense. One more strike like that and you're off the operation, arrested. I'll make it my personal mission to make sure you get the maximum penalty for striking my officers. I'll find another home for our crocodile, understood?"

"It won't happen again, sir," Michael assured him, trying to sound as apologetic as he could. "I don't know what got into me."

"It better not," Dawson said with a rigid frown. "Okay, Willie. How are we getting up this hill?"

Bolasco and Dawson wandered off. As Michael was about to offer a personal apology to Jeff, the officer bumped past him, stopping when their eyes locked once again.

"Pull that shit again, please," Berman whispered, just low enough that Mila couldn't hear him, before following the other officers back up the cliff face.

Michael's heart raced. Suddenly, the crocodilian didn't seem to be the biggest threat.

22
AN EDUCATED GUESS

The remainder of the day seemed to fly past. By the time he made it back to the ship, Michael was fatigued and confused, ashamed of his actions taken against his old best friend over a situation that he wasn't sure about. Now his relationship with Berman was even more fractured than it had been before. He chose to leave Berman alone for the rest of the day, choosing not to confront him any further about his trigger-happy shooting spree.

To make matters worse, the skies above continued to darken throughout the day, indicating the storm was still approaching.

The *Anglerfin* continued down the river in the Everglades, sailing slowly over the alleged territory of the supercroc. The RB-S boats and airboats scouted ahead, frequently leaving the immediate view of the flagship from behind the cypress trees and slash pines. Ahead, the orange sun began to cast jagged, oblong shadows over the swamps, covering certain pockets in darkness.

Occasionally, Michael noticed pairs of red eyes watching the flagship from the swamp before sinking back down to the depths as the ship's waves washed over them. They were quickly losing the daylight. Already a few stars were peeking through the ominous storm cloud cover.

"Alligators," Michael said. "You see them? They love watching the boat."

"Just as long as they don't love it enough to climb up on it," Mila laughed.

He stood with Mila on the back deck of the *Anglerfin*, watching the waves churn as the ship slowly continued its predestined course. Cranes and birds occasionally flew overhead, cawing before finding perches somewhere away from the Marine Protector ship, but close enough to observe.

After the encounter with Berman, Dawson felt that it was best to keep Michael and the officer separated, so he transferred the shifts.

Berman and Bolasco were sent to one of the airboats, while Graham and Adrienne were brought on board the *Anglerfin*, at least for a few hours until another shift rotation would commence.

"Heard you had quite the afternoon," Adrienne said as they walked along the rail, smoking a cigarette and staring out at the sunset through the mangroves.

He didn't picture her as a smoker.

"It was my fault," Michael admitted. "I overreacted. I still think it was wrong what he did. Just handled it in a poor way."

"Don't be too hard on yourself," the officer replied. "We've all wanted to take a shot at him one time or another. He gets under my skin, too."

"What's his problem?" Mila asked. "We were on the beach coming up with a plan, and he just takes off. We try calling out for him – he doesn't answer. We find him on the other side of the island. He shot and killed an American crocodile. And presumably several other alligators. What made him do that?"

"He's been a little fidgety lately," Adrienne confessed, flicking the cigarette into the water, which quietly irritated Michael. After the trouble he already got into with Dawson and Berman, he assessed that saying anything wouldn't be smart.

"Fidgety?" Mila asked. "I'm not sure that's very professional for a law enforcer."

"Yeah, he's just been very irritable," Adrienne said. "A few of the other officers have noticed it, not just me. So his behavior today doesn't surprise me. It's been growing continuously worse ever since he started hitting the gym hard. Bolasco is his only continuous loyal friend."

"Shouldn't going to the gym relieve all that stress?" Mila asked.

Adrienne shrugged.

"You would think. But still, striking an officer? You're lucky he didn't lay you out!"

"Trust me, he wanted to," Michael assured her.

The events in the swamp continued to loop in his mind. Running through the jungle towards the sound of raining gunfire. Tumbling down the cliff and face-planting in the sand. Seeing Berman with his smoking M4. Punching the officer in the face, resulting in swift condemnation from Dawson and Bolasco. And Berman's final, fateful threat in passing.

Pull that shit again, please!

It was a challenge – a warning.

He decided not to tell Mila or Adrienne about Berman's final remarks, figuring they were probably uttered out of anger and self-restraint from not beating the living daylights out of him. Michael assumed Dawson and Bolasco's presence there may have spared him an ass whooping.

He hoped, if given another chance, to apologize to Berman again and try to smooth over the brewing conflict. The thoughts of their senior year of high school and their abrupt falling out briefly came back to haunt him as Graham's voice broke out of the cabin.

"Hey, Hulme," Graham yelled down. "Hey, you down there?"

"I'm over here," Adrienne replied, shouting over the boat engine and the churning water. "What's up?"

"Bolasco called from the airboat. He and Berman are having difficulties with some of the controls. Can you come up here and help me guide them through it. They're talking gibberish – I don't know what they're talking about?"

"Can't Ryan and Clarence help them?"

"They're not in the same area and they're not answering their radio."

Adrienne frowned, unhappy to be leaving the gossip and shuffled up the stairwell to the cabin.

"What kind of cop just shoots an American crocodile?" Mila asked when Adrienne left. "He's a grown man! He could've just run away."

"He was always a hot head in high school, but not like this."

"Wait, hold the phone," Mila stopped. "You two went to high school together?"

"Yeah. A million lifetimes ago." He laughed nervously.

She was about to comment further but stopped. Mila could sense that he didn't want to talk about their time together, and changed the subject.

Michael still had his nose buried in his wildlife encyclopedia. She noticed that this chapter had a lot more dinosaur illustrations than crocodilian ones.

"What's that?" she asked. "Are you thinking it's a T-rex?"

He laughed. The comment cheered Michael up, momentarily forgetting about Berman and the American crocodile incident.

"No, not exactly," Michael smiled. "Could you believe if someone really found a tyrannosaurus down here? That'd be national news! I'm looking at prehistoric crocodilians, primarily searching for helpful facts of the coastal predators."

Mila read the title of the book.

"Prehistoric Wildlife of North America," she said, admiring the cover art. "Wow, impressive book. I know this croc is big, but it can't be 'dinosaur big', can it?"

"Well, you'd be surprised," Michael said. "North America was once home to many diverse species, as you know. Not only just dinosaurs like tyrannosaurs and ice age mammals, but also crocs. One species in particular caught my eye earlier when I was reading over this in the cabin. I can't get it out of my head."

"Which one?" Mila asked as Michael flipped through the encyclopedia.

"This one," Michael said, finally arriving on the terrifying illustration.

"Deinosuchus – a thirty to thirty-five foot long prehistoric killer that lived right here on the East Coast around the Late Cretaceous period. It was such a formidable apex predator in this region, that it was capable of taking down big dinosaurs. Look at the artist's drawing. Tell me that doesn't look strikingly similar to the video shot by Owen just yesterday."

The pencil illustration that hugged the top right of the page, featured a large crocodile with an enormous head and a long, muscular tail. A small human adult male and pet dog silhouette stood beside the drawing, indicating the animal's dominating and tyrannical size.

"It does look similar," Mila admitted. "But the colors are all wrong. The artists drew it brown, and our animal was green and yellow."

"Well, even so," Michael argued. "Obviously, the artist has never seen a real deinosuchus before. It's unlikely that the illustrator would nail the right colors on an animal presumed dead for 70 million years."

"Don't go using logic on me," Mila snapped, pushing him playfully. Michael pretended to swat her away, but secretly craved the attention. He hadn't socialized this much with a woman outside of work for years. He thought that after all of this Everglades business had solved itself, he would make a point to ask her out after he gave her his personal tour of the sanctuary.

"Well, what do you think of my theory?" Michael said finally, squinting to block out the setting sun over the swamp.

"Well, what exactly is your theory?" Mila asked, mimicking his voice playfully. "That this deinosuchus crocodile has survived in the Everglades for millions of years, somehow avoiding mankind all these years."

"To summarize, yes," Michael said, impressed that the veterinarian had nailed the animal's scientific name on the first try. "Also, it's technically not a crocodile, but actually a relative of American alligators. Look, even the snout is very alligator-like."

He held up an illustration.

"Yeah, yeah. So, what's this theory?"

"Basically, my theory so far, if one can call it a theory, is that if indeed this animal is a Deinosuchus from the Cretaceous period, that somehow it survived here all this time – right here in the Everglades.

When Florida became gradually colonized and settled, in the 1800's, the wildlife was gradually pushed out, just like the American crocodiles. Currently, Florida is the only state in the United States that has American crocodiles, a species that was recently considered very endangered.

"I believe that the same may have been true of the Deinosuchus. Since the Late Cretaceous, maybe by some divine intervention or simply a twist of fate, the species survived extinction. Assuming by now, millions of years later, only a handful of the animals remain, right here in the Southern Glades. And now with Palm Grove continuing their urban expansion with Sunset Ridge in the rural areas, the remaining deinos, however many there are, now feel compelled to defend this entire area."

"You think there may be more of them?" Mila asked, hanging onto his every word.

"Well, who can be certain," he said. "The saying 'where there's one, there's another' may not apply here. From what we know already, we can discern that the animal is critically endangered, as it has never been discovered anywhere else but here in the Southern Glades. It's just like you said earlier – it's a pretty big mess of a jungle out here, there may be dozens of undiscovered species just waiting to be found. I have to hope there can be more of these massive crocodilians, but who can tell?"

"And you really think the United States government will let you keep this thing if it is that endangered *and* an undiscovered species?" she asked.

"Why not?" Michael suggested. "I happen to run a crocodile sanctuary right near its original habitat. I'd say, I'm the best person to rescue it. They have to keep it somewhere."

"So this crocodilian is a 70-million-year-old super predator?" she asked, still having a hard time fully conceding to the idea, despite how interesting it was.

"I'm going to continue reading up on deinosuchus facts in this book," Michael said. "But other than that, I can't think of any other possible explanation for what we're seeing. I read that they tended to congregate in estuarine areas and coastal regions, so the Everglades makes sense. Only prehistoric crocs reach sizes like our animal, so it's either a deinosuchus or a close modern day relative. And modern crocodilians for the most part are half that size, even less. Look, here's another diagram showing how small modern day crocs are compared to the ancient deinosuchus."

He held up the book again, showing her a diagram featuring deinosuchus next to a Nile crocodile. The deinosuchus illustration was over twice as long.

"Now tell me that isn't the same size animal that we saw on the video," Michael said, confident in his argument. "And look here. This section refers to the deino's noticeably enlarged osteoderms. I recall seeing similar scutes on the animal in Owen's video."

"Osteoderms?"

"The spikey things on the deino's back," Michael said, trying to dumb it down. "They're a prominent trait in both present day and extinct crocodilians. But look closely near the snout. This is how we'll know for sure if the animal is a deinosuchus."

"How's that?" she asked.

"Look at the tooth," Michael smiled, pointing at the illustration and summarizing the blurb. "It has a noticeable pair of teeth that stick out of its mouth near the front of the bottom jaw, just beneath the enlarged snout. If we see that, we can pretty much assume it's a deino."

"Did you see that in Owen's video?"

"I was looking for it, but no I didn't see it. But the quality of the video and the auto-focus feature was to blame for that."

"I must admit, it certainly looks to be the same size," Mila said finally. "It's a miracle that it's survived all this time."

"There was probably a good amount of them until the urbanization skyrocketed," Michael went on. "It's possible that they are also in the ocean, swimming between Florida and Cuba, although it's currently unclear in paleo studies if they could thrive in saltwater."

"Well if this is the last one of its kind, I think it will be going to the right place," Mila said.

There was a certain genuineness about her that made her beauty transcend into innocence. If anything good were to come out of the expedition, he thought, it was meeting her.

"Hey!" Graham yelled from the cabin. Michael and Mila rose to their feet, dropping the encyclopedia on the deck.

"What is it?" Michael yelled, scooping up the book "Did you find the animal?"

"Maybe," Graham replied. "Something just ran into Berman's airboat. We have them on the radio. The RB-S boats are far upstream, so we're en route to get them."

"Get them?" Mila asked.

"Yeah," Graham said. "Whatever ran into them packed a hell of a punch. The boat's sinking. And worse. The storm's supposed to break any minute."

23

SINKING

"Berman, come in, over! Can you hear me? What's going on over there, over?"

"It's Willie, sir," Bolasco replied over the *Anglerfin's* cackling radio. *"Jeff is down underwater, trying to dislodge whatever we ran into. Don't worry just yet. He thinks it may just have been a fallen tree. He should be back up soon. Over."*

"I understand. Tell him to watch his back down there. We're en route to your location and should be there before the RB-S boats arrive. How slow is the ship sinking?"

"It's just a small dent on the right side, sir," Bolasco replied. *"Sinking slowly, I'm not worried. Over."*

"Hang tight, Willie. We're coming. Over."

"Thank you, sir. I'll be in touch. Over."

"How long till we're at their location?" Dawson asked, turning to Nico who was driving the *Anglerfin,* while continuously checking the sonar and other controlling mechanisms.

"Five minutes," Nico replied. "Maybe ten, tops."

"What do they figure ran into the boat?" Michael asked, coming into the cabin.

"They're not sure," Dawson replied, shooting Michael a cautionary glance after what they had been through earlier. It was their first conversation since the fight with Berman. "Bolasco guessed it was probably a dead tree, but we're not taking any chances. The boat's trapped upstream, and sinking slowly. We're coming to extract them."

"The other boats won't be there sooner?" Mila asked.

"No, the RB-S boats are too far out, and we're having trouble reaching them with our other airboat. Ryan and Clarence aren't responding. We're the last line of defense."

"Ryan and Clarence aren't responding?" Mila asked, concerned.

"The radios are acting up from the weather," Matty replied. "The storm's about to burst down on us any second. I'm just hoping we can get there. The swamp is getting shallower. Our ship might have to stay back. We can still reach them with the landing boat."

"Shit, Sheriff," Graham said from the corner of the cabin. "You don't suppose they ran into that thing out there?"

"I hope not," Dawson said. "At least not until we arrive."

"Michael has a theory on what this thing is, Sheriff," Mila said, stepping to the front of the bridge.

Michael was completely unprepared to talk about his theory, which he considered very much in its infancy. He found that he needed more evidence to back up his claims that a Cretaceous massive crocodile was somehow alive and flourishing in the Southern Glades. Now the spotlight had turned to him, everyone waiting to hear him speak.

"Well, speak up," Dawson said. "That's why we brought you along."

Michael could feel Adrienne and Graham's eyes fixated on him. Even Nico and Matty were listening, turning away from their assigned duties.

"I believe this creature may be something known as a deinosuchus," Michael said, trying to collect his thoughts. He wasn't sure where to begin. Already, he could tell that they had no idea what he was talking about.

"Deinosuchus?" Dawson said. "You mean that ancient crocodilian you were talking about when I brought you on board this operation? I thought you said that was completely off the table. You said it was impossible."

"That's correct, sir," Michael replied. "But honestly, up until now I didn't know that it may be more possible than I thought. At the time, I only knew a few facts about deinos, but the possibility of an animal surviving that long made me shrug off the whole idea. But I've done some research, and now I think this may be what we're dealing with."

"What are you basing this on, Robinson?"

"Well, mostly it's just speculation," Michael began. "The deinosuchus was a super-sized crocodilian closely related to alligators. It hunted across coastal regions of North America, over 70 million years ago. Given a large swath of swampland like the Everglades, it would be a perfect place that this animal could hide all these years. My idea is such: when your urban expansion plan started, you forced the animal from its territory further south, making it increasingly aggressive to passing boats or backpackers, usually with deadly results."

"Are you serious, Michael?" Dawson said, uttering a laugh. He thought Michael's idea was preposterous, looking around the room to see if anyone else would find the theory ludicrous, but the others were listening closely to Michael.

"Is that all you're basing this on?" Dawson said, after failing to get any laughs from the others.

"No," Michael said. "The most obvious similarity is the size of the animal. None of us have personally seen the deino, other than the shaky handheld smartphone clip from Owen's father's death yesterday. But from what we saw, I can conclude the animal is at least twenty-five to thirty feet long. That puts it in range of the deinosuchus' suspected length.

"And then there's the coloration of the animal. Again, from what the video revealed, the animal has yellowish, gold stripes descending down the animal's back. Now none of us were around in the Cretaceous when these crocodilians thrived and reached their peak, but we're all around now, and we know that there are no other crocodilians alive in present day with that description.

"Thirdly, and this is something I didn't think about until talking with Mila, but I'm pretty sure I saw enlarged osteoderms on the animal's back. Deinos had very large osteoderms, which are the bone plates on the backs of crocodilians.

"There's virtually no way to prove my theory unless we capture the animal, after which we will compare its bones to known fossil samples from deinosuchus, my guess is with a tedious x-ray scan."

"It's some theory," Dawson said, unimpressed.

"You don't believe it, do you?"

"Not exactly, Mr. Robinson. It sounds like it belongs in a bad Syfy channel movie."

Suddenly the radio came back to life, causing Nico to jump at the controls.

"Holy shhh – Dawson. Are you th – re. Come in! Over."

Bolasco's excited voice erupted through the cabin's radio. Sloshing noises were heard over the static, overlayed by sounds of boot shuffling and crunching of metal. The poor reception made the message hard to decipher.

"Willie, we're still here," Dawson said, picking up his microphone. "The ship is almost in range! What's happening? Are you all right?"

"Sher.– if, you... get... under the – water..."

"Willie! Come in, over!"

Bolasco's call was quick and short. The officer's voice, although distorted, was audibly frantic and panicking. Something was happening at their crash site.

The radio went dead.

"Damnit! How close are we?"

"It should be around the next bend, sir," a soldier informed him.

"Adrienne, go and get the shotguns. I think this big bastard is trying to take our boys on! We're gonna have to bring the hammer down. Shit! I hope they're all right."

"Shotguns?" Michael said. "Sheriff, you can't kill it. If it is a deinosuchus, it will be the find of the century. Hell, the discovery of ten lifetimes. Since the internet. Use the tranquilizers!"

"He's right," Mila said, backing him up. "The tranquilizers should knock it out."

"Michael, shut the hell up," Dawson commanded. "I've had enough of your shit for one day! If you wanna stay on this operation, then you sure as hell better start playing ball."

"You kill that thing and you're violating the Endangered Species Act," Mila informed him. "And don't think I won't go blowing the whistle on you and this whole operation if the animal is killed."

Dawson turned, enraged and confused that Mila had so strongly sided with Michael. He had been beaten.

"Go and get the tranquilizers," Dawson yelled at Adrienne. "Hurry!"

Adrienne smiled, relieved that the sheriff had changed his mind.

"Yes, sir!" she said, running down the interior stairs.

24

BOLASCO

The swamp was dark.

Willie fidgeted in his seat, fiddling with the radio controls on the airboat, hoping to revive them. In the past half-hour, the sun had vanished over the tops of the cypress trees, leaving the entire wetland in shadow. It didn't help that the electricity in the boat had failed, after the colossal jaws of the unseen carnivore crunched down on the circuitry.

The rain shower was close – he could sense it.

He had a small glimmer of hope, remembering that he had a utility flashlight attached to his belt, flicking on the light and trying to find any trace of salvaging the damaged radio. His smartphone had fallen into the swamp during the creature's second attack, rendering his only other potential form of communication useless.

"Hit a tree, my ass," Bolasco said, casting off Berman's initial analysis.

He shined his flashlight over the muddy surface of the swamp water that raged around him. Berman's bubbles from his scuba gear had stopped pumping from below. Bolasco ruled out the idea of swimming down to him to inform him that there was no tree that struck the boat. With that monster swimming around down there, Berman was as good as dead.

He scanned the radio transmitter with the flashlight.

The whole device was screwed up. The abyssal mouth enclosed on the device five minutes ago, to which Bolasco ducked quickly to survive, narrowly avoiding the crocodilian's fatal bite. After the beast crashed into the radio transmitter, it vanished back into the bog, as if playing a deadly game of cat and mouse with Berman and Bolasco.

Several times after the attack on the radio, he could see the creature's large sharp scutes drifting above the water before plunging back down below, reminding him of the shark's dorsal fin from the movie *Jaws*.

All he could think of was one thing.

The sheer size of the creature's teeth, hinted at by the gentle moonlight that filtered through the canopy and storm clouds. Even in almost complete darkness, Bolasco knew it was the same vengeful animal from Owen's video.

His foot splashed through swamp water that sloshed over the floor.

Oh yeah, he thought. *The boat is sinking.*

Through the cypress trees, Bolasco could see the lights of *Anglerfin* coming around the bend. He could see two seamen on board the deck, shining flashlights around the water, searching for the airboat.

From the distance, he thought they may be Sheraton and Matty.

He shouted twice to them, but found that they couldn't hear over their waves and the *Anglerfin* engine.

The splash of a closer object made him freeze, flipping the flashlight again over the water. The large crocodilian scutes had surfaced again and swirled around the front of the boat, before dipping back below the surface, taunting the stranded officer.

"Shit!" Bolasco cried, grabbing for his hip. Then he remembered – He set his service pistol on the *Anglerfin* bridge before Dawson transferred them to the airboat. He had never felt more alone – more vulnerable. His only hope now was rescue, but deep down he knew that the ship would never make it in time.

Water began to creep up his ankle as the floor of the airboat continued to dip under the bog. On the bank he could see the glean of dozens of red eyes – baby alligators watching intently as the super predator moved swiftly around the sinking ship, ready to claim another life.

Bolasco jumped up on the seat, scrambling out of the rising water that engulfed the craft. He turned around, checking the distance between the airboat and the approaching *Anglerfin*. The cutter was still too far out of earshot range. He found himself waving his arms frantically, uttering panicked phrases that he couldn't remember a second after mumbling them. Matty and Sheraton continued to search, with no success.

Bolasco found himself wondering if the ship would even be able to reach the airboat. The Everglades weren't as deep where their boat had wrecked, and the *Anglerfin* could only go so far into the shallows.

Again, he could feel the water creeping up his boots. As he reached the top of the airboat fan, he realized he was trapped. To his horror, there was nowhere left to climb.

Bolasco looked up.

Above, the branch of a cypress tree hovered just out of his reach. Bolasco jumped, his fingers just inches below the branch as he crashed back down on the boat, a foot skidding down the metal edge of the fan.

He caught himself before he slipped down – but realized it was useless to escape.

Behind him, the scales descended again below the water level, before the crocodilian surged out of the swamp, jaws spread open like an unsprung bear trap. It took only two seconds before the crocodilian enclosed around its victim. Blood spattered like a volcano down Bolasco's head as his skull was crushed under the incredible bite force of the monster, his soul and sanity escaping his body.

The predator dragged his corpse off the boat and into the blackness of the darkened swamp, just as Graham's flashlight located the shipwrecked airboat.

25
THE DEPTHS

Berman shifted under the log, feeling the weight of the dead tree pinning his body to the floor of the murky river. The log wasn't hurting him. The current was partially supporting the weight of the trunk.

Berman chose to keep himself under the tree as a hiding place, trying to remain absolutely still to blend in with his surroundings. He had managed to find a small burrow in the sandy floor of the swamp, using the hole for cover and the tree as a door. He breathed only when he had to, shooting small bursts of bubbles up to the watery barrier at his own risk.

Through the moonlight glow that radiated from the surface, Berman could see the horrific attack on the airboat happening just above him. At first, he debated on swimming to the surface to help his colleague, but the amount of crocodilian silhouettes swimming nearby made him change his mind. Especially the large, dinosaur-like crocodilian with the large scutes that swam back and forth like a cyclone, appearing intermittently within the cloudy water, carefully calculating how to attack Bolasco.

Seconds after submerging, Berman realized that there was no tree that hit the airboat, but rather, the big super-sized crocodilian from yesterday's attack. Although the creature moved in shadowy silhouette, the size and length of the animal told Berman all he needed to know – he had come face to face with the man-eater of the Southern Glades.

Ironically, the animal looked more like an alligator than a crocodile, contradicting what he himself and many on the Palm Grove PD thought the monster really looked like. Even in the shadows, Berman could see the widened snout and pearly white jagged teeth, searching the wilderness for human flesh.

He kept his breathing to a minimum. The oxygen tank could last another forty minutes. All he had to do was stay put long enough to swim for rescue, whenever that would be.

Where were those RB-S boats? And the other airboat – where are

Ryan and Clarence? Surely by now, Bolasco must have made contact with Anglerfin.

But now that the lights of the airboat had gone dark, Berman had his doubts. The big crocodile must have damaged an important electric component of the little craft.

A smaller alligator drifted past Berman, who was surprised that the creature didn't look over and attack. Instead it drifted peacefully past, scurrying on the ground floor into some seaweed, kicking up the riverbed as it landed on the watery floor, out of sight.

Berman yearned for his M4 that he foolishly left back on the cutter. But underwater, the rifle would do no good. He recalled the old horror film, *Creature from the Black Lagoon* from the 1950's and how Richard Carlson and Richard Denning hunted the creature with large spearguns. Even one of those weapons would do. Without a gun, he felt powerless.

He still felt irritable, pissed off from the encounter earlier in the day with Michael. Quietly, he claimed part of the responsibility. His quest for perfection and athletic prowess had recently pushed him into experimenting with steroid use, where he developed an unhealthy addiction to power lifting at the gym. He knew the 'roids were responsible for his increasing insubordination and distrust with his peers, except Bolasco. Berman made an oath with himself – if he made it out of the swamp alive, he would quit the steroids cold turkey. His muscles ached often, and now when he needed them most, he felt fatigued and exhausted, knowing if he passed out, he'd never make it back to the surface.

Still, seeing Michael after all these years provoked his irritability. It was over fifteen years since they had last seen each other, and it had not ended on good terms. If he managed to survive this ordeal, Berman made a promise with himself to get drunk later that evening, with a bottle of scotch he smuggled on board, and confront Michael about their senior year. It had been weighing on him all these years, and now faced with possible death, he felt he had nothing to lose.

Another regret – not punching Michael back on the beach. But showing some self-restraint was important to show Dawson that he was still an officer who could control his temper. Berman continued to brood on the swamp floor as a large shadow passed overhead, heading swiftly towards the airboat.

It was the damn Godzilla alligator again.

Other crocodilians parted away and scooted off into the dark as the big behemoth approached like a silent tornado. The form was so large that it often blotted out the moonlight when it crossed above him.

The air boat above continued to dip forward, reenacting the Titanic disaster on a miniature level.

Berman could see that most of the front of the boat was now submerged, drifting slowly towards him far below. Although the rippling surface distorted his view, Berman thought he could see his colleague shouting for help on top of the seats.

No, it was the fan. Bolasco was on top of the boat's fan.

He appeared to be jumping up, presumably trying to get the attention of something.

Rescue isn't far away!

The *Anglerfin* must have been approaching, Berman thought. More light was glimmering on the surface, bouncing off trees and shrubs until it gently touched on the rear of the airboat. The coloration of the new lighting was tungsten, indicating artificial light from flashlights.

Hurry, you bastards!

Suddenly the overgrown crocodilian swung itself around, underneath the boat, shooting up to the surface where the vessel was half-sunk. With speed that made Berman freeze with fright in his underwater fortress, the crocodile bounced on top of the boat, causing the vehicle to dip further down.

There was a quiver in one of the shadowed ripples, and then an explosion of blood that gushed over the airboat, coating the surface of the pool, turning the moonlight red.

With a tug, the animal yanked Bolasco's corpse over the decking, dragging the body into the abyss. Other alligators scooted away as the titan flew over Berman's log, with an agility that disturbed and reshuffled the seafloor.

Above, the airboat dipped forward vertically, bubbling as the vessel sank completely below sea level, descending swiftly down to the bottom in a vacuum of bubbles and Bolasco's blood before crashing on a large boulder several yards away from Berman.

He looked around.

The other crocodilians had all slipped away, leaving Berman alone in the moonlit lagoon. Above, the artificial lighting continued to grow, until eventually it glowed so brightly that it washed out the surface. Ripples churned up the surface, and Berman could see the white and red coloring of the *Anglerfin* hull as it drove above him, filling his vision.

It's now or never, he thought.

With a massive push, that he credited to the steroids, he hurled the log away and kicked up the ground as the officer propelled himself up to the surface, refusing to look back. His muscles were killing him, and his head throbbed painfully behind his transparent visor.

In the murky depths, the massive crocodilian turned, abandoning

Bolasco's corpse in the bog and turning for Berman who kicked out from his hiding place towards the ship lingering above. Berman kept his eyes fixed on the salvation on the surface, ignoring the prehistoric terror lurking behind him.

The terror with the protruding lower teeth on the bottom jaw.

26
SUNKEN

Michael could see the tail end of the airboat as it slipped below the swamp into darkness, even before Sheraton shined his flashlight over its glistening edges. Violent bubbles shot out from the place where the boat went under, pushing up traces of red liquid. Immediately, he knew that it was diluted blood. The bubbles stopped flowing shortly after the boat disappeared, replaced by the red coating that shimmered under the moonlight.

He gathered on the bow of the *Anglerfin* with Dawson, Adrienne, Graham and Mila. Matty and Sheraton continued to light up the area of the attack with the flashlights, searching for any signs of submerged human life – or signs of the elusive monster croc.

"Where are they?" Dawson shouted, grabbing one of the soldier's flashlights and moving it frantically over the marshes. "What the hell happened? Can we get any closer to the land?"

"No," Matty said in a matter-of-fact tone. "The sandbars are getting dense. We will run aground and damage the ship. We're going to have to stick to the middle."

"Berman!" Graham yelled, trying to shout over the roar of the ship's engine.

"Cut off the engine!" Dawson shouted to Nico, who remained in the cabin.

The *Anglerfin* was quieted, stopping its forward motion.

Under the quiet rustling of the wilderness, the scene was eerily calm. The place where the airboat vanished had settled into a delicate whirlpool. Several small alligators swam off in the distance, over to the beach, turning to watch the scene unfold like stadium spectators at a football game.

In the darkened skies, a thunderclap broke through the tranquility. A storm was on the horizon, and in a few minutes, it would the raining violently.

"Did anyone see what happened?" Nico shouted from above.

"No," Michael yelled back. "We thought we saw one of them, Willie or Jeff waving at us, but by the time we rounded the bend, the boat was sunk."

"Graham, get on the radio and see if you can get a hold of the RB-S boats," Dawson ordered. "And where the hell is our other airboat? They've been out of radio contact now for a while. See if you can find where they're at and get them back here. This mission's concluded. We need more manpower and daylight to take on this thing."

"Are you suggesting we go back?" Graham asked. "But we've come so close! The animal must be around here somewh–"

"Damnit, Graham, don't argue! Just get up there and do it. Men are dying!"

"Yes, Sheriff," Graham said, running back up to the cabin and cursing under his breath.

"It must have been our creature," Michael noted. "What else could take down an airboat?"

"Down there!" Adrienne pointed down below the ship. "Bubbles. Something's about to come up!"

A trickle of bubbles began to ascend from the darkness, breaking at the top and growing more tumultuous as the visitor approached the surface. As the bubbles grew quicker and larger, Berman broke through the waves, ripping off his respirator and grabbing at the ship frantically.

"Hey! Pull me up!" he yelled up at them. "The son of a bitch is coming right for me!"

He pounded at the ship's hull, coughing up water that washed over his head.

As Sheraton threw down a rope to the officer, rain suddenly began to pound down on the wetland, turning the swamp into dancing artful waterworks. The soldier secured the rope to one of the ship's railings, and Berman started to scramble up, tossing off his oxygen tank into the red waves of the bloody swamp.

Through the rainstorm, a large body of scales began to rise up from the marshes, gliding through the waves directly at the officer. A pair of red eyes washed upward on the surface in front of an enlarged snout, locked onto Berman's struggling form. Michael could see the animal coming, gracefully navigating through the rippling surface like a skillful Olympic swimmer, shooting forward with deadly precision.

"Shit!" Dawson yelled. "Do you see that thing? Adrienne, get the guns!"

"There's no time," Adrienne told him. "Quick, pull him up!"

Michael's hand closed around Berman's. With a forceful tug, Adrienne and Michael pulled Berman over the railing onto the metal decking. As he rolled over the top of the ship, the crocodilian surfaced, snapping in frustration that the target escaped, the jaws snapping inches away from Berman's foot.

The animal jumped so far out of the water that most of the reptilian head banged up over the side of the deck. The onlookers watched in amazement at the monstrous size of the prehistoric animal, marveling at its magnificent existence and strength. Michael looked admirably at the green and yellow coloration, confirming it was the same creature from the video.

Roaring a primordial call of irritation at the humans, the crocodilian fought to stay above water as gravity pulled the animal swiftly back into the swamp, preventing another agitated snap of the jaws. Fortunately for the boaters, the animal wasn't tall or strong enough to hang onto the deck, cutting the horrific first encounter abruptly short.

"What the hell is that thing?" Adrienne yelled through the torrential rain, as the others stared speechlessly at the falling titan.

"It's a deinosuchus," Michael informed them with a terrified confidence. "A male, judging by the size."

Michael watched as the giant reptile fell back into the water, confirming the presence of the outward protruding teeth on the bottom jaw when the mouth was closed before the entire figure dissipated again below the bog.

His theory had been correct. They were dealing with a super predator from the Cretaceous.

27
COMMUNICATIONS FAILURE

The survivors congregated in the bridge of the *Anglerfin* tower, as Graham and the seamen attempted to troubleshoot the radio. It wasn't long before they concluded what the obvious problem was: weather interference from the storm. They couldn't pick up any of the other boats on the radio – but the radar provided the crew with their estimated positions.

Michael had a brief momentary lapse of memory to call for help on his smartphone, before remembering the poor phone signal and lack of internet access. He checked his screen, failing to see any bars on the upper left edge of the welcome page, and clicked the phone back off.

The radar indicated the RB-S boats were close, although not moving, and thus probably had scooted off onto the land to avoid the fierce waves that pummeled throughout the Southern Glades. The remaining airboat was farther away, also not moving, probably on land.

The *Anglerfin* didn't have the luxury of heading to land. The environment around the cutter was littered with obstacles like cypress trees, rocky outcroppings, and marshy sand dunes. One of the soldiers dropped an anchor off the side, so at the very least the ship would stay put, keeping it out of harm's way from banging against the numerous obstacles.

The world outside the cabin windows had gone from calmness and tranquility to stormy calamity. The trees were shaking in the wet winds that tore off the branches, sending some of them perishing down into the blackness of the waves. The wildlife on land retreated from the weather, scattering into the dampened foliage. Far away, a bolt of lightning touched down somewhere in the Everglades, lighting up the sky for a moment before leaving the world once again in the dark.

Berman was taken down to a medical setup below the bridge. During his ascent from the swamp, he scraped his leg on a drifting rock, tearing through his wet suit and leaving a nasty scar.

"We're screwed," Dawson said, looking out the window at the

horrific storm that converged on the cutter. In the last half-hour, the fate of the entire mission had shifted. What started as an animal rescue operation now became an evacuation. Only now, they couldn't radio for help, and couldn't communicate with the missing boats.

"That thing was remarkable," Adrienne said, reflecting on the deinosuchus attack that occurred a half-hour earlier. Shock was still resonating throughout the ranks, shock of what they were up against. Shock of Bolasco's sudden death.

The vision of the crocodilian was still fresh in their minds. "What did you say it was again, Michael?"

"It's a deinosuchus," Michael said. "An apex predator from the late Cretaceous period. Millions of years ago these animals flourished along these same wetland areas throughout coastal prehistoric North America. Now, all this time later, there's possibly only a handful of these beautiful animals left, but only one that we know of for sure."

"Beautiful, my ass!" Dawson commented under his breath.

"So that thing's like a dinosaur, right?" Adrienne asked, ignoring the sheriff.

"Prehistoric crocodilian, but more or less, some people might say dinosaur," Michael laughed nervously. "It's bigger than a lot of dinosaurs. I wouldn't be surprised if that thing took down tyrannosaurs. Evidently, it had a bite force that could rival a tyrannosaur. We're talking a bite force of almost 20,000 newtons! The one we're dealing with is definitely a male."

"How can you tell?"

"Its size. Male crocodilians are usually considerably larger than the females. This animal is even larger than my textbook indicates."

"That thing killed Willie," Dawson said, watching the fierce rain descend on the cabin window, collecting in little puddles on the deck below. "We have to put an end to this."

"You're not suggesting killing it, are you?" Mila demanded.

Dawson was quiet, pausing before he answered. He could feel the eyes of the bridge on him, waiting to see what he would do.

"He killed Willie. Willie Bolasco was one of our best men on the force..."

"Well we're not killing that animal, Sheriff," Michael said firmly. "I won't stand for it. It needs to be brought to a zoo, studied. It could be the last of its kind. My heart goes out to Willie and his family, but we owe it to science to further examine the animal. There might be more to gain from it, including further insight into evolutionary barriers, deinosuchus hunting techni–"

"Michael, shut up!" Dawson roared. "I've had enough of you for the remainder of this trip! Keep your mouth shut and stay out my way."

"Sheriff, I don't think we could kill it if we tried," Adrienne said gently from the corner of the cabin. "It looks like it spends most of its time underwater. And I don't think any of us are willing to go down there, not after what happened to Willie. I'm not. I know Graham won't – he's terrified of normal-sized alligators as it is, let alone an adult deinosuchus. Maybe we should come back with more manpower."

"Believe me, we are," Dawson shot back. "But after some thinking, Graham's right. We're not going anywhere until we confirm that the other boats are all right. Leaving them out here with that animal swimming around alarms me."

"It will surface eventually, Adrienne," Michael corrected her. "It probably has a place nearby that it will go and sunbathe, or maybe somewhere to escape the rain. But we're certainly not killing it. We'll tranquilize it. In fact, I'll personally volunteer to go after it when we find out when the deino is land bound."

"What makes you think I'm letting you go out there?" Dawson said, folding his arms. "You have no experience with this kind of crocodile. And I'm willing to bet no experience in firearm safety and gun handling."

"I don't have any experience with firearms, but I know I have more experience dealing with crocodilians than anyone here. And it's not a crocodile. Deinos are more closely related to alligators, Sheriff."

Dawson fumed at Michael's terminology correction. Before Dawson could comment further, a voice replied from the stairwell entrance in the far corner of the room.

"He won't be going alone," Berman said, lumbering into the room. "I'll be going with him. And yes, Michael, before you ask, I'll bring the tranquilizer guns."

The room was surprised at Berman's sudden appearance and swift recovery. One of his legs were bandaged so thickly that it looked like a cast. He moved slightly sluggishly, as if worn out from the ordeal underwater.

"What makes you think I'll let you go either?" Dawson replied. "You have to be sore from your little wilderness excursion from earlier. You two aren't going out there alone. And I'm sure as shit not in any authority to tell the seamen to go in there with you."

"I'm the only one that's seen this thing take a life," Berman replied. "It killed Willie, and it's gonna keep killing until we get it the hell out of here. The storm should be letting up soon, and we'll have our chance."

Michael was shocked that Berman was suddenly siding with him. It was a complete one hundred and eighty degree change from the officer he knew only hours earlier, who was shooting like a crazed active shooter at the alligators. Michael figured something was up, but chose to play along. He was confident that Berman's true motives would reveal themselves soon enough.

"Well, the crocodile is secondary at this point," Dawson said, shaking off any further plans to apprehend the animal. "Our first and only objective is to link up with these other boats. Then regroup back at the docks, before coming back out with more men. And better weather – today was a bad choice to start the operation."

"Where are they?" Berman said. "I could take the motorboat out of the back and try to make contact with them."

"Absolutely out of the question," Dawson replied. "The storm is only growing worse. And from what the radar says, all three boats are very far. And that's a Coast Guard boat. You aren't qualified to operate it."

He pointed down at the swirling green radar and sonar screen which sat on top of a console next to the wheel. Three blinking dots emitted from the screen, all far away from the central dot that represented *Anglerfin*.

"I'll operate it," Sheraton spoke up.

"What?"

"I'll drive them out," Sheraton continued. "It's no problem, really. My superiors are expecting us to drive that thing around anyway. What good is it having the Coast Guard with you if you aren't going to let us do what we do best? Saving lives."

Nico and Matty nodded, causing Dawson to rethink his standpoint.

Suddenly a white light shined through the cabin, burning through the thick rain and shimmering over the glassy wall.

"Damnit!" Dawson bellowed, shielding his eyes. "What is that?"

"It's one of our utility flashlights," Adrienne said. "It's probably Clarence or Ryan. Maybe they are trying to signal us for help from their location!"

They gathered up to the glass of the cabin, trying to get a better view at the light-bringer. The illumination was definitely artificial, coming from a flashlight as Adrienne assumed. The waver of the light was far away through the thundering showers, obscured from view by many mangrove patches and cypress trees. The light would shine for equal increments of time before ceasing all together. Seconds later, the bursting sequence of light would repeat.

"They must be attempting to duplicate Morse code," Graham guessed, squinting through the raindrops. "It's a distress call. They need help!"

"It looks like it's probably half a mile through the rain," Berman assumed, studying the glow through the trees. "I can make it there in the motorboat with no problem, if Sheraton comes with me to help."

"No problem," the seaman replied. "I'd be glad to. *Semper Paratus* – always ready! That's the Coast Guard motto."

The sheriff looked wearily out the window, trying to determine just how much danger the stranded officers had gotten into. With the roving dinosaur crocodilian on the loose, his decision process didn't last long.

With a quick nod, he gave Berman the green light.

"Get out there, Berman," Dawson said. "Bring our men home. The rest of us will keep an eye out for the other RB-S boats – and hopefully, Willie's body. We owe it to his family to reclaim it, if the animal didn't eat it."

"Yes, sir," Berman said, as he turned and walked up to Michael. "Care to put your money where your mouth is, Mikey?"

28
THE RESCUE TEAM

"Carfentanil sedative darts," Berman said, holding up a transparent delivery syringe inches in front of Michael's face. "Capable of sedating large animals like elephants with ease. Also a deadly street drug. To safely take down an animal the size of the deinosuchus, it's our best shot, since you're holding us hostage to not use our shotguns."

Michael gently pushed the dart away from his face.

"Sorry, Jeff. The animal is protected by law. I figured you as a police officer would understand that."

The dart looked like the stereotypical poison dart seen in crime films or animal documentaries – a long, glossy tube with a sharp metallic needle on one end and a red puffy plume on the other. Berman took the dart and safely shoved it back into the foam laden Pelican case, setting it on the table before producing another sealed compartment. He unlatched the opening, revealing a pair of long rifles. He picked one up and handed it hastily to Michael.

"Pneu-Dart branded G2 X-Caliber tranquilizer projectile," Berman said, giving Michael a brief run through of the safety functions and trigger features. "I shouldn't really be giving you one of these."

"I'll be careful," Michael said, annoyed that Berman was trying to sound like a weapons expert, while treating him like a child who just discovered his father's shotgun.

"You better."

There was something odd about Berman. He moved a little sluggishly, and his eyes were narrow, beyond tired. Michael suspected that he may have been drunk, detecting a faint whiff of liquor when Berman spoke, but kept his theory to himself.

The two of them were going over supplies and safety protocols below the cabin near where Michael and Mila were supposedly to sleep that night. Outside the open door ahead, they could see Sheraton waiting near the *Anglerfin* stern, preparing the motorboat for another trek to the land while doing a maintenance check on the departure craft.

"You're gonna need this too," Berman said, handing Michael a dark blue rain-slicker before putting one on himself.

"Thanks," Michael said. "Good thinking."

"We're going too," Adrienne yelled, running down the interior stairs with Graham behind her. They were already dressed in rain gear and armed with their G2s.

"You may need some backup."

"Unless it's anything underwater," Graham said sternly. "Land rescue operations only!"

"Like anyone would volunteer to go down there anyway after we all got a good look at the son of a bitch," Adrienne commented. "I wouldn't go near that thing with a ten foot pole."

"Are you sure?" Michael said. He remembered the fright in her eyes when she saw the deinosuchus for the first time, watching as the indomitable reptile almost tore Berman's leg apart. It wasn't the face of someone he'd expect to want to go out during a monsoon over a swamp full of alligators.

She nodded, firmly zipping up the rain slicker.

"Don't make me change my mind," she reprimanded him.

"Plus, it's Dawson's orders," Graham smiled. Adrienne struck him on the shoulder for exposing her lie.

"Let's just get on with it," she urged, heading down the hall to the stern outside. "I have some walkies in case the weather breaks, but for now I'd expect communication with the *Anglerfin* to be non-existent. Let's just get in and get out. I'll be relieved when I'm back on board in one piece."

They walked out to rear deck, where Mila and Sheraton were waiting. Mila, who was watching the seaman perform safety inspections on the boat turned and walked over to them. Through the wall of rain, Michael could discern her fears and anxiety about the rescue mission.

"You're not planning on going out there, are you?" Michael asked her, shielding his eyes from the pelting rainstorm. She too was huddled in a Coast Guard branded rain slicker. She moved away from the boat as the other officers loaded in their weapons and gear, stepping into the craft and trying to get the best seats.

"I don't think I'd be much help out there," she said. "I just wanted to say I think you've been handling this whole situation really well. You've kept it grounded, keeping lethal weapons off the table, even after Willie's savage death. Keep it up, and we still may be able to rescue this thing."

He gave her an awkward hug, understanding that there were some potential romantic inclinations between the two but they hadn't had any time to thoroughly explore those thoughts. The urgency of the operation would have to shelve their feelings until they reached the mainland again.

"We should be back soon," Michael spoke up, his voice straining over the ceaseless thud of raindrops storming the deck.

After a short pause, Mila said, "just don't end up like he did."

Michael nodded, knowing that she was referring to Willie Bolasco.

"I don't intend to," he managed.

As the water broke over his cheeks, Michael looked out over the side of the *Anglerfin* at the wilderness beyond. Cloudy waves raged around the sides of the boat from the harsh winds. The final images of the adult deinosuchus crept back into his mind, making him second guess the trip, realizing the unimaginable Cretaceous terror that lurked somewhere below.

"Mr. Robinson," Graham called from the boat. "We're ready. You coming?"

"Yeah," he replied, stepping gently into the motor boat beside Adrienne.

The access door to the rear of the *Anglerfin* opened, and the soldier guided the small boat out onto the waves.

Michael felt his heart palpitating as the motorboat descended onto the surface, crashing into the first swell. The boat tossed and turned briefly as the seaman fought to compensate with the current. Waves crashed over the sides, splashing into the passengers as the motor propelled them around the anchored cutter.

As they rounded the side of the *Anglerfin*, Michael waved up at Nico, barely visible behind the watery glass of the bridge. Mila waved goodbye before rushing into the cabin, out of the pounding storm.

Michael found it difficult to hang on, trying to anchor himself to the boat by gripping at the sides and using his feet to cling onto the seating support beams. All around the water sloshed onto the boat, misting over their rain slickers with the ebb and flow of the dreaded swells.

"Can you still see the flashlight?" Graham asked, yelling over the rain and motor.

"Not yet," Adrienne called. "Wait! There! Right through those weeds. See it?"

Illuminating the soaked undergrowth, a light began to flicker through the shrubs on the shoreline ahead, past the mangrove trees and over the area where the other airboat sank – where Bolasco was ripped apart in front of Berman.

The light was pulsating more rapidly now, as if its owner was trying to project urgency through the message. With a brief flick, the light turned sideways, and was no more.

"What happened?" Michael asked, his eyes squinting to block out the shower.

"Maybe his battery ran out," Sheraton suggested, steering the boat through the swamp as best as he could.

Berman pulled out a set of tactical binoculars, adjusted the digital settings for night vision, and looked out from the front of the boat.

"I can see the other airboat," he claimed. "It's crashed on the beach, just beside where the light was coming from. I think I can see Clarence. He's on his back on the beach. I think something's wrong. Full speed ahead please, Sheraton!"

"Aye, sir!"

The motorboat forced onward. Soon the lights and security of the *Anglerfin* melted away into the darkness until it was a blurry blob through the storm. Gradually the second airboat came into view, just as Berman had indicated. The boat was washed up on one of the beaches. Beside the ship, Clarence Quarles slumped beside the ship, half buried in sand and jungle sticks that were washing up from the swift waves.

"I think he's injured," Graham said, squinting through the rain.

"Whoa!" Adrienne yelled. "Michael, what the hell –"

Without warning, an incredible force from below crashed into the boat, forcing the ship upwards off the surface of the water. Luggage and equipment began to float as gravity fought to regain control. Through the splashing of waves and ceaseless barrage of rain, Michael could hear the shrieks of everyone on the boat as their world flipped over, careening towards the uncertain depths.

Michael wasn't sure what had happened, but grabbed onto his Pneu-Dart tranquilizer for comfort, knowing it was no use. He could feel his footing slipping out from the seating beams. Beside him, Adrienne began to lean forward. He could see Graham and Berman fumbling for something to hold onto near the front of the boat as the watery wall approached beneath them.

"Aw, hell!" Adrienne cried.

"Brace yourselves!" Sheraton called. "We're going under!"

As the boat prepared to descend back to the water, the bow dipped forward, crashing vertically into the waves, and sending everyone on board and all the supplies into the vicious swamp. Michael took a deep breath as he saw the others go under the waves before he himself was cast to the darkness.

The water under the tumultuous surface was black. Visibility was near zero until a lightning bolt broke through the clouds, illuminating all the shredded trees and branches that were floating behind the rippling portal above them. Through his blurry vision, he could see that the swamp floor was only a few feet below, swirling around in a mess of muck and jungle debris that the storm cast down.

For a moment, Michael thought he noticed the sunken airboat beside a large rock, hidden behind the clouded wall of churned Everglades mud that the raging swamp kicked up.

He turned and kicked forcefully to the surface, not wanting to spend another second in the perilous tides.

When he broke surface, already there was confusion being shouted from the others. He caught the dialogue halfway through, unsure of what they were talking about.

"– is he? He didn't come up?"

He heard Adrienne coughing up water as she struggled to stay afloat, splashing to and fro with her hands. Berman surfaced beside her a moment later, gasping thankfully for the tropical air.

Michael realized that Adrienne was talking to Sheraton, who treaded the raging water expertly, putting his Coast Guard training at Cape May to good use.

"Graham!" she yelled over the storm.

"We need to head for shore," Berman urged them. "It isn't safe here. That animal is down there!"

"Graham!" Adrienne shouted again. "Jeff, we aren't leaving without him!"

Michael kicked his feet against the current, trying to stay with the others to avoid being pushed further from the group. He could feel himself staving off a panic attack. They were helpless, floating in the swamp with no way of telling what was around them. Although the disappearance of Graham alarmed him, he wanted nothing more than to touch down on the distant sandbar, where security and equilibrium could be properly restored.

Ahead, the beached airboat remained where it was, slumped lifelessly on the shore. Over the rising and falling waves, Michael could see Clarence, frozen in his spot. He appeared to be coughing and shouting something. In between a thunderclap, the officer's voice finally broke through the ambient noise.

"It's coming!" Clarence called, nearly falling over on his side to get the message across. They turned as his cryptic words carried over the tumultuous swamp.

What's coming?

"What the hell did he mean by that?" Adrienne said, the fright evident in her rapid breathing.

Then they saw it – the rising of the enlarged osteoderms several yards away.

Like a surfacing submarine, the deinosuchus emerged yards behind Adrienne. A second after, the pale, helpless form of Graham appeared in the jaws of the animal. Blood poured from his mouth as he tried to plead for help, but his glossy, sunken eyes told them that the officer had already given up hope.

The crocodilian shot between the group with its prey, knocking them apart like bowling pins before diving back below. Berman, who still had his tranquilizer in hand aimed at the animal but sank immediately, needing his arms constantly paddling to stay afloat.

"It took Graham!"

"Head for shore!" Michael yelled, paddling towards the dark silhouette of jungle ahead. "It will be coming back for us!"

29
CLARENCE

With a final swing of his hand, Michael felt the wet clumps of sand grain between his fingers as he grabbed the sandbar. A final wave rushed over him, sinking into the ground as be pulled himself out of the chaotic water, thankful to be feeling the earth beneath him once more.

By some miracle he managed to hold onto his Pneu-Dart G2 X, throwing the weapon onto the damp dunes. He rolled over on his back, out of breath and staving off a panic attack from the brutality of what he'd seen. Despite the humidity, he felt cold. His body was soaked, even under the rain slicker.

The seaman sloshed up to him, extending a helping hand to lift Michael back off the ground.

"Thanks."

"Are you all right?" Sheraton asked. The man was covered in tangled seaweed and his face was smeared in mud. He knew the soldier had made it to the beach before the others. Coast Guard soldiers were excellent swimmers, trained thoroughly in water lessons at Cape May.

Adrienne's coughing broke the conversation. She washed up next to Michael, spitting on the ground and out of breath. Berman was behind her, pushing her up the coast until they were all together again.

"It just grabbed him," Adrienne said when she finally caught her breath. "He's dead, Jeff."

"Look at the airboat," Berman pointed.

Several yards away, the remains of the airboat sat half embedded in the swamp. Part of the front was dented inwards as if a locomotive had crashed into it. The left sides of the vehicle were crunched down, revealing several leaky holes. The deino broke the vessel enough that the officers had to head for land immediately.

Officer Clarence Quarles was on the ground, leaning against the side of the mangled airboat. His pants were tattered. His right leg was slightly twisted at an oblong angle, and blood gushed from behind what remained of the fabric. The officer's skin and his eye were closed – he was unconscious. A lonely flashlight remained at his side half buried in the sand, the battery drained.

Officer Ryan Gray was nowhere to be seen.

"That thing got him too," Berman said, stooping down next to the officer. "Do we have any walkies left?"

"I have one," Adrienne said, turning the device on and speaking into the receiver. "Dawson, come in. This is Adrienne, over."

"Adrienne, th-is-s-s is Dawson. Wha- status over?"

His voice was garbled and distorted. Michael was surprised the reception was working at all.

"We've made contact with Clarence. He's been mauled, but we think he's alive. Ryan is missing and the airboat is shot. Our boat went down in the waves. Graham is dead."

"Are you fu-i-i-i-ng serious? Damn... St-st-ay put. We've finally been able to contact the RB-S b-. The-ey-ey sho-ou-ould be... your location. Over."

"It sounds like the other coasties are coming," Adrienne said, studying the message. "He wants us to stay here. How long until they're at our position, do you estimate?"

"Ten minutes, maybe," the soldier guessed. "The weather seems to be lightening up a little, so it could be sooner. The waves are calmer, so they'll be able to shuttle us back to the *Anglerfin*."

"Hey, Clarence," Berman called, bending down and lightly smacking Clarence's face. "Clarence, are you alive, buddy?"

Seconds later, the pale officer coughed up a little bit of water, pivoting against the airboat before realizing his dire situation.

"Shit, Jeff," Clarence said, disoriented and grabbing his leg in agony. "I've never been happier in my life than to see you right now. That croc ran us aground and ripped my leg apart. It grabbed Ryan and took off into the woods. I'm thankful that you saw my signal. I feel like I'm dying here man, I need medical attention."

"RB-S boats are inbound," Berman assured him. "The soldiers will take you back to the ship. How long ago did the croc take Ryan into the jungle?"

"Jeff, I have no idea," Clarence replied, starting to slouch and lose consciousness again. "I've been coming in and out. It was, shit, it was probably a while ago now."

He fell over, again losing consciousness.

"Adrienne, can you bandage up his wounds?" Berman asked. "Maybe tie off his leg to stop the bleeding? I think there's some rope in the airboat."

"I can but, Jeff, don't tell me you're going in there?" she said. "After what happened to Graham and Bolasco. Gray is as good as dead. Please, let's stick together until the Coast Guard gets here. It could be coming back!"

"I can't afford to wait for the RB-S to get here," Berman said, checking to make sure his three carfentanil delivery darts were still in his secure case that he stored in his soaked pocket. "Stay with the boat and Clarence and Sheraton."

"Jeff, it's suicide to go in there," Adrienne pleaded. "Please, I know we've had our differences this past year. Don't go after it. Wait for backup! The weather will calm down and the RB-S boats will be coming."

"Gray may not be alive that long, Adrienne. Besides, I'm not gonna let the Coast Guard clean up our problem."

"I'm not going in there," she replied, trembling. "Jeff, I'm ashamed, but I'm terrified. I can't go in after it."

"I'm not asking you to," Berman said. "You don't have a weapon anyway. Do you still have your carfentanil case?"

"Yeah."

"Okay, give it to Mikey. He still has his tranq projector. Mike, you're coming in with me. We're going in there and bringing our man back. Adrienne, stay here with Sheraton and guard Clarence until the cutter sends backup. Wait for the RB-S boats to get here. The weather should be breaking soon. When you get back to the ship, tell Dawson to contact the mainland and get us some backup."

"I don't feel comfortable letting a civilian go in there and do my –"

Berman interrupted her.

"Adrienne, you're the only one here with anything relating to a medical background. It makes the most sense for you to stay here with Clarence. Didn't you say you spent three semesters in a nursing program in Tampa?"

"Four semesters," she corrected, trying to light a cigarette in the rain storm. "Until my money ran out."

"Perfect. Stay with Clarence and do what you can. Mike, let me give you a crash course on this thing before we go in."

"Okay," Michael said, confused as Adrienne unwillingly handed him her ammunition case.

"Put the butt up against your shoulder until you're ready to fire. Obviously this is the scope, look through there and line up the cross hairs with the target. Everyone knows that. Load the dart through this shaft. Keep the weapon pointed at the ground until you're absolutely ready to fire. Don't ever point it anywhere in my direction. Last thing, stay close, and we just might make it out of this."

"Okay," he repeated himself, loading one of Adrienne's carfentanil darts into the gun.

Michael wasn't sure what else to say. The idea of going into the jungle with Berman alone after an adult deinosuchus was giving him a splitting headache. He could feel his hands starting to prune in the endless rain as he tried to steadily hold the weapon.

"Still looks pretty fresh to me," Berman said. "What about you?"

He gestured up the beach, pointing at a similar set of crocodile drag marks that tore through the sloppy mud. The trackway fed up into the shrubbery before vanishing into the darkness of the night jungle. It mirrored the crocodile tracks from earlier in the afternoon – only they were twice as wide and had preserved better, shielded by wide overhead palm fronds.

Pressing his hand into the sand, Michael noted the size of the animal was both accurate to Bolasco's photograph from days earlier and the estimate based in his prehistoric fauna encyclopedia book. He was about to embark on a hunting expedition against an apex predator of the Cretaceous.

30
SHADOW TRAILS

A wet palm frond smacked against Michael's face, leaving cold droplets gently cascading off his face. He pushed it aside with the barrel of the G2 X before lowering the gun to the ground before Berman turned and saw him holding the weapon improperly. But Berman was already ten steps ahead in the jungle, carefully creeping around the pockets of obtrusive weeds that the deinosuchus trail weaved around.

"You know, Jeff," Michael said, whispering through the jungle, "this trail could actually be pretty old. Remember, between the time we were attacked on the swamp, the deino had already grabbed Ryan. For all we know, it could still be back in the river."

Berman continued undeterred, shining his flashlight over the trackway at his feet.

"Well there's no way to tell for sure, right?" Berman grunted. "So that means there's really nothing to lose. I owe it to Bolasco and Graham to finish this expedition, before anyone else turns up dead."

"Well, no," Michael said. "It doesn't really change anything. Just saying it's possible that the trackway might lead us back to the water, and we'll be back at square one. Or worse, it might lead us around in circles."

"Just try not to shoot me in the back, Mikey," Berman said, sliding carefully between two trees, checking his corners around the trunks as the rain washed over his rain slicker. Michael noticed the officer still wobbled from time to time, reinforcing his theory that the officer had been drinking before they left the *Anglerfin*.

The rain continued to drizzle down from the canopy, splattering over their rain coats and making it harder to see. Occasionally, the moon would peek through the thick fronds, but often only a fraction of the light filtered through, illuminating the knotted trunks before disappearing again behind the storm clouds.

Michael expected the trackway to eventually break through to another river, like the American crocodile footprints from earlier. But the jungle kept going, stretching endlessly inland in a massive Everglades island. What light there was from the *Anglerfin* way back in the swamp had long faded away, leaving the two men alone in the bleak wilderness.

Their journey was met with long periods of no speaking, save for Berman's expletive comments when he would lose and relocate the trackway. Michael sensed that Berman had something on his chest, wanting to say something but was holding it back.

Michael knew it could only be one thing: the incident on the beach. Now that they were alone, he wondered if going into the wilderness with Berman was the wisest choice.

Finally, as they rounded a large vine that hung across the trail like an enormous spiderweb strand, he hit Michael with the question.

"So, why did you do it?" Berman asked abruptly, cutting right to the chase.

Well, damn, Michael thought, not expecting such a brazen question.

"What?" Michael asked, taken aback by Berman's direct approach.

"You know what."

"Jeff, these creatures are disappearing from our ecosystem every day. Sure, American crocodiles are around in other parts of Central America, but only a handful remain in Florida. I don't know what got into me back there, but honestly, I apologize. I apologize for hitting you and embarrassing you in front of your police buddies. I was in over my head."

Berman glared back at him from behind the wet leaves, pausing shortly for dramatic emphasis, before turning back to continue the trek.

"I told you, the son of a bitch jumped out at me," Berman said in a brooding tone. "Maybe I was a little rambunctious with it once I got started, but you went too far Mikey."

"I'm sorry, Jeff."

Berman continued chopping through the branches, not turning around to accept the new apology. He kept his gaze fixated on the crocodile trackway, that fed into a muddy valley, leading deeper still into the forest.

"You know that shit you pulled was out of line," Berman said finally, hacking a branch off with his police baton. "But that wasn't what I was talking about."

"What are you talking about then, Jeff?" Michael asked, getting annoyed by Berman's passive aggressive nature during the hike.

"You know what I'm talking about," Berman replied. "I'm talking about what happened in high school. The reason why we haven't spoken in over fifteen years. Why our friendship fell apart."

Michael stopped walking, staring after Berman. After a few steps, the officer stopped walking, noticed that Michael wasn't following, and turned back to him.

Since their senior year, when their friendship had fallen apart, Michael had eventually put the incident out of his mind. When he graduated from Miami, Michael had placed the problems with Berman out of his mind, making room for new memories like academics and post-college opportunities. Behind the scenes, Michael and Jeff's families stopped talking. A year into college, Michael heard that the Bermans had moved to Orlando. That was the last time Michael thought or cared to think about that eventful day their senior year.

He thought for a moment, staring at Berman, whose eyes were ablaze with anger, previously unseen but now unleashed. Through the rain, Michael could see his infamous scowl forming over his brow. Michael wasn't expecting a confrontation like this.

Shivering in the rain, he waited a second before he spoke, sensing the volatility of the delicate situation. Although the conflict was ancient history, it was still a fiery subject, even after seventeen years.

"Jeff, I'm sorry about that too. I didn't know what the ripple effects would be. I was too young to understand all that. It was a mistake."

"More like you were a self-righteous asshole," Berman shot back after a momentary laugh.

"Jeff, you were dealing narcotics to students. If I hadn't done what I did then, you may have been arrested a year down the road, putting your adult life in jeopardy. Only then you'd be eighteen or older, and wouldn't have got away with just a slap on the wrist and expulsion from the school."

"It was more than that, Mikey!" Berman screamed, his voice echoing so loudly that Michael was sure that Adrienne and Sheraton heard it back on the shore. He set the tranquilizer rifle against the base of a palm tree, and started walking towards Michael until their faces were nearly touching. "I had to quit the football team. I missed all the talent scouts. The college revoked my entire scholarship that would've been completely FREE!"

Michael backed up, making Jeff lower his voice. His knuckles were balled into fists, but he was still restraining himself from hitting Michael.

"Not only that," Berman continued in a lower, but equally threatening tone, "my father practically disowned me for a year, before sending me to a military school for that entire summer. That little incident was on my record ever since. You did that. You and your little private 'heads up' to the principal, which led to my locker raid."

The day flashed into Michael's mind briefly. He could remember police canine units with sniffer dogs successfully identify Berman's locker, retrieve the contraband and place Berman under arrest in front of everyone in the hallway. He watched from a distance as Berman was escorted off the school grounds in the police cruiser, his life forever changed by Michael's unforgiving actions.

"How did you ever find out it was me?" Michael asked. "I never could figure that out."

"The principal let it slip during a lengthy lecture, before he expelled me," Berman revealed. "I had to get my GED over the summer. Do you realize how hard it was trying to find a job after that? I was lucky they accepted me into the police school."

"I'm sorry," Michael said again. "Jeff, you were right. I was a self-righteous asshole. If I had known all the damage it would have caused, do you think I would have done that? I was expecting you to get suspended, not expelled. I didn't even know all that other shit that happened!"

Berman was silent, still seething. Michel could tell this had been wearing on him for years. He sensed that Berman had been anticipating this conversation for a long time, probably since their paths had first crossed again several days ago, but now that Michael had apologized, and apologized sincerely, the grand finale was hard to imagine.

"If you want to hit me, hit me," Michael said. "Jeff, I know you want to. You owe me a good one, especially after the shit I did today."

Berman hesitated. The fists remained balled, shaking slightly in the cooling rain. The thunder started to rumble again and the wind was making the trees and canopy writhe in frantic arcs.

"Jeff, no one's around, just –"

Wham!

Michael's reflexes forced his eyes closed as Berman's right hook slammed into him. He saw stars briefly, feeling his head tilt up as his legs wobbled, trying to keep himself vertical. The rain seemed to converge on the bruise, quenching the pain but at the same time sending it into a burning frenzy.

He teetered sideways, grabbing onto a branch to stabilize himself before he could fathom entirely what happened.

"Okay, Jeff," Michael said. "You have a nice –"

Wham!

Another hook, this time from the left – a hook that Michael hadn't granted Berman.

Suddenly, Michael realized the predicament had gone from awkward, to bad, to life-threatening. As he tumbled down sideways, he discovered now that both of his cheeks were burning. He hardly noticed that he let his tranquilizer projector rifle fall from his hands, striking wet pebbles on the ground below. Mentally he had made the transition from apologetic to self-defense, scrambling back to his feet seconds after he struck the muddy jungle floor.

He could feel his heart rate accelerating, adrenaline flowing through his flexing arms before flooding into his knuckles. Amid the rain, he could feel a single tear fall from his eye, a reflex to the emotion and Berman's punches.

"Okay, Jeff. I guess this is happening," Michael managed, wiping a smear of blood from his swollen lip.

"It's been a long time coming, Mike," Berman replied.

Michael didn't want to fight Berman.

Jeff wouldn't be the same scrappy quarterback from the Miami High days. He was now an officer of the law, and thus had undergone rigorous combat training. And Michael couldn't determine an end result: was the goal to attempt to beat Jeff into submission or was it just to hit him back a few times for self defense? Or a third option – was it to come out of an ass-beating alive.

Either way, it would be seen most likely as assaulting an officer, and that wouldn't be good.

It didn't matter. There was no time to determine right from wrong – only time to stay upright and keep the battle going.

Jeff swung again, his fist ripping through the rain.

Michael blocked this time, countering with a quick shot to the officer's exposed ribs. Berman wasn't expecting such a quick retaliation, doubling over and vomiting bile all over the jungle floor. Michael used the time to back up and regather his strategy, massaging his cheeks where the bruises inflamed themselves.

Now his fist throbbed from the punch, adding insult to injury. Berman had an incredibly strong midsection, and Michael's counter punch also struck part of the officer's soaked holstered flashlight.

Michael frowned as Berman recovered quickly, racing towards him in a furious raging stampede.

"Jeff, wait –"

Berman crashed into him, forcing them both splattering through the leafy barrier behind the trail. Although Michael was initially busy warding off Jeff's blows, the focus of the battle shifted from fighting to confusion as they slid quickly down the slope of an unseen hill. Momentum sucked them both downward through rows and rows of saturated ferns and weeds. Berman tumbled over Michael, no longer concerned about the fight and more preoccupied with trying to grab hold of something for support.

Michael's hands dug into the mud, only to have inertia force the fingertips out from the earth, resuming the slide. His elbows and thighs ached from where various exposed rooting systems banged into him. The rain slicker was coated completely in mud. He knew Jeff was in an equal or worse condition, regardless of what he landed on, hearing the officer groan and grunt as he fell beside him.

With a sloppy, wet slosh, he landed in a cushioned layer of moss. Berman rolled beside him, stopping his flight when his body thumped swiftly into a rotted, waterlogged tree stump, bringing an end to their noisy descent.

"Shit," Berman remarked, using the tree trunk to steady himself, spitting blood onto the mulch below.

The battle had ended. The environment had beaten them both, putting their ugly past friendship woes on hold.

"You all right?" Michael asked, out of breath and searching with his hand for something to stabilize himself with. The area was dark and ominous. The moonlight was diffused above them, barely making it through the thick canopy. Even the rain had a hard time getting in, appearing only in little trickles where the leaves failed to join together.

"Yeah," Berman said with a groan. "You okay?"

"I think so. Hell of a fall."

His fingers suddenly grabbed something in the dark, cylindrical, and clearly man made.

Must be an old Coca-Cola bottle, he thought.

He brought the object into the waning lonely patch of moonlight, discovering the true identity of the object. It was a G2 X tranquilizer projector rifle, covered in mud and badly dented on the stock. The barrel and trigger looked fine. Michael assumed it was still operational.

"How did you manage to hang onto that?" Berman asked, wiping his face off and rising to his feet.

"I didn't," Michael confessed. "I dropped my gun up there on the path when you hit me. I have no idea whose gun this –"

He gasped, rocking backwards on his heels before centering himself.

The clouds above slid by, revealing Graham's pale lifeless face in the blue circle of moonlight, just several yards away. His sinister face had contorted to an ugly grin, and the eyes remained frozen in his final state. He had been bitten in half from below the waist. Intestines and broken bone matter hung down from his belly, painting the ground beneath with the sliding organs.

"Shit! Graham!"

Around the corpse, an array of other human bone elements remained, collected over the past months from other victims of the deinosuchus attacks. Some of the other flesh fragments were badly decomposed, indicating to Michael that there may have been more victims than previously identified. Chunks of eradicated boats lay scattered around in between the sawgrass patches, placed spontaneously through the weeds as if the creature was arranging living room furniture.

"Looks like I was correct to assume it's been attacking boats," Michael observed, studying the wreckage that dotted the pit. "Maybe it's been relocating them here as trophies or for territorial markings. The fact that it dragged such heavy objects here through the jungle is unbelievable, and a new trait for crocodilians. It must have unimaginable stamina."

"What a sick son of a bitch," Berman remarked, sifting through the mossy debris.

The clouds shifted again, causing passing glimmers of light to reveal a large set of red, curious eyes, watching from underneath the bottom end of a flipped boat directly ahead. Rows of elongated dinosaur-like teeth jutted out of the creature's head – a head the size of a John Deere lawn mower.

"Uh, Mikey?"

"Jeff, remain absolutely still," Michael silenced him. "We've found its lair."

31
LAIR

The deinosuchus pulled itself through its hiding place, bringing its full, lengthy form out into the gruesome, muddy pit. With a flick of its tail, the deino let out a sharp, lengthy hiss, bringing itself upward. Even in the lack of light, Michael could see the sheer bulk of the animal, the sharpness of the scales, the width of the tail. Standing with its bulky head aimed straight towards them, the creature was still taller than both Michael and Berman.

Even in the monster's aggressive state that would soon be unleashed on him, Michael couldn't help but speculate the length of the animal: thirty-five to forty feet – several feet longer than he anticipated or that the encyclopedia estimated the species to top out at.

"Mikey, you through admiring the thing?" Jeff asked. "We need to get up the hill."

"Jeff, we'll never make it that far. It's all uphill and too slippery."

"What's it doing?"

"It's...it's examining us."

The deino took another step towards them, sniffing at the air before spreading its terrible jaws again with another guttural savage groan.

"Shit. It's coming. Run!"

Michael's plan for standing still was immediately ruled out.

After the hiss, the deino charged, lumbering at first but soon galloping forward at a full on sprint. Michael turned, already seeing Jeff's scrappy form taking off up the hill, clawing at the muddy slope only to slide back down.

With a running leap, Michael tossed himself at the hill beside Jeff, but the slope was too slippery, lubricated by the rain and wet leaves. They slid back down, just as the murderous jaws of the deino clamped at them.

"Whoa!"

Kicking off the sloppy ground, Michael propelled himself to the left, watching Jeff do the same thing in the opposite direction. The crocodilian narrowly missed Michael's leg, although the bite was close enough that he could feel the creature's hot breath burning against his calf, even through the saturated rain slicker.

He hit the ground running when he felt mud again beneath the boots. From his peripheral vision, he could see Berman's silhouette sprinting around the ruins of old boats, eventually disappearing behind a patch of overgrown grass.

He was on his own now.

Michael searched through the rubble halfheartedly, his mind pounding with each calculated step he took, knowing the Cretaceous predator was nearly on him which made focusing on long term escape an afterthought.

His first and only idea was to hide. The entire area sloped down from above like a gladiator arena, ruling climbing out of the pit off the table.

He knocked through the boating debris, feeling his feet touching down on old brittle human and animal remains. Behind, the deino pushed through the fractured pieces of an old rowboat, knocking the crumbling vessel away and splintering it over the earth as the animal tirelessly pursued its target.

Michael's heart stalled after he rounded his next obstacle.

Ryan Gray.

As he bumped past another boat fragment, the death stare of the young officer appeared. The cadaver had been chomped in half before being put on display, draped over the bottom of an overturned old rowboat. Seeing his own approaching death in the officer's lifeless eyes, Michael hurried past, trying to prolong his excruciating demise as long as he could.

Everything in the past few days leading up to the expedition flashed through Michael's mind. He found it ironic that he was about to be crushed to death by the very thing that he fought so hard to rescue. He prayed for a chance of escape – or at the least, a swift death.

But as he rounded a corner around a knotted trunk, he thought fate had given him a second chance.

Ahead, buried into the adjacent hillside but sticking out due to years of erosion, was an exposed rooting system, crawling over the earth like prowling octopus tentacles. The roots hung forward like a bird cage, acting similar to the jail bars at a prison.

He took off for them, doubling his efforts in this final, slim chance for survival. Above, the moon began to peek through the clouds and canopy, finally shedding some light. He could feel the rain lightening up. Maybe the storm was about to break.

Quickly, he threw the thoughts out. They weren't important – the only important thing was survival at all costs.

If I can just hold off until the Coast Guard gets here...

His fingers grabbed around the first root. He threw himself at the opening, wiggling between the widest gap. The area inside the natural cage was wide, but not wide enough that the bulky predator could fit through. Michael sensed that many animals probably held out in here as long as they could, trying to tunnel their way to escape, which would explain why it was so well dug out.

When he turned around, the deino was right at the root opening, chomping and thrashing at the coarse wood. The old roots shook, but remained stuck in the ground, refusing to budge. With every move of the creature's clunky head, Michael could feel the earth around him vibrating, as well as the quivering of the ancient tree above.

Now he felt free to admire the creature in security, knowing that at least temporary safety was granted him.

The head of the animal resembled, for the most part, a modern American alligator, but the coloring was off, just like it appeared on Owen's camera. Yellow stripes began behind the creature's red eyes, continuing all the way down the back until they tapered off near the tail. Two teeth near the front of the lower jaw were exposed when the creature's mouth snapped down, backing up the deino theory. Overall, Michael was surprised that the bulk of the forty foot animal was not enough to break through the small root system.

He thought of Berman, and how, with some stroke of unforeseen luck, he could make it up the hill and send for help, now that the creature was distracted.

But would Berman think to do that, or would he assume Michael to be dead, considering their brutal fistfight that just occurred moments earlier.

Michael shook the thought out.

No, he's going for help. He has to.

Suddenly, he realized what he still had in his right hand.

Graham's G2 X. And the ammunition from Adrienne!

It was still tucked safely behind his rain slicker. After all the fighting and rolling and running, he still had the package of three tranquilizer darts, ready to go. Suddenly, salvation seemed to present itself – and the operation was back on.

He rummaged swiftly through the coat, pulling out the little box of drug induced darts, careful not to prick himself with the exposed syringe.

"Now how did Berman tell me to do this?" he mumbled to himself, frantically trying to relearn the loading process. He maneuvered the dart around in the dark, until he finally figured out how to insert the ammunition into the projector rifle. He threw the stock against his shoulder after triple checking to make sure he had operated the weapon right. After looking through the scope, he realized he didn't need it.

The animal was right in front of him, chomping its menacing jaws inches from his foot.

The deino moved its head back and forth quickly, forcing Michael to wait for a clean shot. He didn't want to risk the dart piercing the creature's eye. The underbelly was the intended target, but with the animal so low to the ground, it would be a chore to successfully strike that area.

No!

Michael's heart stopped when his finger squeezed the trigger accidentally, sending the carfentanil dart whizzing towards the deino. In the last second, his arm flinched, forcing the barrel to the left, thus deploying the round into the shadowy jungle, missing the target entirely.

The creature didn't understand the discharge of the weapon, continuing to thrash at the roots, crunching through the wood and sending little splinters sprinkling into the mud. Then, to Michael's disbelief, the creature backed up, raised its belly over the roots, attempting to crush through with the animal's immense weight.

The underbelly!

His moment was now.

Michael reached for another dart, nearly pricking himself with the needle as he jammed it feverishly into the projector. The deino started to squirm and move above him, blocking out the moon and covering the root prison in darkness. He could feel the roof beginning to lower. The deino was becoming successful in pushing the roots to the ground, and the earth above along with it. Soon, Michael would be crushed if he didn't make his move.

Shit, just push the damn trigger, Robinson!

With a gentle breath he squeezed the trigger, emitting a *kerplunk* sound as the dart rocketed upward. The needle struck the deino right in the center of the underbelly, quivering slightly on impact. With another deafening hiss, the animal backed up, stepping off the log into the moonlight.

Michael loaded the final carfentanil dart into the G2 X, unsure if one dart would be enough to neutralize the animal. He knew from past research that these darts were strong enough to tranquilize elephants, and he figured an elephant probably was relatively close in weight with the adult deino.

The animal wearily stared through the roots at him, still snapping its jaws but no longer trying to crunch through the obstacles. Smaller, weaker hissing sounds came out from the deino's mouth. The crocodilian began to wobble uneasily before crashing to the earth on one side.

The operation was suddenly a success.

32

AIRLIFT

Michael waited a few minutes before emerging from the rooting system. Above, the clouds had moved away from the moon, letting the light shine down on the canopy above, covering the lair in diffused, blue lighting. The rain continued to eek down through the leaves in gentle streams, but the storm for the most part had ended.

He walked over the muck towards the creature, finally able to admire the prehistoric crocodile in safety, watching the gentle rise and fall of the creature's breathing through the colossal scales.

The deino only had a few territorial slash marks on its scales, indicating that there were a handful of other crocodiles who may not have been happy that the animal moved into their territory. Michael doubted that they lived to fight the creature again.

He stretched out his hand and placed the palm on the animal's belly, smiling that the breathing seemed normal, comparing it to what he knew from his own crocodilians at the sanctuary. He couldn't help but manage a faint smile, appreciating this incredible moment in his life, touching the past like no man had before.

Instantly he pictured the animal in his sanctuary, adored by families for years to come. The research he could do on the deino would surely lead to groundbreaking results, understanding how a predator hunts at the top of the Cretaceous food chain. And although he wasn't a paleontologist, and knew nothing about paleontology, he couldn't help but think – maybe it will lead to further insights from other extinct life.

A light from the trees broke his daydreaming.

It was Berman with a flashlight, running up at the hill's summit that they had tumbled down only minutes earlier.

He must've found a way out, Michael thought.

Behind him, other silhouettes came into focus, carrying flashlights and shotguns. It was the Coast Guard soldiers from the missing RB-S boats.

"Mikey!" Berman called. "You alive down there? I've brought

backup, man!"

"Yeah," Michael called, hearing Berman and the soldiers sliding down the hill. Berman continued to talk as he slid skillfully down the hillside.

"Looks like Clarence is gonna pull through. He and Adrienne are back on the *Anglerfin*. Holy – what happened?"

Berman stopped, staring at the sleeping form of the deinosuchus that was lulled to sleep on the mud. The sheer mass of the beast dwarfed them both, curling around their perimeter from the snout to the tail. The officer leaned in, touching the scales in utter disbelief.

"How did you do it?"

"Graham's rifle. It still worked! One dart was all it took."

The Coast Guard soldiers slipped down the slope and arrived at the pit, lowering their firearms as they realized what they were looking at. They were speechless, uttering statements of amazement between each other.

"Wow, way to go Mike," Berman congratulated, patting him on the back and forgetting about their struggle from earlier. "What do we do now?"

"The storm's basically over. Is your walkie working?"

"Yeah."

"Radio Dawson. Tell him we have the animal. It's safe, alive but tranquilized. We're gonna need that airlift, but we need to clear this canopy first. These old plants shouldn't be hard to chop down. We can signal by flares. What do you think of that, Jeff?"

Berman smirked, impressed how Michael took control before turning to the soldiers.

"Let's start cutting down this jungle," he said. "We need to cut enough away for the chopper to lower a harness down. I'm not sure how long the drugs will last on the croc, so let's get this moving."

33
NEWS CREW

Michael pushed his way out of the doors to the Redland Crocodilian Sanctuary, mentally overwhelmed and only moderately prepared for the hordes of newscasters and onlookers that gathered outside the building. An array of cameras and microphones angled towards him as he came out of the doors. A small podium was placed where the visitors wanted him to speak at.

He heard his name mentioned a dozen times as he arrived in the sunlight just outside the front of the sanctuary, followed by "crocodile" and "dinosaurs" and "new species". All of the local news stations in southern Florida had gathered, putting his little zoo on the map in a big way. Even in the distance at the end of the parking lot, Michael could see more crowds gathering on the street and at the parking lots on the other side.

The airlift from the swamp had happened three days ago. It was now Saturday. The deinosuchus had been transported by cover of darkness to the zoo, where Sandra helped Michael cover the windows of the pen where the deino was temporarily being housed to block spectators from viewing the animal. The creature's grand opening was officially slated for Monday, so Michael was forced to go to extreme measures to conceal the animal until the weekend was over.

The pen was only temporary, until Michael could raise enough funding to build the animal a proper enclosure. The deino would need a fairly large territory to roam around, much larger than the other crocodilian exhibits. Thankfully, there were many more acres towards the back of the property where additional pens could be installed. Michael initially planned for a gharial exhibit, but after the expedition, the gharial venture would have to be rethought, and potentially canceled. The capture of the deinosuchus had changed everything about how he would do business – hopefully for the better.

He paused at the podium where Sherry, his receptionist, was already waiting to help organize the questions so the interview didn't become a disorganized shouting match. An ocean of camera flashes and swaying bodies awaited him.

Word about the deino's capture started two days ago, when Sheriff Dawson released an official press release about the adventure to CBS Miami. Dawson himself was featured in a minor interview the day before that aired on the evening news. Dawson didn't reveal much in the televised interview, other than a large rare, critically endangered crocodilian was captured and currently being held at the Redland Crocodilian Sanctuary. He confirmed that there were a couple of casualties that occurred that would need to be addressed, but that the mission achieved the objective. When they pressed him for further questions, he declined, saying that Michael Robinson would be interviewed on the following day formally, where he assured that all questions would be answered.

Michael's initial reaction to Dawson's comments was irritation. He felt the pressure was all on him to deliver an eloquent, scientifically accurate speech to the press. All eyes would be on him to deliver a correct analysis on what had been happening. He spent most of the morning praying that his voice didn't crack.

Fortunately, Mila called and calmed him down with a pep talk, which led Michael to believe that it was probably better that way. He knew much more about crocodilians than Dawson or the Palm Grove Police Department, and it might give him a sense of validation and expertise in his field.

He felt tense, wearing a suit and tie – a decision that he later agreed was too formal for a zookeeper news interview. His muscles still ached from the conflict in the Everglades earlier. He was exhilarated that some makeup managed to cover Berman's punch bruises.

With a brief nod, he informed Sherry that he was ready to make a statement. The crowd hushed as he began to speak, reading off a paper that he typed up laboriously the night before. Michael cursed under his breath when he noticed the ink has begun to run low halfway through the letter, rendering the typography at fifty percent transparency.

"Hello, I'm Michael Robinson – owner and founder of the Redland Crocodilian Sanctuary. About a week ago, I was approached by the Palm Grove Police Department to assist in the capture and containment of an unknown animal from the Everglades. I was familiar with the recent attacks down there from the radio and news reports. The police narrowed down the attack radius to a certain area. After the fifth victim, John Sanders, was killed a few days ago, his son Owen managed to bravely film the creature around the time of the attack. Through the video quality and framing, we were able to discern that the animal was unlike any that mankind has encountered before – or at the very least, an undiscovered, endangered species."

Michael paused, allowing a few startled sounds to emit from the crowd before speech resumed.

"After the video surfaced, a larger operation was organized when we realized the size of the crocodilian was massive, larger than any crocodilian ever caught before. In the Southern Glades three days ago, we made contact with the creature. At the ultimate sacrifice of three police officers' lives, William Bolasco, Sherwin Graham, and Ryan Gray, we were able to tranquilize the creature and bring it here as our newest exhibit. Another officer, Clarence Quarles, was wounded but is said to make a significant recovery after the animal inflicted significant wounds to the officer's leg. I'll take any questions at this time."

The audience was enthralled, eager to ask a slew of questions that they had scribbled down on their notepads or typed out in their smartphones.

Sherry pointed to the front row, where a young blonde woman with neatly combed hair awaited with her notebook and middle-aged cameraman.

"Go ahead," Michael told the woman.

"Can you describe the animal you brought back? How big is it? What does it look like?"

"Sure," Michael replied. "The animal is a forty foot long prehistoric predator from the late Cretaceous period known as a Deinosuchus. The coloration is very different from modern crocodiles and alligators, in that it has a pair of golden streaks running the length of its body, from the head to tail. Just like the fossil record tells us, the deino has a pair of teeth that stick out from the lower jaw when the mouth is closed."

The crowd paused, rethinking their questions and scribbling onto their notepads. Sherry pointed to another man, a young millennial social media reporter near the middle.

"Yes."

"Mr. Robinson, with all due respect, how can you possibly assume that this jumbo-sized crocodilian is a prehistoric specimen from the time of the dinosaurs? Don't you think it's much more likely that it's more closely related to modern alligators?"

"Yes and no," Michael replied firmly. "No, for a couple of reasons. One, there are no modern crocodilians on record that are known to grow that large. Second, there are no crocodilians with markings such as this animal. Deinosuchus was an incredible hunter of awesome power, and perfectly matches the descriptions that I've been reading up on. Additionally, deinos were known to have hunted in coastal areas around the Everglades back in the Cretaceous. If the crocodilian isn't a deinosuchus, then it's a very closely related modern relative. But to confirm, I am having a representative from the Smithsonian coming down next week to help me verify my theory. As far as the alligator theory goes, the deinosuchus is closely related to the modern alligator, so you are correct on that assumption. They are more closely related to the American alligator than they are to the American crocodile."

A flurry of photographer camera flashes ensued. Sherry pointed to a thin woman in the second row, leaning against a street lamp.

"Suppose this animal is a deinosuchus from the Cretaceous," the woman began, which impressed Michael that she remembered both the name and geological period, pronouncing both correctly.

"Okay, go on," Michael replied, waiting for her to continue.

"Well, if it is a deinosuchus, then how did an animal that large go unnoticed for all this time? By the way you describe it, an adult deinosuchus sounds like a very hard animal to miss. Surely a hunter or boater would have noticed one by now, don't you agree?"

"That is another question that I only have a theory for, not a concrete answer. My idea behind that question is that urbanization of the southern Palm Grove area drove the creature further south, forcing it to compete with other crocodilians. When the urbanization push continued, the creature felt compelled to attack civilians as they crossed through its new territory. It's a big world of crocodilians in there, and it easily might have blended in with the other alligators and crocodiles for all these years."

"Are you referring to the Sunset Ridge development in Palm Grove?" asked a young man.

"Yes," Michael replied.

"Do you think there may be more of them?" asked an older female reporter with long brown hair. "If there are, do you suspect this may continue to be a problem with the Sunset Ridge developments and other southern Florida settlements close to the Glades?"

"It's impossible to say right now," Michael said. "But given what we know so far, if there are more of these magnificent animals, than there are not many left. The deinos are critically endangered, and possibly near extinction."

"How about this gentleman up here?" Sherry said, pointing to a young intellectual looking man near the front. He had large framed glasses and a tucked in shirt. He had a baseball cap with a few collegiate letters on it, illegible from the distance. Michael guessed he may have been a graduate student.

"There's a rumor going around that you found out where the animal lived?" the man asked.

"I did," Michael answered with a nod.

"Can you describe the creature's den?"

"Well, it wasn't far from the area of swamp where most of the victims were found," Michael elaborated. "It was pretty far back in the jungle, in a small pit-like area. There were many boat fragments and human remains there, which leads me to believe that there may be more victims than previously identified by media reporting and police investigation. This is actually something that I speculated all along. My speculation was that the animal was preying on fishermen or hitchhikers for years, unbeknownst to the police departments. It's a wonder we didn't track down the animal sooner. Of course, the boat fragments could also just be from various sunken ships that the creature found, taking them back strictly for animal amusement."

"Were you in the pit when the creature was there?"

"I was."

"How did you survive?"

"Well my – uh – police escort, Jeffrey Berman and I went in together. We sort of stumbled on the area by accident, not knowing that the deinosuchus was already there waiting for us. When we fell into the pit, immediately we recognized the animal was watching us. It gave chase and we got separated. I hid in sort of a little burrow, and managed to tranquilize the animal safely which led to its capture and relocation via a Coast Guard helicopter."

More camera flashes and chattering erupted from the crowd. Several more news vans were pulling up into the parking lot, as well as teenagers from the edge of the pavement that were drawn in by the overwhelming press coverage.

"Why do you suppose it attacked so many times?" asked a female reporter, out of turn.

"Again," Michael went on, "I speculate that it may have been prompted to attack out of aggression from territory loss. I have spoken with Sheriff Dawson about the ramifications of extending the southern expansion project of Sunset Ridge any further, fearing that if there are more deinos down there, they could retaliate just like this one did. It would be a tragedy for more lives to be lost, especially after we were aware of the danger and risks."

"What are your plans for the animal?" asked an older male businessman who had wandered in from the street.

"Well, I've only had a few days to think about that. For one, we will be attempting to gain funds to secure a more size-appropriate enclosure for our deinosuchus. We still have a few unused acres of land here, and intend to use it for the deino. The second is to partner with biologists and paleontologists to see what we can learn from this creature. Research could lead to a better understanding of the Cretaceous world, how this predator hunted, and what its mating habits were. Finally, an additional goal is to continue exploring the Southern Glades more closely, and see if we find any additional members of the species, with an overarching goal to save them from extinction."

Sherry pointed to another man, eager to ask his question.

"Mr. Robinson, were there any eggs in the lair?"

The spectator's question produced much rabble in the crowd, angry that they hadn't thought of the perfect question. The audio operators angled their microphones closer to Michael for better sound, anticipating a juicy answer, causing Michael to smile.

"Sorry to disappoint, but there were no eggs found in the creature's den. We can confirm that the deinosuchus is a male – a very temperamental one at that."

"Mr. Robinson, if there are any eggs or nesting sites found by another deino, will you bring them here?"

Sherry was getting irritated at the lack of respect for her question selection process. The spectators were now shouting questions at will, often yelling out over one another.

"That's an interesting question. From what we've seen in the Glades, the deinosuchus can be aggressive towards other crocodilians, so I'm not sure how an adult deino will react against another deino's offspring. That's assuming that there are eggs from other deinos out there, waiting to be hatched. By the way, I've been requested to inform you that the Palm Grove Police Department has officially closed the area to tourists, hikers, boaters and all forms of civilian interference, other than traveling through Dixie Highway to Key Largo. Anyone found in the Southern Glades without an approved request from the police may be punishable by prison time, until the region can be properly secured from danger."

"You mean the area could still be dangerous?"

"Well, it's always dangerous in there, even without from the possibility of more deinos. You have American crocodiles, American alligators, all kinds of snakes like pythons and anacondas."

"So you're saying that you do believe in the presence of additional deinosuchus packs in the Southern Glades?"

Michael thought a moment before answering.

"I'm saying it's possible," he addressed them, "but we've seen no evidence so far that there are other deinos lurking around. So as to what I believe, yes, I believe it's possible. But currently unconfirmed. If there are more deinos discovered down the road, rest assured, I will do everything in my power to save them."

Sherry pointed at the back, where a group of college kids had gathered for their school newspaper.

"Seeing as how this animal has allegedly killed so many people, are you concerned with how your facility will be viewed, considering that you helped rescued it? I'm sure a lot of Palm Grove residents would have rather seen the animal poached."

"No, I'm not concerned," Michael replied. "Regardless of this animal's man-eating past, it is still considered a protected animal by the Endangered Species Act. My main objective when opening the sanctuary was to promote and save crocodilians, especially ones that could be considered endangered, like the American crocodile. As I've said, that we know of right now, there's only one of these deinos around, making them virtually extinct or approaching extinction. My heart goes out to the relatives of the victims of the Palm Grove attacks. I saw one of the deaths happen first-hand, and it was terrible – an event I'll never forget. My understanding is that several heavy-hitting non-profits will be donating heavily into a relief fund for the victim's families. The Redland Crocodilian Sanctuary will be making several donations as well. But my main concern is and will always be to preserve these species from the brink of extinction as much as I can."

"Okay, we have time for two more questions," Sherry said, followed by lamenting moans from the audience. "Mr. Robinson has a busy day today, getting ready for the animal's official release on Monday. How about you?"

Sherry pointed back to the blonde woman who asked the first question. Michael eased up in his suit, happy that the interview was almost over. He was happy that Sherry was so regimented about his daily schedule. Public speaking was never his forte, and Sherry knew that.

"Mr. Robinson, it's been a few days since you brought the animal back. How is the creature doing now?"

Michael smiled.

"Well, he's getting accustomed to his new enclosure, although I can confirm he's not very happy about it at the moment. If I could describe it in one word, I'd say he's brooding."

"Okay, final question," Sherry said, scanning through the sea of waving arms eager to speak.

"You."

It was another college student, wearing a University of Miami polo shirt. Michael presumed it was another freshman reporter for the school paper. The man pushed up his dark rimmed glasses and cleared his throat before speaking.

"Mr. Robinson, have you come up with a name for the animal?" came a youthful voice.

The question prompted a reaction of hand waving and additional shouting for attention, which Sherry waved off before directing everyone's attention to Michael for an answer.

"Well, not officially," Michael replied with a smile, happy that the question was finally asked. "As of now, we are simply calling our new addition to the sanctuary, *Deino*."

34
CAPTIVITY

Michael walked back into the lobby of the sanctuary as Sherry closed the door behind her, locking it off from the reporters. When he was safely behind the glass and saw the reporters and spectators begin to disperse, he wiped his forehead with the handkerchief from his pocket, thanking Sherry for her helping hand in the interview. He hadn't sweated that much since the creature nearly had his guts for dinner several days earlier.

The sanctuary would be closed for visitors until Monday, giving him a day and a half to get the deinosuchus enclosure area ready. He was going above and beyond for the release of the creature, going as far as to hire a makeshift spokesperson to stand by the exhibit and rattle off data about what the world knew of deinosuchus from the fossil record. Another request that Sherry had in mind was to have a professional graphic designer compile a cinematic promotional poster for the animal comprised of stock photos and clean typography, which was slated for completion by Sunday afternoon – just enough time to get a batch of them printed at Staples.

He would be preparing the exhibit tomorrow, but told Sandra to help him work overtime at night just in case he needed help to get a head start. After a dinner date later that evening that he had made with his new flame, Mila Madison, he would return to the office and begin prep work.

Regular business hours would be spent mostly taking precautions to make sure the remaining enclosures were clean, presentable, and taken care of. He wanted to have the best presentation possible. Charlie and Sandra had already been a big help for him in successfully moving all the caimans out of their first pen to make available space for their new house guest. There was a lot to do, and he had only a few hours to do it before he had to leave for his dinner date.

"Do you need anything else right now?" Sherry asked, seeing him prepare to shuffle on down the stairs towards where his office and the zoo were held.

Michael took one last look out the glass doors, watching the last of the news vans and onlookers disperse from the sanctuary parking lot.

"No thank you, Sherry," Michael replied. "Thanks for all your help out there today – I couldn't have done it without you! You know I'm not the best at public speaking. Just ask my college Advanced Communications professor, Ms. McKean. After my final speech, which I thought I nailed, she cornered me outside in the hallway only to tell me the entire presentation was 'D Material'. Then she got in the elevator and left me standing there, speechless."

"And then she drops the microphone," Sherry laughed. "She sounds like a real bitch, Mike."

"She was," Michael smiled. "I doubt she's still alive. The old crow was a dinosaur even back then. Anyway, I'm surprised at how fast the whole ordeal went. Much faster than I thought!"

"Me too," she replied. "You had a good group of reporters out there. By the way, the emails are flying in from all over the place. Word seems to have circulated the U.S. pretty quickly about your new exhibit."

"I know," Michael said, raising his eyebrows in surprise. "All of the publicity is what prompted me to hire a night watchman plus have those surveillance systems installed. I just downloaded the app on my phone last night. They work great and the HD clarity is stunning. They're totally worth the investment."

"Well at least now you won't have to camp out and wait for teenagers to sneak in," Sherry nudged him.

"Very funny, Sher."

"You'll have a lot of mail to go through," she continued, moving her mouse to wake the receptionist computer from sleep mode. "Just today, you have inquiries from the New York Times, TIME, Smithsonian, NBC – wow – the list continues to grow. I have to keep checking spam because a lot of these messages from producers are going there, too. I could be here all day just sorting through them."

"I'll try to read a few tonight," Michael said, quietly debating on if he should hire a publicist or an assistant for Sherry. He thanked her again and continued down the stairwell, veering past his office and into the zoo.

As he moved down the mulch trail, he couldn't help but fend off a million questions that railed into his mind. For one, should he hire additional security for the event? There were quite a few folks down south that wanted to see the creature dead. He found it unlikely that any of them would try to harm the animal, but then he remembered that the deinosuchus was a known man-eater, one that had deprived happy families of their mothers and fathers.

He thought of Owen, and how he must be feeling after his father's mauling in the swamp. He found it unlikely the youth would ever visit the sanctuary.

Several of the proceeds from opening day should go to him and his family, Michael thought. *Maybe I can dedicate the exhibit to Owen's father and the other victims from Palm Grove.*

Another alarming question – what legal red tape had been broken by bringing the animal to his facility?

The Palm Grove community owned the part of land where the deino was harvested from, but would there be some shadowy, unknown government agency or law that demanded that the animal be handed over to a more established zoo or accredited scientific institution? He had no qualms about sharing custody of the animal with other organizations, but after what he and the police had gone through to personally apprehend Deino, he would fight tooth and nail before he let the government confiscate the animal completely.

I should probably hire a lawyer about this, he thought.

He opened the metal door to the rear of the caiman exhibit, through a utility hallway only accessible by sanctuary employees. He found Sandra and Charlie talking near the front of the caiman enclosure where the deinosuchus was being temporarily housed. On second glance, he discovered that Charlie was talking. Sandra was ignoring him, mindlessly scrubbing at the glass pane and hoping he would leave her alone.

"Are you sure –?" Charlie was asking her, cut off by Michael's approach through the tunnel.

"Charlie," Michael said. "You don't appear to be doing anything."

The youth turned, perplexed and agitated.

"Well actually, I was –"

"I was just talking to Sherry up at the lobby," Michael continued, ignoring his employee's rebuttal. "If you can, please go up there and give her a hand. She's having difficulties keeping all these emails organized that are coming in about our breakthrough discovery. Maybe see if you can vet the emails from important to unimportant inquiries, so I can read them later. Print them out if you have to. And you two haven't taken any pictures on your phone of the animal, have you? The official release isn't until Monday."

They shook their heads.

"Okay, just making sure. Charlie, please go see if you can help Sherry. She's very overwhelmed."

Charlie groaned and walked away, slamming the metal door and heading back out to the mulch visitor trail.

"Thanks, he's been a little hard to handle recently," Sandra confessed. "I think he wishes he was twenty-one. He keeps trying to invite me out to go party tonight up in Miami."

"Just what every boss wants to hear," Michael laughed. "That his employees are gonna go drinking and gallivanting up in the city. But you're still going to help me tonight, right?"

"Oh yeah, most definitely," Sandra assured him. "I made it known to him that I would be working late and would be unable to hang out. I don't want to hang out with him anyway – he's gonna get himself in trouble."

"Okay, good because there's a lot we have to get done," Michael said with relief. "By the way, you don't have to scrub this glass back here. The visitors can't even get back here. I'd rather you concentrate on weeding the area in front of the enclosure. The crabgrass is getting pretty bad."

"Already done," she smiled. "I'm just cleaning here because it was bugging me. These greasy fingerprint smears have been on the glass forever."

He smiled, quietly celebrating her excellence in his head and contemplating giving her a raise in addition to a Christmas bonus later that year. She was becoming an invaluable employee, and one that he didn't want to lose.

"You are an outstanding employee, Sandra. You're the best worker we have down here."

"Aw, shucks," she smiled.

"How's our newest addition doing today?"

"See for yourself," Sandra said, pointing through the glass. Michael looked through the pane.

At first, Michael saw nothing but the darkness of the interior enclosure, completely vacant of the former caimans. The dark room, which had been remodeled years ago to look like a dark cavern, seemed empty.

"I don't see it?" Michael said. "Did it go to the outside enclosure?"

"No, it's in the pool, over there."

Michael looked over, his eyes finding the animal's thick osteoderms waiting just below the gentle waves. The deinosuchus remained completely submerged under the dark water, the burning eyes radiating outward like two welding torches. Even through the protective glass, he could feel the animal fixated on him – planning an attack and calculating an escape.

"Wow, he's really staring you down," Sandra noted. "We should have made this a one-way window like the cops have."

"I'm not surprised. That's how he's been for the past couple of days. We didn't exactly end it on good terms back in the jungle."

"You never told me about it. What happened down there?"

"What happened is that thing almost had my guts for dinner," Michael answered. "I stumbled across the den by accident, and Deino didn't take my trespassing very well. I managed to find a tranquilizer gun off one of the corpses. If I didn't find it, we wouldn't be having this discussion right now."

"Wow, all by yourself?"

"Not exactly. My police officer friend was with me."

"Oh, the guy who stopped by earlier in the week?"

"Yeah. Jeff Berman is his name. Thankfully, he made it out too."

"I can't imagine how horrible the place must have been," she said.

"Oh, Sandra, it was terrible," Michael informed her gravely. "The entire den smelled like rotting flesh that had been sitting in the sun for too long. There were bones everywhere... If we find out there are more of these animals, I'll be insisting that we bring on additional manpower to capture them."

"Unbelievable, I'm glad you made it out!"

"Me too. I didn't think I was gonna, to be frank with you."

"So, I only caught a little bit of the interview. I was sweeping the rear sidewalk, but I was trying to listen in through a live YouTube feed, but it was going in and out. Wi-Fi sucks back there. Do you really think there may be more of them out there?"

"Deinos?" Michael asked. "I wouldn't doubt it. The Everglades are an extraordinarily large jungle, and my theory is that much of the ecosystem remains unseen, under the water. Also, think of the other swamps in the neighboring states, like Louisiana. There are habitats all over the coastal states that could support animals like deinosuchus, and who knows what else. There may be quite a few of them in there and we may never know it."

35

REUNION

Michael stared blankly at his computer screen, watching the mouse cursor blink on and off. His email draft was blank, other than the obligatory 'To whom it may concern' headline. The email was addressed to a generic .org address for the American Zoo and Aquarium Association, with the headline entered as *Funding Opportunity for Florida Zoo with New Crocodilian Species - Deinosuchus*. He thought it came off as mooching, but right now it was his only idea.

An hour had passed since the video interview, and already clips of his speech were playing on local news stations on his office TV. He wasn't sure why he insisted on listening to his own voice: he hated it. Eventually, he decided the primary reason he was watching his news story was to see if any of the information he delivered was inaccurate. Thankfully, all of his statements were factual. He even liked his posture.

Eventually he turned off the TV and resumed his email draft, struggling to conjure up an impressive body of the text. Unsure of where to turn, he looked out the window, observing the alligators lumbering around below. Behind a fountain feature, he could see Buck swimming around, taunting the other smaller alligators as they tried to float away from him.

Not the king anymore, buddy, he thought, watching the large alligator continue to circumnavigate the pool. Buck and Sinclair had been dethroned – there was a new tyrant in town.

As he began to daydream, he snapped back to the present and faced the computer. The funding would never come if he kept zoning out and fantasizing over his five-minutes of fame.

Would it be worth it to cut to the chase and immediately reveal the motive, or would a brief introductory paragraph be proper? The problem with an introductory paragraph was that he had already introduced himself in emails for prior requests for funding. The only reason he considered it was because often times he would reach different people at the organization. It would rarely be the same person that would reply. He considered having Sherry come in and help him with his draft, but remembered how swamped she was in incoming emails. Bothering her now wouldn't be a good idea.

As he wrestled with the dilemma, a knock came from his door.

Who the hell could this be?

Relieved, he turned off his monitor and yelled a friendly, "Come in!"

Surprisingly, Jeffrey Berman came through the door, with a neutral, if not friendly smile on his face. He held in his hand a paper bag with a hot dog icon on it, setting it down on Michael's desk before taking a seat. Michael was stunned. He hadn't spoken very much to Berman since their fist fight back in the jungle.

"Hey, Jeff," Michael said, uneasy about the officer's sudden reappearance. "You're making a habit of these random visits, aren't you?"

"Your kind receptionist let me in," he said. "I hope it wasn't any trouble. I know how busy you must be, with the release of your new exhibit and all the press coverage your sanctuary has been getting."

Michael sensed a certain sincerity in his tone – a personality trait that Michael hadn't truly witnessed since their high school days, before he ratted out his best friend for the selling of illegal drugs to students.

"No, no it's all right," Michael assured him. "To be honest, you're distracting me from something that I needed distracting from. I need to send an email for some funding and grants for facility improvements. If I'm gonna house our Godzilla crocodilian here, we're gonna need some additional space, and it's space that I currently don't have the liquidity or savings for."

"How much are we talking?" Berman asked, sauntering up to the desk.

"Whatever I can get," Michael said. "I'd hate to have to ask the bank for another loan. Animal exhibits can get expensive, like a couple hundred dollars per square foot expensive depending on the materials, decorations etc. We saw what the deinosuchus can do in the wild – the thing takes down boats. We'll need additional reinforcement for the enclosure, plus multiple access points to the exhibit for ease of cleaning and maintenance without provoking the animal."

"I can put a request to raise some funds down at the police department and the Palm Grove town hall. Dawson might be weird about it, after what happened to Willie, Sherwin and Ryan, but it's worth a shot. Oh, and the community center. I could probably put up a notice there as well. You'd be surprised how many people down there actually care about the damn thing, regardless of how many lives it's claimed."

"Oh, thanks Jeff, but you don't really have t –"

"It's the least I can do," Berman interrupted. "I really screwed up back there, Mikey. Hell, I've been screwed up for a while now. It doesn't matter. Anyway, I'm not really good at apologies. But if I had to summarize, I'd say that I have a hard time letting go of the past. You were right to do what you did back in high school. If I would've gone down after I graduated, I probably would have done hard time – ruining my life and record. And you were right about what you did in the swamp. I didn't have to kill the damn thing. I felt shitty about it ever since. I don't know what else to say. I'm sorry, Mikey."

"Are you serious?" Michael asked.

"Yeah, why?" Berman replied, obviously confused.

Michael laughed.

"Do you know all the anxiety I've been carrying ever since you first walked into my office a week ago?" Michael said. "All this time, I've been trying in my mind to forgive myself about that stupid high school incident. And what happened in the swamp – you know I'm sorry for hitting you. Plus that bullshit in the jungle."

"That was my fault," Berman said. "Listen, I went in there looking for a fight. I was drunk and with the steroids I've been experimenting with lately, well, let's just say it made for a mean Molotov cocktail. I'm glad we ran into the crocodile when we did. We were headed for trouble. But near death experiences change people, Mikey. I've changed. No more living in the past."

"I thought we were goners," Michael added, leaning back in his office chair. "My jaw is still killing my, by the way. You hit like a tank. I had to put on some makeup to diffuse the bruises."

"You're not so bad yourself," Berman laughed. "Anyone who can take down a deino – dino – whatever the hell it's called, is one tough son of a bitch in my book!"

"Deinosuchus," Michael smiled. "You were close. Not many people can pronounce that without hearing it a few times. You would get a kick out of the weird names my staff has come up with while they butchered the real name."

"Have you thought of a name for it? I know you like to name the animals here."

"We're calling it Deino for the time being. I know, real original, right?"

"I like it," Berman said. "Clean, simple and easy to remember. Listen, Mike. I don't want to waste another twenty years being mad about the past. What's done is done, and I've made my peace. Let's pick up where we left off, wherever that was – I can barely remember. Let's start fresh, right here, right now. Now that I know you're just a half-hour up the road, why not?"

Michael managed a smile.

"I'd like that a lot, Jeff. I could use a good friend – my time as a business owner has made me run short of those. This time, I'll try and be a better one!"

"Don't get too warm and fuzzy with me," Berman said, causing Michael to laugh. After so many years, it appeared that their silent feud had finally mended. They had shaken hands like adults.

"So, how have things been up here?" Berman asked. "Oh, by the way – enjoy the hot dogs before they get cold. I bought you three from Palm Grove. I know how much you liked them from the shop."

Michael nearly tore open the bag. He had skipped breakfast for the news speech, deciding that eating while nervous may upset his stomach.

"Thanks for lunch," Michael replied, wolfing through the first one. "You didn't have to do that. Anyway, it's been a little weird. Most of the staff members are excited and confused as to why they're not allowed to take pictures of the new exhibit and share them with their friends or on social media. They don't understand why I'm being so secretive – it's all for marketing really. Basically, I'm trying to make it seem like a grand unveiling, and all they wanna do is vlog about the deino."

"How has the press been?"

"A little hard to handle, not gonna lie," Michael said. "Thankfully, my receptionist is awesome at her job and is handling it really well. She's a little overwhelmed by all the email traffic though. I had to send one of my younger guys up there to give her a hand."

"Has anyone in the dinosaur community rebuked your deinosuchus theory?"

"You mean any paleontologists?

"Yeah, them."

"Some have come out in support of my idea, which I read online in multiple news forums. But yes, there are skeptics as well. My theory won't be confirmed until I have time to get a panel of paleontology experts down here to study the animal."

"Has anyone tried to sneak in and see it?" Berman laughed, expecting a resounding no.

"Well, you'd be surprised," Michael replied. "The first night after the news broke when Dawson went on camera, I did get some drunk teens in the parking lot wanting to see if they could see over our fencing. Thankfully, I was still around at the time, came out and they drove away. I'm actually thankful it happened, because it made me hire a night security guard."

"I think you'll need more than that," Berman noted.

"Why's that?"

"Well, suppose that thing down there breaks loose. I'd hate to have a total repeat of what happened in the Southern Glades."

Michael stared at him, not amused.

"Just a joke," Berman said. "A bad one, I know."

"Very funny," Michael said. "We would never reopen."

"Don't worry. There's a bigger chance of us finding a pterodactyl down there in the Everglades than that croc escaping. By the looks of all the security measures you have around here, that thing's here to stay."

"You better believe it," Michael said firmly.

"Well, Mikey, I better bounce. I'm gonna be up near the north of town today so if you need anything, don't hesitate to call."

He got up and prepared to leave, turning one final time as he reached the door.

"What are you up to tonight?"

"Dinner date with Mila," Michael said with a smirk.

"You schmoozer. I knew I should have made a move on her when I had the chance. Okay, Mikey. Have a great time and keep in touch."

"Will do, Jeff. Hey, just one more thing."

The officer had prepared to leave, stopping at Michael's request.

"Yeah?"

"Assuming you've been down there for a few days clearing things up. How's it been going?"

Berman paused at the doorway, leaning against the frame and letting out a deep breath before beginning.

"*Uh*, well it's pretty bad, Mikey. You remember the smells – the whole place feels like death. We've found all types of remains, both human and animal. We're still not sure of many details of the attacks, but I can confirm that you were right about the boat attack theory. Some of the boats that we've identified have been listed in government databases of missing persons, some in the case of years earlier, in different locations all over southern Florida. Many of the victims may have been attacked further out or years in the past, possibly in various areas throughout the Everglades and dragged for miles. Several of the boat fragments were remains of ships whose owners were still alive, so that's a bit of good news. The creature must love to collect scrap."

"How many bodies have you found so far?" Michael asked.

"Five additional ones so far, not counting Ryan's corpse that we found there when we fell down during our scuffle. The majority of the bones were actually animal remains, mostly alligators. Still, its discomforting to know that this was going on in our own backyard, and for how many years I wonder? Who knows?"

"Well, let's compare it to the American alligator," Michael said. "American alligators live for about forty years – sometimes fifty. They are fully mature around ten to fifteen years. Now if we compare it to the deinosuchus, who it would seem is at least twenty years old and a fully grown adult, it might have been years since the human attacks started."

"It would seem that way," Berman said. "We're still prodding through the area. I'm just grateful the nightmare in Palm Grove is over, and people can start rebuilding their lives – myself included. I'll let you know if we find anything else. See you, Mikey."

"Thanks, Jeff. Take care and good luck."

Berman let the door close gently, offering a final wave as the door separated them.

Michael reflected on their friendship as the sound of the officer's boots dissipated down the corridor, grateful that they had finally patched up their problems and could resume their brotherhood.

With a subtle grin, he turned the monitor back on and resumed his email draft.

It was shaping up to be a very good day after all.

36
CELEBRATING

The dim lighting of *Summer's End*, an upscale restaurant just south of Miami, illuminated an angelic halo over Mila's crystalline champagne glass. She sipped the drink sparingly, Michael noted, hoping to make it last the evening. It was Dom Perignon, a very expensive brand of champagne, but Michael didn't care. They were celebrating.

Although they had just recently met, the adventure in the swamp had brought them together in a way that Michael never thought possible with romance. They had survived a terrifying ordeal, and Mila had only witnessed a fraction of horror compared to what he saw in the river with Graham's final grisly moments – and with the ghostly cryptic den in the jungle.

In the moments after Deino's capture, the RB-S boats picked Mila up from the ship, taking her and Dawson to shore where Michael was waiting at the beach. He explained everything, just as the sounds of the helicopter approached and airlifted the animal out of the jungle and off to the dock erected miles upstream.

After the Coast Guard had cleared out, the police department began the horrid task of examining and removing the corpses and sending them off to the coroner, while Michael returned to the mainland, where he orchestrated the animal's arrival at the sanctuary. After it was safely transplanted inside the secured enclosure, Michael slept for most of the day, waking up around four in the afternoon. He showered, groomed himself, and texted Mila about dinner.

She met up with him, they went out, and hit it off. Fortunately, even a few days later, she was still interested, intrigued by his knowledge and restless passion for crocodilians and preserving their way of life. After they exchanged backstories about their upbringing, high school and college adventures, and finally their professional lives, Michael found himself out of topics to discuss, switching back to where he felt comfortable and the most intellectual – crocodilians.

"You sure do love those things," she smiled, eyeing him from over the table after listening to a lengthy tirade by Michael about Buck, an alligator from the sanctuary.

"I owe my career to them," Michael replied.

Her veterinary background enabled her to have long, detailed talks about animals with him. Michael was relieved that someone finally could relate to his profession. She taught him quite a few things he never knew about working with mammals from a veterinarian standpoint, everything from grooming, cleaning, and hygiene to more intricate things like administering medicine and animal lodging. All in all, he was incredibly impressed by her equally matched affinity for wildlife, and found her increasingly irresistible as the date progressed.

"I like your suit," she commented abruptly, scanning down his dark blazer.

"Thanks," he smiled. "Armani."

"But that wasn't for me, was it?"

"Well, it was half for you," Michael said, defensive but playful. "I had to look my best on camera. I'm surprised my voice didn't crack or I didn't sweat through the collar. Did you watch it at all?"

"How could I not?" Mila said with an offended laugh. "It's been on all the news stations and the local news websites. People at the clinic today were talking about it, joking of course that when Deino gets sick that you should bring him to my practice. I laughed – like that thing would ever fit through the door! Several of my staff asked for your autograph."

"We would need an eighteen wheeler to bring Deino down," Michael said, continuing the make-believe scenario. "So far, I think most of my staff are terrified of the thing. They know what its reputation is and the aggression level the animal possesses. I'm still going over plans on how we're going to clean the enclosure. I don't trust any of my employees going inside without me being there. It's always watching, waiting for an escape. I've learned a lot about the deinosuchus in just a few short days of observation and documentation – from what I can tell, it's eager to get back to the wilderness."

"What makes you say that?"

"It may sound weird, but the animal's body language. It's incredibly irritated. I tried to go into the enclosure to coax it with some food the other day, after my employee Sandra told me she thought that Deino looked dead – because it wasn't moving really at all, you see. I barely made it through the door and the animal was already on me, charging for the door in a split-second. Plus, the damn thing never seems to sleep. It's very opportunistic."

"It does have an odd internal clock," she said. "Some of the victims, like Owen's father, were killed during daylight hours. But when we went on the expedition, it had no problem snapping at us at night. I still can't get over what happened, Michael. Officer Bolasco and Officer Graham. The other cop, Gray I think his name was – Ryan Gray. I keep replaying it in my head over and over. How have you been dealing with it all? It's a hell of a lot to process."

"I try to keep my mind off it," Michael said. "To me, it's just an animal – an animal with a ravenous appetite. Unfortunately, humans are on the top of the deino's snack list. And hell, you should have seen it, Mila! The way it just pushed effortlessly past us, with Graham locked in its jaws while tossing us aside in its waves like we were nothing. It moved with such ease, such prowess. And the look on the animal's menacing eyes as it sucked him under. It was a look I'll never forget – it still haunts me."

She was captivated by his words, putting a hand up as if to silence him but still listening intently with her eyes, wanting to know more about the deinosuchus but terrified by what the mysterious creature was capable of. He knew she was picturing the fateful scene in her head.

"I was powerless to stop it," he added.

"Oh, I know," Mila said. "I'm just happy you escaped when you did."

"Graham had the last laugh," Michael went on. "It was his tranquilizer gun that I found in the den. My own tranquilizer slipped out of my hand when Jeff and I fell down the hill. It was because of him that we were able to capture the deinosuchus and make it back to Palm Grove safely. After all that's happened, I'm seriously considering donating a large sum of the money from the deinosuchus opening day event to the families of the victims. I figure it's the least that the sanctuary can offer, if nothing else."

"That's a good idea," Mila said, pausing before she went on as if she didn't want to ask the question. "Have you been getting any hate mail?"

"You mean for capturing the animal alive? I'm not sure yet, because I haven't gone through all the emails that have been pouring in. I think Sherry and Charlie got through most of them before I left. I'll be going over them tonight. I'm hoping this shit doesn't bring me into the spotlight in a bad way."

"Well, whatever happens, just remember it's because of you that these attacks stopped. Think of the lives you saved. The deino is out of Palm Grove now, safely in captivity where it can't harm anyone again."

"I hadn't thought of it quite like that, Mila," Michael said. "Thanks, I needed that."

"Oh, watch out, here it comes!"

Their food arrived by a pair of white-gloved waiters, prompting them to pause the conversation and begin the dinner. Michael had ordered steak with a bowl of lobster bisque and Mila ordered a salmon. As he forked through the meat, Michael noticed some eyes around the room looking at him, whispering questions to their friends under their breath. He knew they were wondering if he was the same man on the news – the man from Redland with the prehistoric, murderous crocodile.

"They're still staring," Michael whispered to her. "Maybe going out on the same day as the news release wasn't such a wise idea."

"You're gonna have to get used to it," she replied in between bites. "You're probably gonna be a big celebrity now. People will put you up there with Steve Irwin and Jane Goodall. You may even have your own show on Animal Planet because of this."

"Well, I don't really care about being famous," Michael said, sipping water. "But if it helps my zoo and my goal of saving and promoting crocodilians, while keeping everyone gainfully employed, maybe it isn't so bad after all."

"It just may take some getting used to," Mila said in a voice that soothed him.

He couldn't help but stare at her. She was wearing a long, elegant red dress, complete with a pearl necklace and dark lipstick. She had caught him staring several times, of which he averted his gaze and went back to his dinner.

"So what are we planning for *after* dinner?" she asked, smirking after she caught him studying her again.

Michael continued eating his dinner, trying to recover from his embarrassment.

"I'm sorry, what did you ask?" he asked, avoiding her eyes. He could feel himself turning red, unsure if it was because of the heat of the bisque or his obvious attraction to her.

"I said what are we doing after dinner?"

"Oh, sorry. I have to run to work. There's some loose ends that need tying up before the big opening on Monday. I asked one of my employees, Sandra, to help me out tonight. You're more than welcome to come visit if you like. But we'll probably be very late."

"Maybe I'll stop by for a bit," Mila said. "As long as you're confident that Deino is secure."

"Trust me, he's secure," Michael smiled. "I wouldn't be keeping him there here if I wasn't absolutely sure about that."

37
LATE NIGHT VISIT

Sandra cracked her laptop open in the employee break room, which offered a nice view of both the animal enclosures below and the lush unkempt acres beyond the facility. The sun had nearly set, and Michael was supposed to be back any minute now from his dinner date with his new flame he met while on the expedition. Sandra looked forward to meeting her – whoever she was.

She enjoyed doing her coursework in the break room. It made it easy to focus, except when the loud fax machine from the late 2000's would randomly churn out paperwork – thankfully that hadn't happened yet. She huddled up in an old diner booth that Michael had bought from a flea market last summer, having it installed near the observation window. It was a favorite spot among employees to have lunch when it was too hot to dine outside.

Below, she observed the American crocodiles in their first enclosure, basking in the final moments of sunlight before slipping away into their pools or back inside to their interior enclosures for the night. Beside her sat a Starbucks mango dragon fruit iced drink that her boss often referred to as 'hipster' and half a sandwich she salvaged from lunch. Earlier in the day, she made sure to run and get food. Sometimes, working overtime at the sanctuary would run very late. But she didn't mind. Sandra loved the sanctuary and wished to volunteer more time there after she received her degree.

A raspy old voice interrupted her thoughts – so raspy and convoluted that she had trouble understanding the words.

"What's that?" she asked.

"I said, do you need anything before I take my smoke break?"

It was Gene, the new night security officer. Sandra didn't know his last name. She figured he was way too old to be a night watchman, but didn't tell Michael that. Most of the old man's teeth were gone, leading to his slurred, muffled word delivery.

Gene was the first of Michael's newest attempts to tighten up the sanctuary, after a recent scare from some local teenagers scared him into taking extra steps to keep the crocodilians secure. From what she heard, it was just one of the many security measures he had planned. She heard from Sherry that Michael also intended to get electrical perimeter fences and more cameras at all entrances and sides of the compound.

"No thank you," she said politely. "Where are you going?"

"There's a little nature trail behind the property," the old man said. "I think I'm gonna go down there and see if I can watch the stars for a little while."

"Oh, yeah," Sandra replied. "I know that trail. Enjoy."

Gene did a little salute before slowly continuing past the door frame down the hall. If Michael came back and found him taking a "smoke break", Sandra figured that Gene may not be employed at the sanctuary for very long.

Quickly, she resumed her homework, as the doorway to the sanctuary lobby down the hall clicked and locked shut. She pulled out a set of notes from class that she scribbled down in a binder and connected to Wi-Fi to begin her research. There was a lot to get done, and she only had a little window of time to do it before Michael returned and began assigning her tasks.

As she was about to stick her earbuds in, Sandra heard a rattling at the front of the building. At first, she thought someone may be trying to break in, but on closer inspection, she thought the clanging resembled more of a friendly, secretive knock. Irritated, she squirmed out from the booth and headed out to investigate.

Naturally, this would happen right after Gene left his post, she thought. Or maybe it was Gene, and the silly old dog locked himself out. As she rounded the bend to the lobby, she frowned. It was even worse than she thought.

Charlie.

Her colleague was standing outside the first entry door, staring into the lobby. He was dressed in what she would refer to as 'teeny-bopper' attire, which was comprised of dark Dickies shorts and a Tapout hat and shirt. She thought the look made him look even more immature than he already was.

What a douche.

Quickly, he spotted her at the corner of the lobby, beckoning for her to let him in. She froze, pissed off that he saw her. Charlie's waving appeared insistent and impatient. He was just as annoying after hours as he was on the job. Begrudgingly, Sandra proceeded to unlock the doors.

As soon as he was inside the facility, she could detect the smell of alcohol and regretted letting him in. He moved sluggishly, nearly colliding with a Redland Crocodilian Sanctuary welcome sign.

"Charlie, you smell like shit," she scolded him, wafting her hand around to diffuse the overwhelming smell of liquor. "Why are you here?"

"I saw that Mike's car wasn't here yet so I figured I'd stop in. Do you want to come out with me? I can drive, I swear. Just a little buzzed..."

"I've been telling you throughout the week," she said firmly, "no. I have to work late tonight. Besides, Michael is gonna be back any minute. If he finds you here when you're drunk, he's gonna be pissed. You know how strict and fatherly he is about underage drinking. He'll probably reprimand you, if not fire you."

"Like I give a shit," Charlie said, bumping gently into the door frame of the lobby. "Oh, come on. Just for an hour? I heard Sherry talking earlier that Mike was saying his date may run late. Who knows, they may have other stuff planned after dinner."

He wiggled his eyebrows seductively, but it came off as goofy and childish.

"You're gross," Sandra said bluntly. "And if you think that's gonna happen with me, you're gravely mistaken. Now get out! You know I'm only looking out for your job."

"Forget the job," Charlie said. "I have another job interview tomorrow at Walmart, and I know I'll get it. They're short on staff. I'll be making a hell of a lot more than I make here, and that's just starting out. You should think about working there too. Plus, easy commute. Way easier!"

"You're leaving?" Sandra said, trying to mask her happiness with phony concern.

"Yeah. I was planning on telling Mike tomorrow, but if I run into him tonight and I get one of his famous lectures on responsibility, I just may have to break the news early."

"That's not exactly giving him a lot of notice, Charlie."

"Like I care. It's just a first job. Adults are used to that from our generation, right?"

"That's only a generational stereotype. You're practically an adult yourself. I think you need to give him at least two weeks' notice. Now please, leave before he comes back and gets pissed at me for letting you in here under the influence."

"Fine, but you have to catch me first!"

"*What?*" Sandra asked blankly. "What are yo– "

Before she could stop him, Charlie started running down the corridor, around the reception desk and down the stairs towards the sanctuary.

"Charlie!" Sandra said. "Get back here!"

She took off after him. When she reached the stairs, she saw him arc leftwards, down to the stairs leading to the visitor trail. She couldn't help but laugh as he nearly skidded into a wall with his alcohol induced momentum, but shook it off, knowing that he wasn't messing around like he usually did. When Gene came back, which she hoped would be soon, he would have to help her escort Charlie off the premises before they both got in trouble.

What the hell is he doing?

She chased him frantically through the mulch trail, gaining on Charlie because of his clumsy mistakes he made, bumping into decorative features and information boards for visitors. The alligators watched as the humans passed, curious as to what was happening and offering warning hisses as Charlie veered by. Normally, no one walked through the visitor trails at night. This was quite the show for them.

Sandra frowned, nearly out of breath when Charlie disappeared into the utility hallway entrance, hidden by landscaped jungle fronds beside the former caiman pen.

He's going for the deinosuchus interior enclosure!

She ran through the opening after him, relieved that she caught him before he did something stupid. He was out of breath too, waiting for her on the outside of the secured entrance to the Deinosuchus exhibit's interior enclosure. Behind the glass, she could see Deino not far away and, for once, asleep.

"Charlie, what the hell are you doing?" Sandra said, noticing that his hand was clamped onto the rusty door latch for the enclosure.

"I'm gonna wrangle the new exhibit," Charlie informed her. "And film it on my phone – it will go viral for sure. I'll be YouTube famous!"

"You better not go in there," Sandra said, mortified as his hand slipped further down the doorway. "You heard those horror stories that Michael went through in the swamp. Do you even know how many people that thing's killed?"

"Yeah, like six or seven," Charlie said in a know-it-all voice. "Relax, I'm not gonna let it out, despite how much fun that'd be for Mike to clean up. I'm just going in there for a second."

"We signed a non-disclosure about it," Sandra said, trying to stall him, hoping that at any time the security guard would come in and put an end to this impossible scenario.

Where the hell is Gene?

"That was about Michael's original trip to the swamp," Charlie replied. "We didn't sign anything about confidentiality once the animal was actually here."

"Charlie..."

"Chill..."

"Don't you open that door! I will call the night watchman."

"Who? Gene? He's like ten thousand years old. And he's in the trail, out back. He'd never get here in time."

Her heart stopped as his hand pressed down on the lock, moving toward the latch.

"Don't."

He offered an adolescent smile before turning to the pen door.

With the hard turn of his wrist, he pulled the door open, letting the misty air from the exhibit leak into the dark maintenance hall. Sandra could feel her heart beating as Charlie turned the corner and began to walk inside, pulling his iPhone out of his pocket and moving to the camera app. She felt powerless. She couldn't run and get help. What if something happened while she was away? She was forced to babysit until he came out from the exhibit. She decided once the door was shut and Charlie was safely out of the enclosure, she would call Michael immediately and report the situation.

He'd better be confident about the Walmart job. He's fired for sure!

From the fogged glass window, she watched as her colleague slowly approached the sleeping giant. She debated on locking the pen door, but decided against it, knowing the risks if Charlie was attacked. He would need a quick escape. When he would finally emerge, she would tear into him like he'd never seen before.

He might be better off with Deino, Sandra thought angrily, tapping her foot impatiently as she helplessly watched Charlie proceed through the dark cavernous room.

The deino was parked on a large boulder, built to look like Pride Rock from The Lion King. The animal was so large, that the tail and head drooped off the stone to the floor below, like a big cat on a kitty tree. With every breath, the scaly armored chest rose and fell, pushing the jagged osteoderms up and down like stegosaurus plates. The creature was in a deep sleep. It craved rest, brought on by days of confusion from the capture to relocation to Redland. Even as Charlie moved closer to the animal, phone in front of him like a weapon, she couldn't believe how small he looked in front of the ancient crocodilian.

"Hey," Charlie called in a false bravado tone. "Hey you!"

Charlie's calls went unanswered. Deino remained asleep as he pressed record on the video app, turning the screen towards himself, selfie-style.

"Okay. I'm Charlie Mundall, a former employee of the Redland Crocodilian Sanctuary. Here we have the famous deinosuchus from Palm Grove. Or, the Everglades I should say. As you can see, he's exceptionally large."

He turned the camera from himself to the deinosuchus. Sandra could see the animal was starting to rouse itself from unconsciousness, disturbed by the new noises in the chamber. The eyes opened partly, confused as to why there was a human lurking about in the enclosure.

"Charlie, get out! It's awake!" Sandra yelled from the glass.

"Yeah," Charlie said, turning back to her. "That's the point. I can't wrangle it while it's asleep!"

He continued walked towards the animal, resuming his spiel to the phone screen.

"It looks like he's awake now, let me show you how to subdue this animal."

Sandra grimaced as Charlie nearly stumbled over a faux rock that served as an enclosure design. He teetered to the left before regaining his balance. By the time he found his footing, the deino's eyes were wide open, watching the boy glide sluggishly around the room, slowly coming towards the sealed, ready jaws.

"Wow," Charlie said, his voice faltering. "I didn't realize it was so big until now, when you're up close..."

Deino stirred from his spot, rising to its full height slowly, stretching from the nap. A low rumble started from the creature's belly, emitting up to the massive neck. The deino let out a menacing hiss that rumbled through the artificial cavern, causing Charlie to freeze in his tracks as the monster stared down at him from Pride Rock.

"*Uhm*, yeah. It's pretty big," Charlie murmured, the mood of the room changing from curiosity to despair.

"Maybe I'll just settle for a first-look video instead. Sandra, I don't think I can –"

The deino took a step off the boulder towards Charlie. Sandra could see his iPhone shaking in his hand, nearly teetering out from his palm. Charlie backed up, almost tripping over the same rock again.

The deinosuchus moved forward curiously, quicker this time, its footsteps precisely placed to minimize the distance between its mouth and the intruder. Finally, Charlie's phone slipped from his hand, the screen cracking on the concrete floor, sending crystalline shards over the callous surface.

"Easy, easy," Charlie whispered, putting his palm out in a futile self-defense.

"Charlie! Come on! It's gonna grab you, you asshole!"

Sandra was beckoning to him from the doorway, but Charlie wouldn't turn around. The deinosuchus moved up to the palm, sniffing powerfully with its imposing alligator-like snout.

"Sandra, I can't move. It's petrifying."

"Charlie! Just run!"

"Maybe it isn't hungry..."

"What? Charlie! I said run!"

The animal stared at Charlie at first with an innocent fascination. It was the first time someone was in the cage without Michael present. It continued to walk towards Charlie, picking up speed as they walked in a grisly duet towards the exit. The animal's sniffing became more intense, egged on by Charlie's beating heart and sporadic, drunken movements. Sandra could feel her heart-rate accelerate as the creature began to open its jaws, pressing her trembling palms against the glass that she had just scrubbed meticulously hours earlier.

"Charlie!"

"Sandra, I think I need your... Whoa –"

With a quick swerve of the head, the deinosuchus' jaws sprung open like a cobra, clamping its gargantuan mouth down on Charlie's palm, crunching the bones and pulling him off his feet and crashing onto the floor.

"Charlie!" Sandra yelled, screaming in hysteria as his frail figure flipped over and was tackled by the murderous primal carnivore.

As Charlie shrieked and slammed into the ground, blood dripping off his arm, Sandra reached into her pocket for her phone, finally able to look away from the life-changing visual she was forced to witness.

She crouched down behind the glass, clumsily scrolling through the list for Mike's number as the sounds of Charlie's untimely death and shrieks raged behind the glass. Her fingers weren't cooperating, shaking and twitching through the apps until she finally made it to the contacts. She eventually descended the contact list, quietly settling a quick debate on whether the police should be called first before Michael. As she pressed the dial, she realized her mistake.

Oh, please. No!

She looked slowly over her left shoulder.

The enclosure door was still open, several feet behind her!

As the phone started to ring, she froze, hugging the grungy concrete wall. The powerful presence moved out of the door, but she dared not turn her head around to greet it. Through the glossy reflection of the glass ahead, she watched as the deino walked out of the room, barely two yards away behind her. With a thoughtful hiss, the animal turned away from Sandra's hiding place and moved towards the exit to the mulch trail.

As the deinosuchus rammed through the doorway, letting the crisp night air flood into the utility hall, Sandra heard Michael's calm voice through the speakerphone.

"Hello? Sandra?"

Sandra trembled as the Cretaceous tail swerved out of the corridor, banging the iron door shut as the animal arrived in the exterior exhibits, free of captivity. Quietly she approached the utility entrance and shut the door, before informing Michael of the terror that just transpired.

38
A DEINOSUCHUS IN REDLAND

The metal door swung open, allowing Deino to stride freely without barrier into the dark visitor trails of the Redland Crocodilian Sanctuary. The reptilian claws dug swiftly into the mulch trail, sniffing malevolently at the Floridian air, searching for another target to maul.

Several days of pent up aggression had roiled up the deinosuchus to an apex of rage. Now that the creature was free, it sought to unleash its fury.

The first scent of savory food came from other nearby crocodilians. Numerous crocodilians, all around the strange maze of man-made trails.

The Deino looked around, discovering there were crocodiles all around him, but obscured by impenetrable cement barriers and conveniently placed cliff drop-offs. Straight ahead, the deinosuchus could see alligators and caimans watching safely from their walled-off exhibits. Some slid into the pools to hide, acknowledging the super predator's unchallenged dominance in the zoo.

Another, beautiful scent soaked into Deino's nostrils after entering the mulch trails.

Human.

The animal had grown quite fond of the taste of tender human flesh, especially in the last week where the creature had now torn apart five male victims. Their bones made for great crunching, and their boats made interesting artifacts to adorn the den with. But this scent was far off, coming from the other end of the compound, trailing lightly on the restless evening breeze.

It was coming from somewhere on the other side of the compound's walls.

The taste of the young clumsy male human was hardly enough. More was needed to appease the creature's appetite. It began to run through the compound in desperation, crashing through the decorative signs and informative crocodilian fact charts that visitors would read casually while walking through the park during the day.

The deinosuchus arrived hastily at a small fountain feature, spraying water out from a rock decoration like a geyser. The water formed a pool that trickled down to a waterfall before flowing down a narrow swamp that served as a beautiful border to a lunch area saturated in picnic tables for the visitors.

The creature lapped up some of the water, reminding its crocodilian senses of the Everglades. The deinosuchus sensed that the Glades were close, yearning for their deepening pools for hiding – and hunting. It longed for the boundless expanse of the jungles of southern Florida.

As he finished drinking, Deino tilted his muscular head upward, perturbed by a random change in scenery that shouldn't have been there. Ahead, a long board fence ran the length of the enclosures, bordered by more alligator exhibits and an entrance to the visitor lobby and administrative building. In the center of the board fence, at the end of the mulch trail, the deinosuchus picked up a brief opening in the wood, watching the gentle weeds sway through the hole in the wind.

It was the damaged portion of fencing that Michael neglected to repair.

Flimsier than boat, thought the deino suddenly.

Can break...

The deino reared up on all fours, charging through the shallow stream and back onto the trail, picking up speed towards the weak point in the fence. A group of birds that had gathered on the trail took off as the giant careened towards them, fearing the stomp of the deino's massive feet.

Snout first, the reptile crashed through the board fence, finding itself in a weed laden area just east of the Redland sanctuary property as the wood fragments crashed into the earth around it. Ahead, the treacherous eyes detected the distant lights of local businesses, and more glows from the streetlamps masked behind palm trees. On the road above the hill, the rumble of evening traffic flew past the sanctuary parking lot, deterring the animal from continuing up to the front of the building.

Vehicles. Maybe Big Swamp Boats. Not nice.

The savory smell of human lingered from the rear of the sanctuary, towards the high grass. The deinosuchus spun around and took off down toward the rear nature trail, hissing a treacherous wail as its tail slipped out from the sanctuary before fading into the night.

As the earth-shaking footsteps of the monster grew fainter, Sandra crept out from the utility door, having observed the entire event from the moment the creature broke into the visitor trail.

Multiple fresh fears raced through her as she wiped the sweat from her eyes, making sure the animal was gone. Behind her, the nauseating smell of Charlie's blood seeped out of the doorway, forcing her to fend off vomiting. She wanted nothing more than to get home and start a new job – anywhere but the sanctuary.

Is it coming back? Is there anyone outside I should warn? It's all my fault. I let Mike down.

The computerized voice of her boss and the muted clinking of background fine-dining dinnerware broke her concentration.

"Sandra? Sandra, talk to me! You sound scared. What's going on?

She contemplated not answering. Not answering, hanging up, getting in a car and driving as far away as possible. This would be all over the local news soon. And all over the national news in the morning. And it would be all her fault.

"Oh God. Michael, it's gone. The deinosuchus is gone!"

"What? Sandra, the deino is locked up. What are you talking about?"

"No. It got out. Michael, I'm sorry. I'm telling you – I promise. I just watched it break through the board fence. It's out now. Deino is out in Redland."

39
CAUSING A SCENE

"What?" Michael could feel his voice faltering, fending off another panic attack. "What do you mean it's in Redland?"

He was standing up in his seat now. Around him, he could see the other guests pausing their meals and staring over at him in confusion. If they weren't sure if he was the man on TV before, he thought, they were definitely suspicious now.

Horrified that everyone around him was eavesdropping on this potentially damaging business situation, Michael lowered his voice and walked out to the patio area, relieved when he saw that it was empty. He could hear Mila come out behind him, closing the sliding glass door behind her as he resumed the conversation. Through the glass, he could feel more curious eyes staring out at him before returning to their dinner.

"Sandra, tell me what's happening," Michael said, trying to lower and calm his voice to not sound like he was scolding her. "Slowly, please."

Mike...I don't know – it was so quick. I'm still coming to terms with it.

He could sense that she was terrified of whatever had occurred, and probably wrestled with making the call herself. She sounded mortified and had definitely undergone some form of trauma.

"It must be contained inside the barrier somewhere," Michael said. "That's what you meant, right?"

"No," Sandra replied. *"It got out. Charlie came over and he was drunk. I don't know. He wanted to film the deino for YouTube. He went into the cage – I tried to stop him..."*

Michael's vision went blurry. His professional life and future of the sanctuary raced past him. Suddenly, he wasn't sure if he wanted to hear the rest of the story. He had a feeling that he knew where the tale would end up. The world around him spun like a cyclone. He stabilized himself by falling into a table, knocking off a pepper shaker.

"It grabbed him, Mike. I – I couldn't shut the door in time. I wanted to make sure Charlie could get out. It all happened so fast. It ran out and went through the door to the outside trails..."

"Is it still there?" Michael yelled. "Are you somewhere safe?"

His brain was pounding. The wind felt cooling on his throbbing forehead as it whipped through the alleyway that bordered the patio area. He could feel his heart jumping around in his chest, worrying for a moment it was a sign of an oncoming heart attack.

"No, it's out Mike. That's what I'm saying. You remember that broken patch of fencing towards the visitor building? It ripped right through it. It was heading for the nature trail out back."

"Head for the visitor building, go to my office and lock yourself in. I'm coming now!"

"Do you want me to call the police?"

"No, I'll handle that."

He hung up the phone and turned back for the restaurant.

"What's going on?" Mila asked.

"The deino's out."

He didn't care to explain any further – Michael knew she understood the gravity of the message. The deinosuchus was loose in Redland, a metropolis just south of Miami, with plenty of potential unsuspecting human targets to track down and tear apart.

They ran back through the dining area. Michael slapped a few hundred dollars on the table and then darted out of the room. The blurry images of confused waiters and people watched as they streaked past, bumping shoulders with a hostess on her break.

Exiting the building, Michael careened through the parking lot to his Taurus. He unlocked his car and dove into the passenger seat. As he started the engine, his passenger door clicked open and Mila slid into the seat, buckling herself in.

"What are you doing?" Michael asked, before shifting the vehicle to drive.

"I'm coming with you," she replied. "We've already been through this once together."

"Yeah, but Mila – you didn't see how this creature moves. How it lives. It's dangerous. I don't know what will happen."

"I'm coming with you," she repeated herself. "Now let's go!"

"Okay," Michael said, shifting into reverse as he backed out of his parking spot. "Sticking with me from this point on may be risky for you. By morning, my face might be all over the news as a huge commercial flop and a negligence cautionary tale on zoo management."

"Just get us to your sanctuary," she ordered him.

There was no more time to redirect her away from the car. Every second he wasn't at the sanctuary was another second he remained in guessing limbo.

Where was the creature? Had it killed anyone yet? How in the hell was he going to get it back? What fines would he have to pay? Would he serve jail time? Would Charlie's parents sue? Was his time as a zookeeper limited? Would the deinosuchus be there, waiting for him to return, as if waiting to exact revenge for their first encounter in the jungle?

"Who do you want me to call?" Mila asked as they swerved out of the parking lot and onto the main road, barely avoiding a fire hydrant.

"First, call Jeff."

"Berman?"

"Yeah," he said, handing her his iPhone. "His number is in there. Call him first, explain the situation. I think he said he may be on patrol today. I'd rather see him right now than anyone else."

"I thought you two were on odd terms," Mila said, scrolling quickly through the contacts.

"Things changed today," Michael said, eyes burning from the sweat of uncertainty and choking anxiety. "I guess life or death situations change people."

The phone rang for only one tone.

"Berman," came a familiar voice through the speakers.

"Jeff, it's Mila. We have a situation in Redland."

"Mila? What's up?"

"We just heard from one of Mike's employees. The deino's escaped. We think it's somewhere in Redland, somewhere close to the sanctuary."

"What? How could this have happened? Are you sure?"

"Yeah, here, talk to Mike."

She handed him the phone.

"Jeff. Hey. I'm freaking out here, pal. Apparently one of my employees showed up and started fooling around. They opened the cage and the deino escaped. I didn't know who else to call."

"Jeez, Mikey. Okay, let me call Dawson and we'll get a few men up there immediately. Once we've confirmed that the creature is no longer on your property, we'll notify the Redland police."

"You don't think we should notify the cops up here?"

"Not until we know it's off your property," Berman replied. *"We don't want to start a panic unless we have to. I know your property's fairly large. Hopefully it's down in the reeds somewhere. I still have my tranquilizer gun on me now. I'm en route. I'll meet you at the sanctuary."*

"Thank you, Jeff."

He hung up the phone and tossed it into the empty beverage holder.

"What's going on?" Mila asked.

"We're meeting Jeff at the sanctuary," he said. "He's gonna meet us there and call Dawson. He thinks the animal probably hasn't got far. He still has his tranquilizer."

He rolled down his window, racing down the main road as fast as he could, trying to gather more wind to smack off his forehead to quell the crushing headache. The champagne from earlier wasn't helping.

"What are you doing?" Mila asked. "I can put the air on."

"I think I'm about to have a panic attack," he said, trying to control his breathing.

"Hey, calm down," she told him. "Breathe. Just breathe normally."

She started imitating how she wanted him to breathe, emphasizing the drawn out, gentle breaths. He mimicked her, keeping his hand on the wheel, rocketing the Taurus down the dark Florida road. It was a wonder that no police saw him burning past – he remembered they patrolled the area often.

Gradually his heart rate began to descend to normal. Mila's nurturing attitude that he discovered in the swamp expedition returned to help him again.

"You're good at that," Michael said. "Mila, how could this have happened? I had so many security measures in place. Ah. That damn perimeter fence!"

"How far away are we?" she asked.

"We'll be there in a few minutes, if I avoid the red lights. Mila, I should've fixed the hole in the fence. I've known about it for so long. And Charlie. I knew there was something odd about him. His aunt vouched for him in the interview, so I felt bad for the kid and gave him a second chance. I should've sent him packing when I had the chance. Now the poor kid is dead, and my business is in ruin!"

"It killed one of your employees?" Mila froze.

"He was a ballsy kid. Sandra said he just showed up randomly. Shit, and where the hell was Gene?"

"Who's that?"

"Gene. He's my night watchman I just hired to keep anyone from getting in. Apparently I should've been more worried about the deinosuchus getting out."

"It might still be near the sanctuary," Mila said, trying to calm him down. He slowed down when he realized she was holding onto the ceiling handle. "Do you think it might still be there?"

"No way of knowing," Michael replied. "I'd have to assume it's going to stay away from the roads and city grid, probably keeping to the wooded outskirts. Okay, thank God. Here we are!"

They pulled through an alley, spying the Redland Crocodilian Welcome sign on their left.

After nearly colliding with a rickety old pickup truck that bumbled past, Michael pulled out of the alley, scooting over the road and coasting toward the parking lot, carefully scanning over the long grasses that bordered the compound.

So far, he couldn't see any large red glowing eyes.

40
DESOLATION

Michael pulled the Taurus under the flickering entrance light of the lobby. The doors to the facility remained barred shut. He was surprised that Gene wasn't there to greet him, giving his trademarked courteous salute and waving his flashlight. As he clicked the engine off, he waited to exit the vehicle. Mila unbuckled her seat belt, but Michael put his arm in front of her, pushing her back into the seat.

"Wait," he said, studying the surrounding shadowy area.

The parking lot was empty, except for Sandra's car and Charlie's SUV, which were parked over on the side near the employee entrance. Gene's car was parked on the far edge, right in front of the untamed crabgrass and weeds that Michael regretted not cutting earlier that week before he set out for the Southern Glades expedition.

"I should've cut the damn grass," Michael cursed, scanning over the dense vegetation, searching for signs of a pair of crocodilian eyes.

Inside the visitor center, the lights of the lobby clicked on. Sandra appeared from around the receptionist desk, shaking in fright and holding onto the counter for support as she uneasily rounded the table. She turned white when she saw her boss parked just outside. Michael waved to her, signaling that he was planning on coming in. Sandra nodded timidly, retrieving a set of keys from her pocket and unlocked the first door.

"Come on," Michael said. "I think the parking lot is clear."

He ran around the car, opened Mila's door and then ran with her to the entrance. Around them, the grasses waved a taunting dance, but still nothing ran out to greet them. Michael suddenly had doubts that the creature was still in the area, dreading where the deinosuchus may have strayed off to.

Finally, after what seemed like minutes, Sandra opened the lock to the second door, letting them in and re-locking it behind them.

"Are you okay?" Michael asked as they walked into the lobby, resting a reassuring hand on his employee's shaking shoulder.

She nodded, eyes and cheeks aglow from drying tears.

"Yeah, I think so," she managed.

"Tell me what happened, Sandra."

"Well, I was doing my homework in the lounge. I heard a knock on the door – it was Charlie. Naturally I didn't want to let him in, but I didn't know what he wanted. After he was in, it was obvious that he was drunk. He took off running down into the exhibits to film the deinosuchus for a YouTube video. Michael, you have to believe me, I knew it was wrong and did everything I could to stop him. I tried to tell him not to, telling him it was wrong! He didn't care. He was going to tell you tomorrow that he was leaving for another job – Walmart, I think."

"Okay. Then what?"

"He went into the cage and started filming. I guess he didn't expect for the deino to have such an intimidating presence so close up. It didn't take long. He got pulled down so fast – it was like a blur. Deino ran out before I could shut the door. That's when it escaped through the fence. It charged through the wood like a rhino!"

"Have you seen it since?"

She shook her head, drying another stray tear.

Michael walked over to the corner where a widescreen TV remained shut off and flicked it on, tuning the channel to the local news. He was relieved when he saw the latest scandal in Washington playing and not anything about himself, his wildlife sanctuary, or the deinosuchus.

"Mila, turn on those monitors, will you? The power button is on the back of the screen."

She stepped around Sherry's desk and pressed on the computer screens beside the printer. Four mini-screens came to life one by one. The screen was revealed to be the layout of a surveillance camera system, portraying two sets of four camera angles every few seconds in repetitive loops.

"It's so dark, Mike," Mila said, studying the video feeds. "I can't really see anything in particular. Nothing like our deino."

He came around the desk.

The cameras were dark, except for the glow of each lens' corresponding overhead lamp that shone down on the area the lens was angled at. All of the cameras revealed nothing, other than the restless waving of tropical reeds and the gravel perimeter he poured strenuously last year. Several mosquitoes hovered by the lenses, streaking by like ghosts as they swarmed around the lights.

"Anything?" Mila asked.

"Nothing," he said, studying the images several times. "It's not showing up on camera, if it's still in the area."

"Michael, I'm sorry," Sandra said. "I tried everything I could think of."

"I know," he said, trying to sound reassuring, but couldn't help but coming off as irritated. Most of his agitation was directed at Charlie for his insubordination. The other part was directed at himself, for not repairing the hole in the fence when he had the chance – and for not firing that little shit earlier. Now he was dead, and Michael felt guilty about that too.

"Sandra, it's my fault," Michael stated finally. "I knew about the fence problem. You all brought it up to me privately and in company meetings. It should've been repaired the second we noticed it. I just never figured any crocodilians would breach out to the mulch trail. Hell, I certainly didn't think they'd break through the fence. But then again, this isn't your everyday crocodilian. Are all the doors locked to the visitor compound?"

She nodded, as the sounds of a distant car engine rumbled near the entrance, causing everyone to turn.

"Someone's coming," Mila pointed.

A pair of car headlights appeared through the brush in the front of the parking lot. As they turned into the lot, the cool blue color of a police cruiser was visible under the streetlights. The car pulled up to the front, parking beside Michael's car.

"It's Jeff. Thank God!"

They congregated towards the doors, unlocking them as the officer exited the vehicle. Berman checked his sides before approaching the compound, unsure if the bloodthirsty animal was waiting in the brush. In his hands, he had a tranquilizer projector rifle, a projector pistol, and a shotgun. Michael frowned at the sight of the third weapon as he unlocked the final door.

"Luckily I was in the area," Berman said when he arrived in the lobby. "I called Dawson. He's en route. Adrienne should be coming too – I think she's pretty close actually. Okay, give me a quick debriefing, Mike. What's the damage?"

"The deino is not showing up on the cameras," Michael started. "I doubt it got too far, but it's certainly not anywhere in the sanctuary."

"What about on your property?"

"I'm not sure, Jeff. I don't own much land to the left and right of the compound, but the property goes back for quite a few acres to the rear into a pretty wild area."

"Define wild?"

"Unkempt. A lot of jungle. Tough to navigate. Jeff, one of my employees was killed."

"Who?"

"Charlie. That kid you saw earlier in the week before we set out on the expedition. I haven't seen him yet. His body is down in the enclosure, right Sandra?"

She nodded, trying to resist the urge to cry any further.

"Shit, Mike. Here, take this."

Berman handed Michael the Pneu-Dart GX 2.

"Thanks, but Jeff, what do you plan on doing with the shotgun?"

Berman looked up, not surprised, but hesitant.

"Mike, it's just a precaution. This isn't the Everglades anymore. This is suburbia. There are residential homes nearby. We know how the deino has a craving for humans. I'm not taking any chances bud, sorry. If it ends up near any houses, I'm using lethal force. It's already killed one person. That's final."

Mike frowned, but understood his message.

"You're right. Keep it, just in case."

Another police cruiser swerved into the parking lot, parking diagonally in between two spots right outside the door. It was Adrienne. They let her in.

She looked tired and drained from the drive. Berman handed her the Pneu-Dart pistol and filled her in on the situation.

"What's first?" Adrienne asked, lighting up a cigarette to cope with the sudden stress.

"First, Sandra, can you take me down to the enclosure?" Berman asked. "We need to confirm that Charlie is dead. If he's not, we need to call an ambulance immediately. If he's still alive, he'll need medical attention ASAP."

She took them down through the visitor lobby and out to the mulch trail. Michael informed them that the visitor paths were technically unsecured, since the deinosuchus could access them, so they took a shortcut through a rear access hall that was concealed behind a faux rock wall. The corridor eventually led around to the former caiman pen, where the incident happened.

As soon as they entered the hall before the pen, the smell of blood and death flooded the room. Mila bent over and threw up on a metal supply cart that was pushed against the wall, dented from the animal's tail during the escape. She wiped her mouth, smearing her dark lipstick.

Charlie's body was planted in the center of the artificial cavern. What was left of the flesh was a gruesome entanglement of shredded organs and jumbled body parts. The head was crushed to the skull under the incredible bite force that the animal had applied to the victim. Blood crept slowly down the concrete slope, collecting in the indoor pool and coating the cavern floor with a crimson tint.

On the ground nearby, the scarlet stained phone remained in recording mode, proving the encounter forever in the phone's database. The auto-focus feature continuously adjusted on the red wave of blood that descended past as it dripped ominously into a floor drain.

That should come in handy in court, Michael thought, feeling guilty for thinking it. He couldn't help it. His ass was on the line now – he would need every shred of ammunition to save his reputation.

Sandra bent down to pick it up, but Adrienne put an arm in front of her, holding her back.

"Leave it," Adrienne barked. "The scene should be left undisturbed until it's properly photographed and logged for evidence."

"Sandra, where was the last place you saw the animal?" Berman asked.

"Towards the far side of the sanctuary near the visitor building, where we came from," she replied. "It was heading for the fence, broke through and then –"

She gasped.

"What?" Berman asked. "Sandra, what?"

"Gene! It was heading for the trail out back. Gene, our night watchman was back there!"

41
THE OVERGROWN TRAIL

The swath of land behind the sanctuary was a flurry of runaway plant life, a combination of thick weeds, tall palms and musa acuminata banana trees. The ground directly behind the building was covered with a thin layer of gravel that Michael poured over landscaping tarp to keep the weeds away from the outer fencing. Over time, some of the gravel made its way into the jungle, which is what gave Michael the idea to pour some more rock down to make a path into the jungle. When he was motivated, he poured about twenty yards of path down until it transitioned to a narrow dirt trail, snaking into the long grass.

"Hey Gene!" Michael called, cupping his hands.

Berman and the others came up behind him.

There was no answer from the foliage, other than the gentle rustling of reeds and banana leaves.

"Mila, maybe you and Sandra should wait in the visitor center," Michael said, after seeing how lush the backyard of his business had become.

"Call me if you need anything," Mila said. "And please, be careful Mike. You need to come back safely so we can properly finish our dinner date."

"Will do," he smiled, happy that she was trying to ease his mind about the disastrous situation.

Without a weapon, they would be virtually useless in the tight corners of the jungle. When Michael heard the door clink for the visitor building, confirming that Sandra and Mila were safe, he nodded to Berman to begin down the trail. The officer clicked on a flashlight, clipped it onto his jacket, and proceeded down the path.

"Hey, Gene!" Michael called, his cries rippling into the night. Still no answer.

"Why isn't your man answering?" Adrienne asked, holding up the rear.

"I don't know," Michael replied. "He's old. He may have hearing problems."

"Anything out of the ordinary here, Mike?" Berman asked, keeping the shotgun trained on the dark wilderness that enveloped them, stretching endlessly in all directions.

"Yeah. The gravel is all spread out. It's all scuffed up. The deinosuchus moved right down this trail. Look up ahead. The trackway is clearly visible on the edges of the path."

The gravel ended, transitioning into the dirt trail. Large crocodilian imprints were on both sides of the trail. In the center, the deino's massive body left behind a gaping indent in the earth, deforming the path by pushing the ground down. The trail continued into the darkness, hidden by outstretched branches.

"Mike, how far does this go back?" Jeff asked.

"I'll be honest, Jeff, I'm not sure," Michael answered in shame.

"You're the owner and you don't know?" Adrienne asked in disbelief.

"I've never been through the whole property," Michael replied. "After the gravel ended, I sort of lost the motivation to venture any further, unless eventually I planned on pushing the zoo back."

"So you have no idea what we're about to walk into?" she asked again.

"Not in the slightest," Michael replied, getting annoyed with her.

The darkness of the jungle and the brightness of the moon that lingered over the top of the foliage reminded Michael of the encounter with the animal days earlier near Palm Grove. The path in the Southern Glades was so dark, that they didn't realize the deinosuchus den was only a few yards away.

In the dark thicket, the animal could be anywhere.

Berman swore as his boot slipped into a slushy pile of milky water.

"Are we sure he's even down here?" Berman said. "Maybe your watchman wandered back to the lobby."

"No, Mila would've called by now if he did," Michael stated.

Suddenly through the darkness of the leaves that obscured his view of the trail ahead, Michael caught a brief flash of white on the ground, blocked by the grass stems.

"Wait!" Michael said, wiping away the plants from his face. "Jeff, shine your light over there!"

Berman moved the flashlight towards the white flash. Two white tennis shoes appeared through the foliage, scuffed with mud.

"It's Gene!" Michael yelled. "I know the shoes!"

Please God, let the old man be alive!

He pushed through the leaves to the body shrouded in the shrubs, discovering Gene to be partially buried under shredded reed stems. Something slammed him off the trail into the jungle with tremendous force, the impact causing much of the plant life to be frayed during the skirmish.

"Is he dead?" Adrienne asked, staying back behind Berman as Michael inspected the body.

"No. No, he's alive," Michael said, checking the pulse. A wave of relief washed over him.

Gene's dirt-stricken face remained frozen, his wrinkled eyelids locked shut. On the side of his head was a large bruise, presumably where he hit the ground. A large muddy smear was imprinted over his button-up shirt horizontally, an indication that he had been whacked with something wide.

"Hey, Gene. You with me?"

Michael lightly padded the man's face, causing him to rouse back to consciousness. Finally, his eyes opened, confused and disoriented. He shielded his eyes from Berman's flashlight, before the officer turned to shine it away.

"Mike," came a groggy old voice. "What happened?"

"One of our exhibits escaped, Gene. It was the deinosuchus, you know, the animal that's been getting us all the publicity. We think you may have been swatted from the path, probably by the creature's tail. Actually, you're lucky to be alive. Are you hurt?"

"*Uhm*, I don't think so," he replied in a raspy lamented gurgle, moaning when he moved his hands over his chest. "But I feel like I got the wind knocked out of me, kid."

"What's the last thing you remember?"

"Smoking a Marlboro. Looking up at the stars. About to head back. I heard something in the brush. Then nothing. Black."

"Michael, let's wrap this up," Berman urged him. "The thing may still be in the area."

"Can you walk?" Michael asked Gene.

"I think..."

Michael and Adrienne helped him to his feet. He wobbled uneasily, stabilizing himself against a palm trunk before catching his balance. He wasted no time producing another Marlboro from his pocket and lighting it up, looking around anxiously at the surrounding wall of plants. Michael exhaled calmly, relieved that Gene's life had been spared from the creature's escape.

"Adrienne, can you take him back to the zoo and check if he has additional injuries?" Berman asked. "I'm not sure how much farther back this path goes. We could be out here for hours."

"You won't be out there too long," Gene said as they started walking back to the visitor compound. "The trail empties out into a lake just through those bushes. I would've kept walking but the path ended. Michael, I'm sorry. I should've been keeping watch and not back here on break."

Ordinarily, Michael would've been in a rage – especially with the death of Charlie that could have been avoided if Gene was properly manning his post. There wasn't time to reprimand him now. All that mattered was tracking down the deinosuchus before they lost it again in the night.

"No one was hurt, were they?" Gene asked.

"Just go back to the compound and lock the doors," he said, leaving Gene confused with Adrienne as he followed Berman further into the dark leaves.

"Okay, be careful Mike," the old man called out as Adrienne helped him through the darkness, taking a toke from his Marlboro.

"You gonna fire him?" Berman asked after they slipped into the next hedge of plant life.

"Fire him?" Michael asked. "I'll be lucky if I'm running the business in the morning. Jeff, it's all gone to hell. A kid died in my zoo today. I don't know what's gonna happen."

"I wish I had an answer on that," Berman said. "But from what I can tell, you aren't at fault for what happened. Charlie went past all the failsafes into the enclosure. His death was his own fault – and stupidity. Who knows how a judge and jury will see it, but if it's all recorded on his phone, you should be in the clear. It's sad what happened, but his flaw by recording the incident might just be your salvation."

"That may be true. But what about the weak point in the fence? That was all me."

"That's why we need to find this son of a bitch before it kills again," Berman told him. "We were lucky he didn't kill your lazy ass security officer. I'm assuming he's not gonna find any more human hitchhikers back here in this vacant wilderness, so you may be in luck."

"Whoa, Jeff, watch your step!"

Berman stopped short of walking off a sharp concrete brink. If he would have taken another step, he would have fallen twenty dizzying feet into the black water.

"What is this?" Berman asked, glancing down over the precipice.

"Gene was wrong," Michael said. "This isn't a lake. It's a reservoir."

The large body of water stretched ahead into the darkness. They could see where the reservoir ended on the other side, lit up in sparse areas by outdated security lights, covered in jungle vines and old graffiti tags. Under their feet in the dirt, the deino trackway ran up to the brink of the wall before ending at the ledge.

"He's in the reservoir," Berman said, shining his flashlight over the water just beneath the edge, but could see nothing under the shadowed waves. "At least we know where it is. I can radio Dawson and see if he can send a few officers up here with boats – we can probably smoke him out in the morning when we can see better."

"I don't think he's in the reservoir anymore, Jeff," Michael said, turning white as a ghost.

"What are you talking about, Mike?"

Before Michael could answer, Berman turned towards the sound of a distant mechanized humming. Across the reservoir, a police helicopter was circling above a settlement of houses. A bright spotlight shone down from the chopper, glimmering over some unseen situation that was unfolding across the moat. Michael instantly knew where the path had ended up and where he was. It was the reservoir for the Windy Ghoul neighborhood, an upscale housing development only two miles from the Redland Crocodilian Sanctuary. His eyes followed the water to the left, noting that it ended by an old fence, fifty yards away from the backyard of the nearest Windy Ghoul home.

Over the water, a human scream erupted from the sleeping neighborhood, prompting some of the lights in the neighboring windows to click on as the residents woke up to investigate.

As Berman scrambled past him, rattling off commands over his walkie to Adrienne while running back to the zoo, Michael slumped forward in horror, uncertain of what had transpired in the village.

But he knew the deinosuchus was there.

42
PREHISTORIC JUSTICE

Clive Franklin gripped the 4K UHD TV with both hands, using his foot to kick open the front door of the empty house behind him. He wasn't expecting how heavy the television really was, and had to set it down a few times before he found a better way to grip it.

Together with his associate, Johnathan Hardy, they continued their quiet raid on 531 Blossom Ring road in the Windy Ghoul neighborhood. For the past two weeks, they had watched over the home, taking notes of the comings and goings of its bachelor owner, Timothy Hornwick, eventually memorizing his schedule with near perfect accuracy.

A year and a half earlier, Clive and Johnathan were contacted through their contracting firm, *Fix It – Build It*, to remodel Hornwick's basement, along with a handful of other hired workers. The basement was banged out in a handful of weeks before the firm moved onto another job. However, during one of the final days of the renovation, Clive made a duplicate key for the rear basement door, knowing that Johnathan would love to one day burglarize the luxurious property.

531 Blossom Ring was a beautiful house in the Windy Ghoul plan – and perfect for a robbery. It was situated at the tail end of a cul-de-sac, bordered on both sides by ten foot tall hedges and small patches of forest, which made it hard for the neighbors to stare directly into the front yard.

After waiting for over a year to return to the house, Clive and Johnathan staked out the premise from afar every night. Clive remembered hearing Hornwick telling them that he had landed a night job which demanded frequent trips to Miami, often times taking well into the morning to complete. For the life of him, Clive couldn't remember what exactly the job was, but he didn't care. The only thing that mattered was that Hornwick was out of the home a long duration of hours – with no dog or home surveillance systems in place.

"Watch the stoop," Johnathan said.

"I see it," Clive snapped back. "Okay, easy. All we need right now is for the sprinklers to turn on."

"Don't jinx it, Franklin."

They clumsily moved the large television down the walkway to the curb where their white contractor van was inconspicuously parked, strategically just out of the streetlight. Through his ski-mask, Clive looked back and forth often to make sure any night joggers or neighborhood watch patrols weren't nearby, relaxing after they finally shoved the TV into the back of the van. From what they witnessed of the neighborhood over the past week, the nightlife was sparse, with most of the evening activity taking place at the nearby country club.

Johnathan shut the back door to the van and pulled out the keys, assuming their lengthy night raid had finally ended.

"What are you doing?" Clive asked.

"Clive, we're done. Aren't we? We have all the main stuff."

"The hell we do. I wanted to check out the upstairs. There might be a safe there we can try to pry into. Or maybe some jewelry we missed."

"There's no safe," Johnathan replied. "I combed through that upper level a few times, even when we were working here. There was no safe – I would've seen it if there was. I think his money is all tied up in the bank and broker investments. And jewelry? He's an unmarried man. Good luck on that."

"Well what about some of the artwork?" Clive asked. "Might be worth a quick look around, don't you think?"

"Clive, artwork? Seriously? You think he has a frickin' Jackson Pollock original in there we haven't seen? Those canvases are just mass produced duplicates. I could find those at any Kohl's store."

"It might be worth something. You never know. Just let me see the keys. I'll be in and out before you know it."

Clive reached for the key set, expecting Johnathan to pull them away. Instead, Johnathan handed them forward, letting them fall from his hand before Clive could reach them. With a clink, the keys bounced off the curb and rattled into a small storm drain, splashing into the water a few feet below the grating.

"Well that's just great, Clive," Johnathan frowned.

"Shit. Do you have your spare set?"

"No, dumbass."

"Can you reach them? It's not that deep."

"Maybe," Johnathan said, stepping back down on his knees. He reached into the grating, withdrawing his hands after his wrist got stuck between the corroded bars.

"*Youch*! I'm gonna need a tetanus shot. Wrist is too fat, I can't get it. Can you?"

His voice was nervous, bordering on panicking.

"Look, calm down. I'll get the keys. My wrist is skinnier anyways. While I'm doing that, can you please go back into the house and grab the artwork. I think the backdoor is still unlocked."

"I'll grab one and that's it. Which one do you want?"

"The three-piece mural in the upper hallway. It's modern and abstract, I bet we could sell that on eBay or Amazon for some quick bucks."

"Yeah, yeah. If it's nailed in pretty deep you can forget it. Just get the keys so we can get out of here."

Johnathan grumbled and headed back around the home, vanishing around a decorative yard boulder.

Pressing his wrist through the opening, Clive fumbled around in the dark. After a few moments of trial and error, he flicked his flashlight on from his phone, propping it over the edge with a pebble. With a glimmer of silver, the keys radiated upward, half submerged under a small stream of residual rainwater.

"Damnit," Clive said, fingering the edge of one of the key rings with his finger, but clumsily pushing them further back into the drain. He gasped involuntarily as the keys began to slide with the watery current, down towards the dark tunnel, threatening to be lost forever in the Windy Ghoul sewage system.

Whoa, hey there...

Clive tilted his head up, distracted by a shadowed visitor.

From the corner of his eye, he thought he saw something stir on the other side of the hedges. He thought it might have been a big dog, but the shape vanished before Clive could categorize it any further. Beneath the hedges, a long shadow ran out, caused by the overhead streetlamp. It bumbled along until it slipped out from the light, melting back into the darkness. Thankfully, whatever the animal was, it was on the other side of the sturdy hedge wall.

Clive shrugged, resuming his task.

Damn Everglades panthers.

He fumbled through the opening, fingering the edge of the key ring but not close enough to get a firm grasp. Clive cursed, straining to retrieve their ticket to escape.

We're burglars. How the hell could we not just hot-wire the van and get out of here? Because this isn't Fast and the Furious, asshole. And where the hell is Johnathan? It was a wall mural, not an entire curated art gallery.

He felt more metal around his finger.

At last!

His fingers closed around the cold keys and he jerked his arm up to the grate. With a bang, the keys rattled out of his hands after striking a bar, tumbling back down into the water.

No!

A brief nightmare scenario flickered through his head; the van stuck there when Hornwick came home from work. With a final reach, he immediately knew that any further attempts would be futile. The keys were now too far out of reach, already scooting under the tunnel. With a quick flush of current and a clink of metal, they were gone.

And to make the volatile situation worse, the mysterious animal had returned, coming towards the edge of the hedges, almost into view. Still only able to visualize a fraction of the elusive creature through the hedges, Clive now debated over whether it was a panther. The animal now appeared to be huge – over twenty feet long.

Is my mind playing tricks on me again? An anaconda? No, it doesn't move like an anaconda. Anacondas don't have legs!

As it came in and out of the shards of light, it now appeared to be lumbering along on four legs. The strange locomotive forward motion told him it had to be some kind of crocodilian. But no crocodile in the world was that long. And yet the strange plates on the back and the glimmer of razor teeth near the snout told Clive otherwise.

"What the fu –"

The words ceased, just as the animal rounded the hedge and walked onto the sidewalk pavement, turning a massive, muscular neck in the direction of the van.

"*Awh*, hell!"

A crocodile? No, alligator. The snout is definitely an alligator snout.

It was a monstrous alligator, probably thirty feet long at least. In the flickering lighting of the streetlamp, Clive could see the odd coloration of the animal's scales, admiring briefly the streaks of gold on the animal's bumpy back. He sat in awe before the stunning, grim realization set in: *your hand is still stuck, Clive!*

"Come on, you bastard. Come on!"

He frantically fought to dislodge his wrist, realizing that the alligator wasn't there to pass through peacefully.

After a challenging hiss, the crocodilian took off, stampeding towards the burglar, the claws *click-clacking* over the concrete and the tail dragging loudly over the sidewalk rivets.

Clive couldn't free his arm, strenuously tugging it around between the bars, tearing and bruising his wrist. The rusty metal burned into his bloodstream, causing Clive to grind his teeth to deflect the pain.

He could feel his head throbbing, matching each step that the animal took in its full on sprint towards him. Finally, his body twitched, turning his wrist and enabling him to free his arm. Momentum pushed him backwards as he stumbled over the curb sideways – an incident that saved his life.

The animal crashed into the rear of the van, denting the back and activating the car alarm that rang out through the night, narrowly missing Clive's poorly executed somersault. The lights of the van flashed on and off in warning, scaring the alligator momentarily before the creature resumed the chase.

With a powerful chomp, the monster lunged savagely at Clive, who teetered sideways, crab-walking in terror backwards down the dark sidewalk. As the animal stepped back onto the concrete, Clive flung open the side door, throwing himself inside just as his attacker hurled its weight into the van. From the inside, Clive could see the vehicle cave in during the impact. The world shook, moving and reshuffling objects around and shattering the prized 4K television screen into a hundred pieces.

Another hard ram and the vehicle wobbled on its wheels, turning diagonally in the air as Clive felt his body begin to fall backwards. The crocodile was trying to turn the van over, which would trap him inside.

With a third violent ram, the vehicle was successfully pushed over, slamming into the road and shattering the driver's side window. From his view in the backseat, Clive could see past the stacked furniture through the front window, where lights were beginning to turn on in the nearby houses farther up the lane. The robbery mission was a critical failure. The only option now was to abandon everything and run on foot. But first, he would have to free himself from the van. And every exit was blocked by stolen goods and broken merchandise.

Where the hell is Johnathan?

The alligator mounted the side of the toppled van, confused as to how it planned to enter the vehicle and resume the attack. The immense weight and steps of the animal further dented the roof. The vehicle began to buckle inward, threatening to squish Clive flat against an overturned couch. He huddled into the fetal position, unsure of how to hide from the debris.

Finally, through the continuous ruckus above him, he heard the front door to Hornwick's home jolt open, followed by a confused voice bellowing from the stoop.

"Hey, Clive. Are you insane? You're gonna wake up the whole –"

Johnathan's voice stopped. Clive could hear the sounds of potentially lucrative wall artwork dropping and breaking on the front stoop as Johnathan realized what was unfolding in the street near the house. Above, only inches through the van's wall, Clive could hear the deafening hiss of the alligator. The vehicle turned sharply as the animal bounded off the roof and threw itself back on the lawn towards Clive's co-conspirator.

He heard Johnathan let out a baffled shriek.

Clive listened for a final agonizing scream, but instead was pleased to hear the front door slam shut, just as the crocodilian rammed into the entrance. The sounds of splintering wood followed, but when another set of groans and roars resumed, Clive assumed the entrance to the house hadn't yet been breached, giving his friend more time to get away.

Run for it, Johnny!

Now able to search for an exit, he squirmed helplessly in the rubble, looking for an opportunity. But the furniture and merchandise prevented any escape that didn't require the van to be flipped back to its wheels. He grabbed the legs of a dining room chair and tried to wiggle it free, calculating that if he were to move it, he could climb into the front seat and kick out the window. But it was useless – the chair was pinned between too many other pilfered obstacles, trapping him in the vehicle's prison.

Through his tilted viewpoint, he could see brave pedestrians beginning to filter out of their homes and onto the sidewalk. A few men with flashlights formed up, proceeding down the sidewalk towards the mangled van. They would be on him in seconds. His only hope now was that the rabid super-sized alligator would chase them away, if it hadn't already vanished into Hornwick's house after Johnathan.

When the sound of oncoming police sirens was heard at the entrance to the Windy Ghoul neighborhood, he made peace with his situation and relaxed in his crammed spot, awaiting the coming handcuffs and jail cell that would surely follow.

43
WINDY GHOUL

Sprinting back up the trail, Michael tried strenuously to keep up with Berman, swatting away leaves and shrubs that stretched out in their wake. The officer ran with conditioned athletic stamina, compared to Michael who was an out of shape zookeeper whose exercise consisted of dragging protesting crocodilians out of their exhibits. In the distance, the hum of the Redland police helicopter continued to churn over the trees. For a second, he thought he heard a male voice over a loud speaker, shouting instructions to the town residents below.

Finally they hit the gravel trail and the rear of the sanctuary was in sight.

"Pick it up, Mikey!" Berman yelled.

"What are we gonna do?" Michael asked, nearly out of breath, grabbing at his gut.

"We need to get over there and find your animal before the shooters get to it first. If it's any danger towards the civilians over there, I could imagine they would use lethal force, unless animal control gets there first."

"You think so? Even for such a rare animal like the deinosuchus?"

"Protect and serve, Michael. Animal safety is an afterthought if lives are at stake, you know that."

"Well what about you, Jeff. Are you saying you'd rather use tranqs? What happened to your shotgun approach?"

"In a few minutes there will be enough guns over there that my shotgun won't matter anymore. So yeah, if you're still intent on tranqing the damn thing, now is the time. But we're running out of it, so pick up the pace!"

They reached the side of the sanctuary, running past the destroyed fencing fragments and back up to the vacant parking lot. They rounded the front of the premise, waving to Mila and Sandra who were in the lobby. After Sandra unlocked the doors, they scrambled inside.

"Where's Adrienne?" Berman asked, looking around the lobby.

"She drove Gene to the hospital," Sandra said. "What's going on?"

"Sandra, you're free to go home," Michael said. "Thank you for all your help. I'm sorry about what happened. I promise, you'll be well compensated for what you went through today. Mila, I have to go with Jeff."

"What's going on?" Mila asked, concerned and gathering her belongings as Sandra shut off the lobby lights.

"The deino isn't on our property anymore. We think it's in the Windy Ghoul neighborhood just down the road. There's a police helicopter circling there. If it's there, it's beyond our control and has become a local problem. I think the cops are gonna try to shoot it."

"You can't be serious!"

"I am."

"Okay, I'm coming with you."

"Mila, it's gonna get pretty dangerous, I'm not sure that –"

"Michael, don't argue. I'm not gonna be of any use here, am I? Let's get moving."

"I'll drive," Berman said, unlocking his squad car.

As they jumped into the squad car, a pair of Redland police SUVs drove past behind them, flying down the road with sirens blaring, flying towards the direction of the Windy Ghoul estates. They swarmed down the road too fast, resulting in several oncoming civilian cars having to swerve off the road, almost crashing into the guard rail.

"Sheriff, come in. Berman, over," Jeff yelled into the police radio, reversing out of his parking spot and preparing to pull onto the road. He let Sandra leave first before pulling out, driving in the direction of the pursuing SUVs. Dawson's garbled voice came immediately through the radio speakers.

"Berman, what's going on up there? Did you find it? Over."

"Negative, sir," the officer answered, speeding down the road with the siren now activated. Michael and Mila sat in the backseat, searching for the police helicopter through the jail divider wall installed in the car. When they passed a large abandoned factory, they found it, still circling over Windy Ghoul. A police officer with a long rifle was perched on the ledge of the helicopter, searching over the rooftops with the scope.

"The animal has escaped the sanctuary property. One fatality so far, possibly more unconfirmed. There is a police helicopter over a nearby neighborhood, and several Redland units are already reporting to the scene. I'm switching to their police frequency and gonna try to get into the action. Are you still coming? Over."

"I am. Which neighborhood am I heading to? Over."

202

Berman looked over his shoulder.

"Windy Ghoul," Michael told him. "It's only a few miles from my zoo."

"Did you get that, sir?" Berman asked.

"I did. Is Michael in the car with you?"

"Yes he is, sir."

"Michael. This is a very serious situation you're heading into. Hunting this thing in the swamp was one thing, but now it might be in a populated area. You better be prepared for them to shoot it down if it's a threat to the residents. Don't get in their way."

"I understand, sir."

"Okay. Jeff, keep me updated. I should be up there in fifteen. Over."

"Yes, sir. Over and out."

"We have to get there before they find it," Mila urged them. "We can still save it. The pen is still secure."

Michael checked the tranquilizer gun, making sure it was pointed away from Mila.

"If we find it," he said. "It might already be out of the neighborhood."

The ride was over in a minute by the accelerated rate Berman was driving. The officer swung the wheel left after Michael pointed to the Windy Ghoul welcome sign, partially tucked behind some overgrown bush landscaping. As soon as he arrived in the entrance road, they were barred entrance from the estates.

Yellow guard rails were set up end to end, only letting outgoing traffic pass through. Three police officers were scattered in the area, shining flashlights at the bushes and wooded areas nearby that bordered the causeway. They were searching for something that was presumably in the thicket. One of the officers, a younger one, had a hand on his pistol as he approached the trees.

As Berman approached, an officer initially pushed him away, before realizing it was a police cruiser, and waved him up reluctantly.

"A little way from your district," the officer said after Berman stopped the car at the barricade, rolling down the driver side window. The cop walked beside the cruiser, eyeing the Palm Grove logo suspiciously that ran along the side. "What are you doing up here?"

"Hey, Ned," Berman said. "Remember me? We went to police school together."

"Holy shit, Jeff? How have you been? Down in the Palm Grove unit, I see. I didn't even recognize you without your beard."

"I'm trying something new," Berman replied, patting his hair back. "Still have the pompadour though! Actually, I've been clean shaven for years."

"Who's this?"

The officer named Ned turned the flashlight to the backseat, where Michael and Mila shielded their eyes.

"This is –"

"Is this the zoo guy from the news?" Ned asked, cutting Berman off of a formal introduction.

"Yes, this is Michael Robinson and Mila Madison. Michael is the owner of the Redland Crocodilian Sanctuary down the road. We're friends from way back. We believe one of his escaped animals may be here, and we're trying to bring it back."

"Oh, it's here all right," Ned laughed. "At least it was twenty or so minutes ago. The gator prevented a robbery and tipped a van over on its side. Half the town's gone stir-crazy over it. When they came out to investigate, it chased them back into their homes. We can't find it now, but rest assured that we will. Hell of a creature, from what the residents were saying."

"Ned, can we get through?" Berman asked. "We have tranquilizers. We need to bring this creature back to the zoo for proper study. You saw the news report from this morning, I'm assuming? It's sort of a rare breed – deemed extinct, before last week. They're saying it's a deinosuchus. They've been around since the time of Tyrannosaurus rex and –"

"No can do, Jeff," Ned said, folding his arms. "That means nothing to me."

"Why's that?"

"Windy Ghoul is now under a sort of police state, you could say, at the moment. Martial Law. Sheriff doesn't want anyone else coming in. We already have all the plans laid out as it stands – no room to brief other police departments on the issue. Sorry, Jeff. You understand, right?"

"What? That's completely ridiculous!"

"Rules are rules, Jeff," Ned said, wrinkling his brow.

"Well what are you planning on doing when you find it?"

"It will probably have to be shot, Jeff. The thing's a menace. It's a danger to the residents here."

Michael fidgeted uneasily in the backseat, straining to keep himself from saying anything stupid. Killing the deinosuchus was a monumental mistake. The animal could be tranquilized. They had proven that before.

"Why don't you switch to carfentanil tranqs?" Mila asked the officer. "They work. That's how we got the croc here in the first place."

"Lady, there's no time for that. We're lucky no one was killed here already."

A news van pulled up behind Berman's car, followed by another two cars that wouldn't fit around the turn, sticking out into the main road. Several of the officers turned from their posts, trying to detour them away from the neighborhood entrance.

"Ned, do you have any idea how important this animal is?" Berman asked. "It's literally from the time of the dinosaurs – and it's right here in Florida. Let us in there, please! We have the tranquilizers needed to bring it down safely. We can get it back to the zoo, and make sure it's properly secured this time."

"Yeah, you should've done that the first time around," Ned scoffed. "Don't think I didn't hear about that ragtag mission you guys ran down in the Southern Glades. Three officers killed – another injured. Now look, you're gonna have to move it along here. There's other people that need blocked and informed."

"Ned –"

"Jeff, move it along!"

"I'll remember this, Ned."

"Yeah, yeah. Tough guy."

Berman scowled, rolling the window back up and shifting into reverse and backing slowly down the road until he was a foot away from the first news van. Grumbling, he turned the cruiser back down the access road and onto the highway, heading right this time, away from the zoo and leaving the blockade behind him.

"Where are you going?" Mila asked.

"Michael, do you know if there are any other ways into Windy Ghoul?"

"That's the only way in. Why?"

"Excellent," Berman said, pulling the cruiser off the side of the road near an old park and ride area. Beyond, the sound of the other sirens was muted, far away behind the walls of trees. Michael turned, barely able to see the tiny vans as they were turned around up the road, under command of the Redland police blockade.

"Jeff, what are you doing?"

"We're sneaking in," Berman said, pointing to the trees.

Michael turned. A tiny hiking trail weaved into the thicket. Through the leaves, the illuminated houses of Windy Ghoul were seen, sitting atop the hill like a peaceful colonial settlement.

He debated on arguing with Jeff, given the legal trouble he was probably already in. But after everything, he figured sneaking into a neighborhood on lockdown would most likely be his least punishable offense.

He turned to Mila to ask her opinion, and she was already unbuckling her seat belt.

44
SHADOWS IN THE TREES

Michael assumed by how narrow and wild the trail wound through the forest, that it must have been conceived from an ancient deer trail, carved out years before the Windy Ghoul blueprints were ever drafted.

Berman led them into the jungle, after parking his cruiser inconspicuously under the shadowed trees, close to the edge of the forest. Michael followed, pushing Mila in front of him chivalrously between the two men.

"You sure you don't want to wait in the car?" Michael asked, stepping over a divot in the earth.

"No way," Mila said, maneuvering through the brush, hiking down her dress. "What am I going to do in there? Wait for you to get eaten? You could use an extra set of eyes. I just wish I would've brought a change in shoes!"

Michael smiled. She was very persuasive when she wanted to be.

"High heels certainly wouldn't be my first choice for deinosuchus hunting," Michael remarked.

The trail led them through the dark trees uphill, crossing over an old rickety bridge built by a hunter long before the housing expansion was ever announced, and gradually leading towards the brightening windows of the outermost street. The red and blue illumination of police lights ricocheted off the trunks as they got closer to the string of connected backyards.

The police presence was the least of their worries.

Somewhere around the dark jungle was a forty foot long prehistoric alligator, probably in a foul mood after all the commotion that it caused during the botched robbery attempt.

Shouting from Redland police officers was heard ahead. Berman pushed Michael and Mila off the path behind some wild ferns, waiting for the noises to break off. Michael stuck his head up, parting the leafy plant life with the barrel of his Pneu-Dart projector to get a better look.

In the area ahead, the forest began to level off, emptying into a less wooded area which gradually ended up running into a worn out board fence. On the other side of the fence, foot shadows caused by the flashlights and streetlamps were visible, patrolling the neighborhood. In the opposite direction, the slow rumble of a police SUV drove down the road. Michael realized that hiding was no longer necessary. The police were on the other side of the fence.

Questions were interchanged between the officers on foot and the driver of the vehicle, but the conversation was so muted by the circling helicopter above that their conversation was severely drowned out. Final words were exchanged, and the SUV resumed the patrol, leaving the officers on foot to continue down the street, hidden on the other side of the perimeter fence.

"How are we gonna get over there?" Mila asked. "That fence looks like it runs the entire duration of the neighborhood."

"It doesn't," Michael replied. "From what I remember, the fence runs the length of a community park, before breaking up when the park butts up against the houses. We can cross over there."

"Which way is that?" Berman asked.

"Follow me," Michael said, starting through the vegetation.

He darted to the right, leading them up onto the ledge of the forest and up to the faded board fence. The other side was quiet – the officers had vacated the area in the hopes of finding the deinosuchus somewhere else. Berman stuck his head through a narrow hole, looking out into the abandoned jungle gym and monkey bars, confirming the Redland patrols had vanished.

"Here we are," Michael smiled, scurrying up to the edge of the fencing as he looked out around the last post.

The area of the park where the fence ended was barren and abandoned, except for some old degraded picnic tables and barbecue grilling stations that hadn't been fired up in years. They prepared to wander out into the neighborhood, only to dive back behind the fence as a Redland police car meandered around the bend, radiant high-beams washing out their vision.

The driver pulled out a flashlight and scanned the park momentarily. With a click, he turned off the flashlight and resumed his patrol, circling around and heading back up the road to survey the other houses. As the vehicle rolled away, a streak of lightning touched down miles away, giving another ominous indication that a similar storm was inbound.

"Not again," Berman cursed, as a drop pelted his forehead. "Again with this storm shit."

Soon many more raindrops began pummeling the park. The storm was only a drizzle compared to what happened days earlier in the swamp, but it was enough to be annoying.

Mila attempted to block her hair from the rain, but it was useless. Michael couldn't help but chuckle as to how ridiculous she looked, in her stunning dress, hiding behind an old fence in the jungle during a rainstorm.

"Something amusing to you, Robinson?" she poked him, rain washing over her forehead, matting her hair. "Sorry, I didn't realize we'd be hunting for Deino after our dinner date."

"Where to now, Mike?" Berman asked.

"I was kind of hoping you were gonna tell me."

"How's that?"

"Well, you're the cop."

"Yeah, but you're the alligator expert. Where do you suppose a forty foot long deinosuchus would be?"

Michael breathed for a second in thought, resting his head against the soggy wood grain behind him.

"I would say it's certainly not in the residential planning grid any longer," he began. "Not after all the attention it's already mustered up. But the way I figure, they must assume that it's still in the vicinity, because they haven't called off the helicopter yet. What do you think about that?"

"I'd say that's probably a good guess," Berman said.

"Hey, Berman! What the hell? I can't get into the plan. It's blocked off. Over."

The radio on Berman's soaked coat rang out. It was Dawson, upset about the Windy Ghoul blockade.

"I'm sorry, sir," the officer replied into the receiver. "I meant to tell you. They aren't letting anyone else into the plan. Apparently they want to simplify the process and keep it contained to the Redland department. I don't know why they're keeping it internal, but my guess is so no one shows up and commandeers command. I tried to persuade them, but they're stubborn sons of bitches. Over."

"Well where the hell are you? And where's Officer Hulme?"

"We're trying to find it, sir. Adrienne had to run someone to the hospital, sir. I don't know where she is now. Over."

"What do you mean you're trying to find it?" Dawson's enraged voice bellowed over the airwaves. Michael could tell how pissed the sheriff was by the lack of his use of the word 'over' after his statements.

"Sorry, Sheriff. You're breaking up. I'll attempt to recontact when we are in a better spot."

Berman clicked the radio to a different channel, fiddling with the controls on his vest until Dawson's abrupt protests were cut off.

"What are you doing?" Mila asked him, bewildered that the officer just lied to his sheriff and was tuning the radio another frequency.

"I just realized," Berman said, "I think I remember the Redland police channel during a brief co-op project I had with them a few years earlier. If I can fiddle with this piece of shit radio, I should be able to tap into their signal. This storm isn't as bad as the one in the swamp. Hopefully these radios work better closer to civilization."

He fiddled with the knob for a few more seconds, finally catching what appeared to be two police officers communicating over the unraveling Windy Ghoul situation. The rain began to pick up as the storm swelled over their heads, scrambling the dialogue in random moments.

"*Reporting from the southern side. Nothing near... park. Returning to northern... Over.*"

"*Julius here. Nothing in the lady's backyard... Maybe a cat? Certainly not... crocodile. Over.*"

"Damn. Jeff, you're a genius."

"Now all we have to do is wait for something to come through," Berman said. "It sure beats trying to go too far inside their perimeter. They'll catch us and just throw us back out."

"*Evans... Going to north. More people and news...break through. Backup...on way.*"

"*Ross, can you...here? It's...pretty ridiculous...*"

"*en route. Nothing to the west...Respond...*"

"*Coming...streets are...Over.*"

"Looks like the press is getting wind of what's happened," Mila said.

"The storm's messing up all the signals again," Berman said. "But it sounds like most of the units are converging to the north, probably to back up the guards at the barricade. I'm sure the press is getting hard to handle. I bet they'll be sneaking in just like us before long."

"What do you suggest we do?" Michael asked, shielding his eyes from the rain as it bounded off the palm canopy over their heads.

"We need to get a little closer," Berman answered, starting to leave the fence in favor of the woodland. "Let's get closer to the neighborhood roads. The signal may improve. You all right, Mila?"

"Yeah," she replied, frustrated by the rain. "Let's just get moving."

Michael felt bad. Her hair was ruined, hanging in clumpy strands over her back. The makeup was smeared on her face, and the lipstick was beginning to splotch. Still her dedication to preserving scientific history outweighed her disdain for the storm.

They trudged through the park, avoiding the sidewalk ahead and darting through the picnic tables to a backyard of a dim house. Michael assumed by the lack of activity, that the owners were probably heavy sleepers or not home. They also didn't care much for lawn maintenance – the grass was uncut for weeks and the wooden garden shed was deteriorating from the inside out.

Berman barred them from passing the shed, hugging the edge as another police cruiser passed by, visible for a few seconds between the gap in the houses. The red and blue lights swirled around the shed before the vehicle passed beyond the next house, leaving them again in shadow. Berman turned down his radio, anticipating that perhaps the communications would resume right when he was trying to hide.

The lightning flashed again, just as the police helicopter flew overhead, partially pausing the rain as it hovered above them, before passing over the nearest rooftop over the next street of houses. The sniper in the chopper's perch failed to notice them crouching in the marshy grass just below, distracted by his rained-out view of the approaching street.

Berman hopped over a chain-link fence into the next yard, trekking into another grassy overgrown area. Apparently this was the lazy side of the neighborhood.

Halfway through the high grass, Berman's radio rattled to life. A high-pitched barbaric yell screamed out from the speaker, making the three of them stop in their tracks. The reception at first was fuzzy, but after Berman adjusted a knob, the speech was delivered eloquently crystal clear.

"Mayday! Mayday! Target spotted just off of Greenridge Street. Heading through front yards. Chopper has eyes on it. Rerouting cars in pursuit. Get those pedestrians at the intersection out of there! Over."

"They found it!" Mila exclaimed, huddling towards the radio speaker.

The sound of reigning gunfire rattled out, echoing over the Windy Ghoul rooftops.

"Where's Greenridge Street?" Berman turned to Michael.

"It's the one right in front of us."

"Target turning. Into front yard heading East. Toward the dinky little community park! Over."

More gunfire. The sounds of stray bullets were heard, whizzing into concrete. One of the rounds broke glass from either a car windshield or distant window by accident. Something exploded, gushing water over the road on the other side of the houses. Michael guessed it was a damaged fire hydrant.

"I see it. Holy cow, that thing is huge, Evans! Tommy, you have eyes?"

"Target heading between two homes just down past the park."

Suddenly the security lights on the side of the house clicked on, prompting Michael, Mila and Berman to duck behind a stack of withered mossy firewood that was piled up beside the chain-link fence. With a frighteningly aggressive grunt, the deinosuchus burst through the narrow gap between the homes, denting the siding with the swing of its massive, walloping tail.

It stampeded toward them, without knowing the humans were there as it shook the earth with every forceful step. Bracing itself for impact as it headed toward the edge of the forest where the backyard ended, Deino rammed into the first row of banana trees into the wilderness. Michael couldn't help but admire the speed and determination of the confused animal, who appeared to finally be on the defensive with the human's counter attack.

The police helicopter soared over the roof after the crocodilian, letting off two quick bursts of sniper fire after the animal as the retreating tail slipped into the plants, osteoderms shredding banana leaves as it tumbled hectically out of sight. The chopper banked right, trying to anticipate where the animal would be heading next, flying over the palm trees.

"We have to go after it!" Michael urged them, his hair ruffled from the helicopter's air surge.

He froze when he saw streaks of blood along the grass, illuminated by the security lights of the house. The deinosuchus had been injured in the hunt.

In the street above, the flurry of police lights began to dance along the siding of the houses as the sirens grew louder. Reinforcements were descending on Greenridge, and would be parked out front in any moment. The animal had left an impressive trackway for the police to follow.

The sound of the slamming of car doors was heard up above, followed by the shuffling of police boots.

"Go after it, Mike," Jeff ordered him.

"Yeah? Aren't you coming, Jeff?"

"You remember how to use that tranquilizer?"

"Yeah? Jeff, what are you –"

"I'll try to stall them," Berman said. "You know where the trackway is now. You can catch up to it. When you tranq it, call Dawson. Hopefully you'll have phone service. With any luck, we can airlift it back to your compound before they blow it apart."

"What are you gonna do?"

"I don't know. I'll make it up. Now get after it. You too, Mila. Unless you both want to spend the night in the Redland police holding cells?"

Michael turned, pulling Mila after him as they took off into the trees, away from the sound of the oncoming officers.

"Thanks, Jeff," Michael yelled, leaving the yard behind and letting the jungle consume him once more.

"Don't mention it, Mikey," Berman said, considering the courageous act as a form of settling the score with his friend for his past behavior and antics.

Shrugging, he raised his hands in the hopes of getting their attention, deciding on luring them over to the far side of the community park in the hopes that they'd believe the deino ran that way. In reality, the animal was heading further into the jungle, towards the eastern edge of civilization.

Where Redland suburbia collided once more with the border to the Everglades.

45
FAREWELLS

"Do you know where we're going or what's down there?" Mila asked as they slid down the slope of the hill, following the fleeing crocodilian through the soaked underbrush.

"The road," Michael said, trying to catch his breath as he brushed through the banana leaves. "And the city limits. I think it's trying to head back into the Everglades."

Knowing what the deinosuchus was capable of, ordinarily Michael would have waited until the creature was further away before tailing it. But the demeanor of the animal had changed from fight to flight. It lumbered swiftly along thirty yards ahead, disappearing and reappearing under the pockets of moonlight and police helicopter searchlights that would occasionally scan through the canopy. The mass of the crocodilian descending rapidly down the hill caused minor muddy avalanches in its wake, causing the creature to accelerate while awkwardly clawing into the ground for stabilization.

Michael noticed blood pouring from the creature's tail, in between the largest osteoderms. Two bullet holes grazed the animal there, although they didn't appear to be slowing the beast down. Deino scurried on as if nothing had happened, determined not to let another gunshot incident repeat itself.

Suddenly the muddy slopes ended and the forest leveled out. Traffic sounds rumbled past just ahead through the wet fronds. With a heavy thump, the deinosuchus broke through the tree line out into the main road, sloshing through the rainwater that collected on the side of the street. With a thud, its collarbone struck the corner of Berman's empty police car, pushing the cruiser diagonally into the roadway. A honking horn was heard, as a car swerved away from the confused deinosuchus, skidding off the wet road before flying towards the adjacent tree line, coming to a grinding halt by ramming an old gnarled tree trunk.

"Michael, what the hell happened?" Mila asked, brushing through the wet leaf wall into the road.

As the deinosuchus carried on into the next stretch of jungle across the road, Michael and Mila hurried out and checked on the driver, just as the wounded tail vanished into the woods.

The front car was dented inward. The windshield glass was cracked, but otherwise intact. Behind the glass, the male driver stirred, frozen in shock.

Michael pried open the driver's side door, cursing as the sounds of the retreating deinosuchus were fading away into the night air.

"Hey man, are you injured?" he asked, surveying the inside of the vehicle.

In the driver's seat was a man in his mid-twenties, confused and dazed about the calamity that transpired moments before. His shaggy head had a bruise where his skull struck the top of the steering wheel, dripping a bead of blood over his white hipster glasses. The airbag had deployed and the bottom part of the car was bowed inward, but the driver was otherwise unharmed.

"Wow, dude. What happened?" the man asked woozily. A strange smell emitted from the vehicle. Michael recognized it as marijuana and realized that the driver was high, probably with no memory of why he crashed.

"What's your name, man?"

"Scott," the man replied, coughing politely into his fist.

"Scott. You crashed, pal."

"I know, did you see that thing?" asked the stoned millennial, trying to pinpoint what it was that ran across the street. "Like a big elephant, or something. *Whoa* – that actually happened. It was as big as a school bus, no joke!"

He glanced through the cracked windshield, noticing the damage done to the front of the vehicle during the impact. The vehicle was wedged into the trunk, bowed around the cracked bark.

"Michael," Mila whispered, pulling her partner away from the window and wounded passenger. "Go find the deino. It's getting away. You need to get to it before the cops catch up with it."

As she spoke, the police helicopter roared over their heads sixty feet above, crossing above the road. The sniper noticed the car accident from his perch, rattled off something into his radio, and the helicopter resumed the patrol for the missing crocodilian over the palm trees.

"Are you sure?"

"Yeah. I can flag down a few of the police. Maybe hold a few up. Scott needs tending to anyway."

Down the road, several of the news vans were pulling out, drawn to the change in course from the police helicopter and the car crash on the curb. A handful of officers were moving away the barricade, letting their own cruisers coast onto the main road, turning to follow the news vans.

"Thanks, Mila– I owe you one!"

"You're lucky I love animals!"

He kissed her awkwardly on the cheek before taking off into the woods, leaving the crocodilian initiated car accident and his new flame behind. Now with Berman and Mila both gone, it was up to him to save the animal – and his reputation.

In the time after the car crash, the deinosuchus had gained a significant lead on him. The trackway was nearly invisible under the multi-layered canopy, appearing only when the shards of light from the helicopter passed over the trees. The animal was far ahead, completely out of sight, with the beast's footfalls quickly echoing further and further out into the Floridian jungle.

Damn, that thing can run!

Michael struggled to close the gap, trying to ponder if they were going to encounter any other pockets of humanity on the creature's hectic flight path. Through his former knowledge of perusing the neighborhood over Google maps during his days of house-hunting on Zillow, he recalled that the Windy Ghoul neighborhood was the furthest westward settlement from downtown. All that was left ahead was a small stretch of forest before the region filtered back into the expanse of the Everglades.

It's like he knows exactly where he's going, Michael thought, following the deino's tracks down through another muddy gulch.

"Whoa!"

He shrieked, nearly colliding with a hidden juvenile alligator, parked quietly beside a fallen slimy log. The reptile hissed, causing Michael to side-step the agitated young carnivore, resuming his pursuit of the deino on a shady side trail. From the darkened nooks of the crooked trees, he could see the daunting red eyes of various other alligators, watching his flight intently but resisting giving chase.

The speed at which the deinosuchus ran impressed Michael. Normal crocodilians were nowhere near as fast, and their stamina would have long worn out by now. Finally, after cresting a small knoll and giving himself half a minute to catch his breath, he saw the deinosuchus' bumbling form running ahead of him, plowing through the wetlands.

The animal had already managed to slide down the grade of the next hill, where the clumpy ground of the woods gave way to a moist, partially submerged grassland – the last remaining barrier to the Everglades. Beyond the lush wetland, the swamps awaited. From there, the creature would most likely be unreachable, especially at the rate it was running.

Damnit!

Michael didn't give himself much time to rest, propping himself up on a trunk and resting the barrel of the tranquilizer gun away from himself. Just as the deino began to slip into the reeds, the police helicopter swarmed overhead, forcing Michael to begrudgingly resume the chase.

He started a full-on sprint down the hill, unprepared by the slippery flattened plant life that the deino had already flattened. His heart pounded laboriously behind his chest. He was breathing loudly through his mouth, cursing to himself for not exercising more. To make matters worse, the storm continued to grow harder, covering his vision in a wall of translucent falling water.

To his happiness, he discovered that the helicopter sniper still hadn't spotted the deino. The searchlights were aimed in the wrong direction, looking over to the left where the grassland began to dissolve back into the forest's edge.

Michael picked up his pace, realizing the deinosuchus was getting further into the reeds, becoming less visible as the animal churned a path through the plants towards freedom.

From the forest behind, he could hear the sounds of police officers shouting through the trees, struggling to find the path as the rain began to wash over the muddied earth, threatening to diffuse the trackway. The helicopter came around for another pass, heading back for the trees to provide light for the men on foot under the dark branches. As he ran forward into the first patch of reeds, he saw the first glimmers of light coming off their flashlights, but doubted they noticed him.

If they did, he wondered, would they try to stop him from tranquilizing the animal before they could shoot it down themselves?

He didn't know. But he knew he had to try.

The reeds overtook him, smacking off his face as he ran carefree through the wilderness. The deinosuchus was already out of view again, despite the matted trackway it left through the brush. The demolished path was so wide, Michael thought it was a miracle that the chopper hadn't spotted it yet. The helicopter banked left over the treetops, narrowly avoiding the overhead power lines before turning towards Michael's direction.

He wiped the water out of his eyes as he continued frantically searching for his missing exhibit. The path weaved throughout the reeds in a serpentine pattern, preventing him from seeing the animal from around the sharp bends.

The ground beneath him began to sink, imploding into muck under his weight – a telling sign of the approaching swampland.

The helicopter circled again, the pilot having finally realized the trackway and readjusting its fight path to inspect the trampled earth. The whirring of the blades began to grow louder. The helicopter was dropping lower to the ground, descending so the sniper could get a clean shot.

Time was running out. Michael rounded another bend of swamp vegetation, coming face to face with the ancient crocodilian in an alarmingly close distance.

His mouth dropped. It would be the sniper's wet dream.

The deinosuchus was wedged in a small swamp pool, trying in vain to stay hidden. At barely two feet deep, the animal stuck out like a sore thumb. The great tail thrashed back and forth angrily, casting water spatter towards Michael as he crept around the last of the leafy barrier, into Deino's vision. The reptile noticed the zookeeper approaching, hissing once, prompting Michael to falter backwards as he prepared the G2 X.

With a horrific growl, the deinosuchus took a step toward Michael from inside the pool. It snapped its jaws once with a defensive stance, a sound Michael had come to learn well in the past week. The red eyes of the man-eater gleamed over, locked with Michael's only yards away as the carnivore examined its target.

Michael raised his weapon, only half-sure that he had properly readied the tranquilizer projector for firing. He aimed the barrel down at the deino's chest as the monster froze in front of him. The weapon shook in his hands, the barrel wobbling uneasily aimed at the creature. Michael couldn't take his eyes off the rows of glinting teeth that awaited the crunch of his fragile bones.

Fire damnit! Just fire the damn dart!

A flurry of conundrums sailed through his mind. Was it really worth it to recapture the animal, after all the property damage it caused – the lives it claimed? Would it be easier to run back now? What if the police caught him? They were closing in. And still, Charlie's grisly body refused to leave his thoughts, forcing him to imagine the lengthy legal proceedings that would undoubtedly occur.

The deino took a step closer. Its vision narrowed in on Michael. The animal was growing agitated, baring its teeth in a challenging display of primordial dominance.

Easy now, old boy...

With a slash of its claws, the animal tried to tunnel into the swamp pool out of Michael's vision and out of the view of the oncoming helicopter, but failed to burrow any deeper. In its efforts, it only succeeded in splashing more water out from its little pool, making concealing itself more cumbersome as it drew attention to itself.

Michael stepped backward, suddenly lowering the barrel, unsure if he wanted to restart this nightmare scenario all over again.

Was this worth all the pressure? All the legal proceedings? More employee liabilities and bad press coverage?

Ahead, the deinosuchus continued to scrape into the earth to no avail. The police helicopter approached, drawn on by the creature's sporadic movements. Michael ducked down in the swamp grass, trying to hide from the oncoming cockpit.

Finally, the deinosuchus prepared to crawl away from the miniature pool, readying itself for another run towards the Everglades just yards ahead.

As he raised his projector rifle again, knowing that this was his last chance to tranquilize the deinosuchus, a final, single thought materialized inside him.

Maybe the animal isn't meant to be captured. Maybe it was meant to be unseen. In a lost world of its own – away from man.

His finger teased the trigger, but he refused to fire, lowering the gun in a submissive stance. The deino took a step out of the pool, capitalizing on Michael's momentary lapse in judgment. With a hop, it bounded out of the pool, sensing the danger of neutralization was temporarily postponed.

Run! Get out of here!

With a loud steady hum, the chopper passed over Michael's head, flattening most of the reeds and leaving the massive crocodilian exposed. With the vegetation forcefully pressed down against the earth, the region beyond the deino's pool became visible, revealing the expanse of the Everglades just through the last patch of reeds.

Deino spun around, noticing the close proximity of the endless swamps and seized the chance for escape, tossing Michael and his indecisiveness aside with an unintentional flick of the tail. The smack threw Michael back into the watery reeds, causing him to temporarily see spots as he fought to regain his stance.

Through his exhausted vision and obscured view from the plants, he saw the animal's tail dive back into the watery surface far away– a mirror image to his first look at the animal from Owen's video days earlier.

The helicopter flew over again. The sniper fired off two rounds, missing the submerging animal by a few yards.

With a final surge of large bubbles, Deino's writhing form dissipated into the swampy depths, and the animal was free again.

Michael couldn't help but smile, ducking down again as the police began to usurp the area from the trees, flashlights and guns drawn.

46

CLOSURE

It was around four in the morning when Michael finally made it back to his own neighborhood, wandering through the trails in the nearby woods that he had come to memorize in recent years during a short-lived hiking infatuation.

He pushed open the latch of the gate to his fenced-in backyard, following the small cement walkway to his backdoor. The neighborhood was mostly still asleep, except for a few early commuters for Miami that he heard pulling out of their garages. Finally, he found his set of keys from his soaked, muddied pockets, opening the backdoor and entering into his kitchen.

Michael pushed up the outdated light switch, shielding his eyes at how bright it was, causing him to immediately flick it back off. There was enough spill light from the streetlamp flooding in through the living room curtains to help him see more comfortably. Kicking off his shoes on the floor mat, he stumbled through the living room, knocking over his vacuum cleaner that he refused to put away earlier, before crashing onto his couch.

Toying with the idea of clicking on the television, he picked up the remote. The images of the fictional news headline: *Zookeeper Fails at Containing New Species: One Employee Dead* appeared in his subconscious. He set the remote down, staring at the blank TV screen.

The events of the night wore him out, especially after the long trek all the way back to his neighborhood through the jungle trail. He figured the proper thing to do would probably be to go back and deal with Charlie's body that was lying cold in an empty caiman pen, so he redirected his course.

On his way back through the woods, he passed by the sanctuary, seeing several ambulances outside with their lights and sirens blazing through the plants. Some news vans were there too, further contributing to his desire not to make an appearance.

It can wait until morning, he figured as he kept heading home. It probably wasn't the right thing to do, but given everything that had happened, he at least owed it to the authorities to be of sound mind when he explained everything that had happened.

A voicemail from his phone earlier from Berman assured him of the situation.

"Mikey? Hey, are you still alive? Give me a call back when you can. I've picked up Mila. There are a few authorities on the lookout for you, wanting a statement from the scene at the sanctuary. I wouldn't be surprised if they come looking for you tonight or stop by your house. Adrienne informed the local authorities about the situation in the sanctuary, so don' worry about getting a hold of anyone now. There was talk on the police frequency that they spotted someone chasing the creature ahead of the patrols. You got some balls, buddy! Not sure what's gonna happen as far as legal loopholes that need addressing. Don't go talking to the press – that's my recommendation as a friend for the time being. Any news reports or contact will probably just lead to bad publicity for now. Dawson and I will be in the area tomorrow, if you want to meet up or if you need help. I'm assuming since you haven't called that the deino was probably gunned down or still at large. Let me know, buddy. Sorry about everything."

The call ended.

After the deino's last sighting in the swamp, Michael decided that after he avoided the police patrols, not to reunite with Berman and Mila, figuring that they were probably already out of the area, herded off for questioning by additional police escorts.

His vision glazed over, mindlessly staring at the glowing blue light of the completed dishwasher cycle from the kitchen.

What will happen to the sanctuary? W I be relieved of ownership?

Or would the situation be simpler and more forthright? Paying compensation for Charlie's family, whom – other than his aunt – he'd never met before, and paying for whatever property damage had been caused. He knew there would be some liability issues for the fencing.

Despite all the negative expectations and uncertainty of his crocodilian zoo, he knew he didn't regret tranquilizing the deinosuchus again. If he tranquilized it, the police still would have shot it down, regardless if the animal was out or not. Another gut feeling told Michael that he didn't want a repeat of what happened in Redland to ever happen again.

If only he would've come to this realization before the expedition ever took place. None of the atrocities would've happened – and he'd still have his reputation.

The deinos were meant to be free, however many there were.

Now that the world knew of their existence, he feared that they might become potential poaching targets. Michael made a mental note that after whatever legal insanity awaited him at dawn, that he would make an honest effort to preserve these beautiful animals and their unknown ways of life for the rest of his career.

His eyes adjusted to focus on the glow of his phone, which had been set face down on the couch cushion. He picked it back up.

It was a voicemail from Mila.

He smiled, happy that it wasn't the police or the press, and pushed the listen option.

"Hey. I just made it home. Jeff and I were out for a few hours looking for you. The guy in the car is better. We dropped him off at the hospital. If you're okay, please give me a call back. Don't worry about anything – we'll figure it out. All of this will turn into something positive. Anyway, I'm sure you're in the middle of dealing with a flurry of issues. There is shit all over the news. I don't even think they know really what happened. Don't bother listening to the reports. They're all speculation at this point. Call me when you get a second. Oh, and hang in there."

She breathed a sigh and hung up.

He found it refreshing to hear her voice again. Michael guessed that she too was worn out from the night's ordeal. It had been nonstop since they left the restaurant. He resolved to call her back after a quick power nap and a hot shower, both of which were long overdue.

As Michael prepared to lay his head on the couch pillow and kick his feet up, the sound of rolling tires bumbled onto his driveway, followed by additional vehicles.

Hell, not yet.

He parted the curtain slowly, looking out over the top of the couch cushion that was pressed against his bay window.

News crews.

Car doors began to slam, followed by the shuffling of tennis shoes as reporters ran up to his front door. The pounding began. The doorbell starting ringing incessantly.

He heard none of it, already dreaming of a distant swamp, filled with breathtaking, hidden

ecosystems that the world had never seen.

EPILOGUE
A NEW BEGINNING

Thirty miles west of the Palm Grove city limits and the edge of the Windy Ghoul neighborhood, a single rowboat banged hard against a rotted pier in the Everglades, splintering into the dock before rocking gently back on the waves. No one was around to see the encounter – the owner of the dock was miles away, asleep in his bedroom, hypnotized by a Spanish language audio tutorial that he listened to through earbuds.

It was hours after the incident in Windy Ghoul, and at last, the first rays of sunlight began to flood over the Floridian countryside from the east. In the aftermath of the encounter in the neighborhood, the Palm Grove Police Department sent several helicopters over the lakes and swamps up to five miles out from the last known sighting of the deinosuchus, but the search showed nothing. Several boaters and Coast Guard Auxiliarists joined in the search, but to no avail.

By now, the deinosuchus had learned the art of blending in with its surroundings, gliding carefully at the bottom of all the swampy inlets, moving among the darkest and cloudiest areas of the water. Along the animal's endless migration toward the eastern part of the Everglades, it wandered into many other ecosystems, forcing the other crocodilians to slither away as it churned through the murky seafloor.

Deino's mind only maintained one goal: move as far away from the villages of man as possible, avoiding the motorized vehicles at all costs. It was a clear contrast to the animal's goals only a week earlier, when it had attacked anything it had come in contact with, with a flawless success rate – until the dreadful night that the Coast Guard cutter crossed through its domain.

Nothing had been the same since that stormy night, causing the creature to rethink its hunting habits. From the moment it hatched in the Southern Glades, it had been an unstoppable force of nature, trained by its primordial parents until they were killed by poachers, sinking to the bottom of one of the swamp pools before their carcasses could be retrieved for trophies.

The animal paused under the dock, scuffling up the sandy floor to tunnel down near the base of the wooden support posts. The deinosuchus was exhausted from hours of endless swimming migration, unsure of where it was headed or if it led to a moment of peace, away from the dangers of man.

As it stared out into the green haze of the deepening swamp floor, something vibrated above the crocodilian. A sliver of shadows meandered over the dock. It was a young girl, playing with her Barbie toys and reenacting a scene from one of her favorite Disney Princess movies.

She sat down on the very end of the dock, letting her feet dangle over the edge, only inches away from the surface. With one hand she operated a toy Jeep, driving the vehicle along the edge as she continuously reenacted her make-believe love story.

Despite her cautious attitude regarding the swamp, the girl failed to notice the large behemoth waiting right under the waves, watching as the girl's hypnotic feet kicked back and forth in the refracted surface, hypnotizing the crocodilian.

Deino stood up on his two hind feet, paddling gently and stealthily up to the surface, inching closer and closer to the swinging feet. The girl continued to play with her dolls, unaware of the growing shadow that was rising steadily closer to her toes. Had she stopped playing and leaned over the edge at the ripples, she would've instantly been aware of the Cretaceous hunter, giving her enough time to run back to the mainland.

But before the carnivore broke through the surface, it stopped, a foot under the water, unsure of what might happen if he broke through the water barrier and exposed himself to the uncertain world of man. Sure, the little girl would be an easy target, but what if there were other adult humans nearby? Humans with boats and guns.

Blowing a defeated bubble upwards, it descended slowly back down to the abyss, letting the little girl go untouched. The child paused as the bubbles burst over the surface, rippling into the dock's edge. Curiously, she leaned in to see if she could see something.

But there was nothing there anymore – the deino was gone again, resuming its uncertain submerged voyage toward a hopefully restful future, back into the lost world of the Everglades.

END

About the Author

Joey Kelly (also known by the pen name *Julian Michael Carver*) is an American film editor and novelist, writing works based in the lost world sub-genre of science fiction.

In 2013, Kelly graduated from the now defunct **Art Institute of Pittsburgh**. Since college graduation, Kelly has worked full time in the world of commercial advertising. His video content has been featured on *Ancient Aliens, Roseanne, Forensic Files 2,* and *The Sinner*.

He is married and lives in Pennsylvania.

CHECK OUT OTHER GREAT DINOSAUR THRILLERS

JURASSIC ISLAND
by Viktor Zarkov

Guided by satellite photos and modern technology a ragtag group of survivalists and scientists travel to an uncharted island in the remote South Indian Ocean. Things go to hell in a hurry once the team reaches the island and the massive megalodon that attacked their boats is only the beginning of their desperate fight for survival.

Nothing could have prepared billionaire explorer Joseph Thornton and washed up archaeologist Christopher "Colt" McKinnon for the terrifying prehistoric creatures that wait for them on JURASSIC ISLAND!

K-REX
by L.Z. Hunter

Deep within the Congo jungle, Circuitz Mining employs mercenaries as security for its Coltan mining site. Armed with assault rifles and decades of experience, nothing should go wrong. However, the dangers within the jungle stretch beyond venomous snakes and poisonous spiders. There is more to fear than guerrillas and vicious animals. Undetected, something lurks under the expansive treetop canopy . . .

Something ancient.

Something dangerous.

Kasai Rex!

CHECK OUT OTHER GREAT DINOSAUR THRILLERS

WRITTEN IN STONE
by David Rhodes

Charles Dawson is trapped 100 million years in the past. Trying to survive from day to day in a world of dinosaurs he devises a plan to change his fate. As he begins to write messages in the soft mud of a nearby stream, he can only hope they will be found by someone who can stop his time travel. Professor Ron Fontana and Professor Ray Taggit, scientists with opposing views, each discover the fossilized messages. While attempting to save Charles, Professor Fontana, his daughter Lauren and their friend Danny are forced to join Taggit and his group of mercenaries. Taggit does not intend to rescue Charles Dawson, but to force Dawson to travel back in time to gather samples for Taggit's fame and fortune. As the two groups jump through time they find they must work together to make it back alive as this fast-paced thriller climaxes at the very moment the age of dinosaurs is ending.

HARD TIME
by Alex Laybourne

Rookie officer Peter Malone and his heavily armed team are sent on a deadly mission to extract a dangerous criminal from a classified prison world. A Kruger Correctional facility where only the hardest, most vicious criminals are sent to fend for themselves, never to return.

But when the team come face to face with ancient beasts from a lost world, their mission is changed. The new objective: Survive.

CHECK OUT OTHER GREAT DINOSAUR THRILLERS

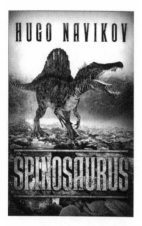

SPINOSAURUS
by Hugo Navikov

Brett Russell is a hunter of the rarest game. His targets are cryptids, animals denied by science. But they are well known by those living on the edges of civilization, where monsters attack and devour their animals and children and lay ruin to their shantytowns.

When a shadowy organization sends Brett to the Congo in search of the legendary dinosaur cryptid Kasai Rex, he will face much more than a terrifying monster from the past.

Spinosaurus is a dinosaur thriller packed with intrigue, action and giant prehistoric predators.

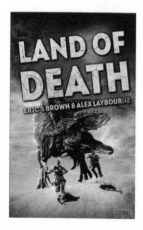

LAND OF DEATH
by Eric S Brown & Alex Laybourne

A group of American soldiers, fleeing an organized attack on their base camp in the Middle East, encounter a storm unlike anything they've seen before. When the storm subsides, they wake up to find themselves no longer in the desert and perhaps not even on Earth. The jungle they've been deposited in is a place ruled by prehistoric creatures long extinct. Each day is a struggle to survive as their ammo begins to run low and virtually everything they encounter, in this land they've been hurled into, is a deadly threat.

Made in the USA
Middletown, DE
23 June 2021